LAUGHING DEATH

A

BLACK MASK

Mystery

RAOUL WHITFIELD

---

introduction by James Reasoner

illustrations by Arthur Rodman Bowker

cover by Jes Schlaikjer

BLACK MASK

2021

Table of Contents

Introduction

WORD SAVAGERY, LESTER DENT called it.

He was referring to the writing style that the iconic pulp *Black Mask* brought out in its authors. Joseph T. Shaw, the magazine's editor during its most legendary period, referred to the type of prose he liked as "a hard, brittle style" and insisted on "authenticity in characterization and action."

One of the authors who embodied the *Black Mask* style—who helped create that style—during the decade in which Shaw edited the magazine, was Raoul F. Whitfield.

Born in New York in 1897, Raoul Whitfield led a life that resembled something out of the pulps for which he wrote. He spent part of his childhood in the Philippines with his father, a diplomat, soaking up the colorful atmosphere of that island nation. He claimed to have been an actor during the early days of Hollywood, an equally colorful locale, and he may well have been, even though there's no real substantiation of that claim. He learned how to fly at Kelly Field in San Antonio during the Great War, as they called it then, and may have seen combat briefly in France. Like his acting career, that dashing aviator part of Whitfield's life history is a little shaky. But he certainly looked the part. There's no doubt that he was handsome, urbane, charming with the ladies, and quick-witted. Good with a turn of phrase, too, as he demonstrated when, after short stints in the steel industry and as a newspaper reporter, he began writing for the pulps in the mid-1920s.

He found considerable success early on, selling almost a

hundred stories to such pulps as *Breezy Stories, Snappy Stories, Droll Stories, Sport Story,* and *Complete Sports Stories* before he ever broke into *Black Mask* in 1926. After that, even though he continued selling to other magazines, *Black Mask* was clearly his spiritual home.

He wrote a series of stories about a character named Chuck Reddington, a police detective who's also a pilot (aviation figured heavily in many of Whitfield's early stories, not surprising given his background), and a similar character named Ben Breed, in a number of yarns that came to be known as the Border Brand series.

Later, he began a series called The Crime Breeders, which eventually was published in book form under the title *Green Ice,* probably Whitfield's best-known novel. His longest and most successful series featured private detective Jo Gar, who operated primarily in the Philippines and whose complete adventures have been reprinted by Altus Press in the volume *West of Guam.*

But between those two sections of Whitfield's career came *Laughing Death,* Whitfield's first attempt at a longer, more sustained narrative. A popular technique in the pulps was to write a series of linked short stories or novelettes that could then be reworked, usually with a minimum of effort, into a novel for hardback publication after the stories first appeared in the pulps. Dashiell Hammett did that with the stories that became *Red Harvest* and *The Dain Curse,* and that approach continued to be popular throughout the Twenties, Thirties, and Forties in several different genres.

The nine stories that make up *Laughing Death* appeared in consecutive issues of *Black Mask* from February through October, 1929. The protagonist is another pilot, Gary Greer, who owns a small airport in Central City, which, given some clues in the stories and Whitfield's own history, may well be based on Pittsburgh. Things are run by crooks who have taken over the city government and the police department, and just about the only honest man in a position of authority is Sanford Greer, the prosecuting attorney—and Gary Greer's father.

When the local mob decides to put Sanford Greer on the spot and sends six gangsters to rub him out, Gary finds out about the attempt ahead of time but can't prevent it. His father is brutally murdered, and Gary swears vengeance on the men responsible for that killing. They laughed at Sanford Greer as he was dying. Gary vows that he will laugh as *he* delivers death—and justice—to them.

Each story is another step forward, or in some cases, a step backward, in Gary's vengeance quest as he attempts to wipe out his enemies and uncover the hidden mastermind behind his father's murder. It's a fast-paced, exciting ride, reminiscent in some ways of such later vengeance-driven characters as Mike Hammer and Mack Bolan. Whitfield's spare style is very effective in conveying the action and painting a vivid picture of a bleak, crime-ridden city that becomes an explosive hellscape at times. He also delivers at least one plot twist along the way that packs a potent punch in the gut.

This series was rewritten heavily and published as the novel *Five*, under Whitfield's pseudonym Temple Field, by Farrar & Rinehart in 1931. But the original stories have never been reprinted until now, more than ninety years after they first appeared. *Laughing Death* is grim, atmospheric, and filled with action, a worthy precursor to Whitfield's more famous later work, and a highly entertaining thriller in its own right. Word savagery, indeed.

—James Reasoner

Laughing Death

1

On the Spot

GARY GREER STEPPED out of the soundproof, hangar phone booth. He walked straight toward the nearest window, one looking out over the level stretch of the South Side Field. His face was very white, his lips were set in a grim, narrow line. He held a cigarette between the fingers of his right hand; the ash and the burning tobacco pressed against his skin. Slowly he spread his fingers, let the stub of the cigarette drop to the concrete floor of the hangar. Mechanically he crushed it with a heel. He muttered to himself in a low, hard voice.

"S.G.—" he muttered—*"on the spot!"*

His face twisted suddenly, his lean, muscular body stiffened. In the distance a siren wailed. A Chicago-Center City air-mail plane was gliding for a landing. It dropped down across Gary's line of vision; his gray, slightly squinted eyes saw it—and yet he did not see it. The words of his father, which had just come over the phone wire to him, were beating in his brain: " 'Whisper' Daley has squealed. They got to him at Headquarters. I'm on the spot. Better come home, son."

Sanford Greer—slated for the lead of gangsters! His father, too square a prosecuting attorney for Center City, calling up the field and telling his son to "come home." S.G. was no fool. Center City was spreading out, sprawling across White River, taking in territory. It was a mill town, a money town. It was a gang town. And Sanford Greer had played the game squarely.

Men had burned, men had gone to the Big House—because gangster money was bad money to Center City's prosecuting attorney. And now—gang vengeance was the answer.

Gary Greer turned away from the window. He moved silently across the hangar concrete. He had a lean face, a lean body. But there was strength in the body. You could see it, and sense it. And there was strength in the face. Suppressed strength. Narrow lips, a firm chin. A goggle-cut over his left eye. Sandy-colored hair, a bit too sandy and rumpled. He moved swiftly, his body erect.

At the wide entrance of the hangar he hesitated. The mail plane was dropping low, leveling off for the landing. A figure rounded the end of the hangar, moved toward Gary. The man was short; he had a broad grin on his face and his blue eyes met Gary's.

"Joe got her in on time for—"

He stopped speaking abruptly. His eyes widened. Pete Ranning had known Gary for years. Only once before had he seen such an expression on the pilot's face, and that had been when Russ Elliott had dropped ten thousand feet in a loose-winged spin—and Gary had turned his eyes away, at the crash-second of his best friend.

"What's wrong, Gary?" Ranning spoke huskily. "What's hit you?"

Gary Greer seemed to be staring through Ranning's body, staring beyond. Then, suddenly, he snapped out of it. He spoke sharply.

"Have the boys roll my ship out, Pete. Make 'em rush it. I want to wing for the Municipal Field. Dad's on—" he hesitated for just the fraction of a second—"*the spot.*"

Ranning stiffened. He started to say something, checked himself. He turned, ran toward the dead-line. Above the exhaust rumble of the taxiing mail-plane Gary heard him shouting for the ground crew. He saw the boys getting into action. His lips moved; he muttered thickly.

"I can make it in—ten minutes. I'll get a message through, telling S.G. to stay in the office. We can wing out, away—"

His voice died; he was moving swiftly toward the Field Headquarters Office. Miss Bailey was at the switchboard; he saw her startled eyes as she looked up at him. He tried to smile; no use letting himself go this way. His face must be strained, twisted. It wouldn't do.

"S.G.'s office, Miss Bailey. You leave my message, please. It's terribly important. Tell him to wait, to stay in the office. I'm flying to the Municipal Field. Tell him—he *must wait!*"

He turned away, moved again toward the field. Tight-pressed lips held back a groan. S.G. wait? It wasn't likely. Sanford Greer was a fighter. Wait for his son to come, to fly him out of a bad mess? He wasn't of the breed to do that. And yet—

Gary halted, straightened. He cried out. The sharp report had come from behind. He turned, his body relaxed. A tiny tractor was hauling one of the pay-load ships out of a hangar. It had back-fired sharply. The sound was not so different from that of machine-gun fire. Sub-caliber machine-gun fire.

The pilot moved on again. The two-place, Ryan-engined Wasp was out on the dead-line now. As he stared at her he saw Ranning climb down from the front cockpit. She was an open job, because Gary liked the rush of air, the feel of the prop wash. She was his pet crate. Her propeller was whirling now, at an idling speed. Pete came toward him.

"Give her a rev, Gary," he advised, his face holding a serious expression. "Don't take her off cold. Things may not be as bad—

Pete Ranning checked himself. And Gary knew why. Ranning was aware of Center City conditions. The South Side Field had furnished planes to fly payrolls, things had been so bad. When a man was slated for gang vengeance in Center City—the dose was administered.

Gary Greer stepped close to Ranning. He spoke in an icy tone. His voice was very low.

"If I'm—too late, Pete—it'll be just the beginning! They can't get away with a thing like—"

He stopped. His own words mocked. They *had* got away with plenty of kills, in Center City. Two months ago the chief of police had gone down on wet cobbles, with a dozen bullets in his body. A month before that, Anton Savoy had gone out. A square lawyer—a fighter. And now S.G. was lined for the mark, on the spot. Whisper Daley had squealed. And Whisper wouldn't lie—not in such a case.

Gary was moving toward the two-place Wasp. He dropped

into the front cockpit, snapped the safety belt across his gray suit. He wore no flying togs. He used no seat-pack 'chute. There would be no altitude gained on this trip, and a 'chute was useless without altitude. From a pocket at his right he extracted helmet and goggles. He advanced the throttle, revving the ship's rotary up.

He tried to relax, waiting for the engine to warm up. His body was tense, his nerves on edge. There was a strong bond between Gary and his father. Neither of the men was sentimental. Strangers thought Sanford Greer hard, even brutal. But Gary knew that wasn't so. His emotions were held under control, beneath the surface—a trait inherited by Gary. Father and son were very close. Gary's mother had died when he was quite young. S.G.—and Gary always called his father by the initials—had raised the son.

The pilot's fingers closed over the metal of the stick rising between his legs. Blood was driven from the surface of his browned hands—they showed white. His gray eyes narrowed back of the goggle-glass. He moved his head, called sharply to Ranning.

"You're in charge of the Field, Pete," he stated. "A Verlaine's due in at five. Get her landing room—she's a sluggish bus. I may not be back—"

He tried to smile again. Ranning nodded and turned away. Gary called toward the ground-crew boss.

"Get 'em clear, Mac!"

The wheel chocks were pulled away from the rubber. Gary advanced the throttle—the plane rolled out from the deadline. He took her off in a steady climb toward White River and the North Side. As she gained altitude he picked up the buildings of the city. It was a summer afternoon; with a murky sky. No wind, and the mill smoke hanging low. It would be a swift flight to the Municipal Field—a graft boner the politicians had put across. The field was close in, near the City Hall. But it was too small. The air-mail had refused to use it. Gary had licked the politicians—it was his field that had the ships, the pay-load business.

But he would land on the other field now—and taxi over to the City Hall. He would talk with S.G. It wouldn't be easy. If he could get his father away from Center City for a week, two weeks, a month—

Gary wiped a smear of oil from the glass of his goggles. He advanced the throttle all of the way. White River was sliding back toward his ship. The exhaust roar was steady. Air-speed—one-forty an hour. The Wasp was a winger! She could travel. She handled like the Nieuports he had flown in France, only better. Twenty minutes from his take-off, and he'd be in S.G.'s office.

His throat tightened. Would his father wait? Would he get the phone message—and wait? Or would he go down to the car, after slipping his Maxim-silenced gun into a pocket, and drive toward their home in the suburb fourteen miles from the city?

Gary Greer kept his eyes on the tall buildings gliding back toward the low-winging plane. White River, as black as coal beneath the ship—ironically named—slid from sight. He could see the low buildings of the North Side, the gang district, beyond the city. Warehouses, terminals, sheds and shacks. A breeding place for organized crime. The birth section of the Terminal gang.

The square of the Municipal Field was in sight. Small, tricky to get a ship into. An emergency landing spot—little more. And the city had paid high for the purchase from private individuals, politicians.

Already Gary was diving the ship, cutting the throttle speed down, gliding. His feet pressed hard against the rudder pedals. There was a gusty, building-spread wind, as the plane lost altitude. He risked a glance toward the City Hall. He could almost see the windows of S.G.'s office. The office of a prosecuting attorney *on the spot!*

Lower and lower the ship dropped. Gary banked her sharply. She nosed around into a tricky landing wind. There were building shadows across the field. He gave the ship the gun— her exhaust crackle startled him. He had a swift vision of a fast-moving car of men using guns, making them crackle. He cried out against the exhaust beat as though he were shouting against gun clatter.

"No—no!"

And then his nerves were steady again. He was setting the ship down for a landing—she was striking turf in a perfect three-pointer. She was rolling, losing ground speed. And as she rolled to a stop, a man closed a door behind him, ten blocks distant. Ten blocks and eight stories distant. The man was medium-sized, with a lean, pale face and dark eyes. Prosecuting Attorney Sanford Greer was leaving his office. His secretary had repeated, word for word, a telephone message, some ten minutes before. But it hadn't seemed to matter. S.G. was going away.

SANFORD GREER STEPPED out of the elevator,

moved toward the main entrance of the City Hall. He saw Mackinson move out from the crowd, walk along behind him. Mackinson was a big man, over six feet and built like a weight thrower. The attorney slowed down, stopped. He half turned; out of the corners of his eyes he saw Mackinson stop, light a cigar. The man appeared unconscious of Greer's existence, but he failed to fool the attorney. Greer moved to Mackinson's side, spoke in a low, quiet tone.

"It's no good, Al. Don't do it. You've got a wife and some kids. I'm going along by myself, Al. Lose me, outside." The big man swore softly. "Forget that line!" he growled. "It's my job, ain't it?"

Greer smiled grimly, shaking his head.

"No man's job—to get himself in the way of—"

He stopped as Mackinson growled again. It was good of Chief Albright, sending the big guard along. Good and clever of him. Mackinson was too honest. He was a scrapper. Albright had no use for the detective.

Greer shrugged his shoulders. He turned away abruptly. There were plenty of thoughts running through his head. As he reached the wide steps leading down from the City Hall he slipped his right hand into the right pocket of his gray suit. His fingers closed over warm steel. He moved slowly down the steps.

A trip, Albright had suggested. And, of course, Gary would favor that plan. He was even now winging toward the Municipal Field, Sanford Greer guessed. He did not look up into the sky—that made no difference. In life he had been hard, had controlled his emotions. In death—

At a newsstand he glanced at the headlines of an early evening edition. It screamed at him, of course. Bradley's paper—Bradley putting before his eyes the words of Whisper Daley. It didn't matter, of course. Bradley was a crook—a shrewd crook. It didn't matter. Nothing mattered much. He glanced back of him. Mackinson was sauntering along. The parking section was across the busy street. Greer moved back toward the guard.

"Listen, Al—drop out of this, will you? You're no fool. It may last for weeks. It may come in a hurry. You can't stop it. Your bulk won't help any. Think of the wife, the kids—"

Mackinson yawned. Sanford Greer stared at him, then smiled.

"I'll lose the cab you tag me in, Al. You'll be sore as hell—and then glad as hell. See you tomorrow, Al!"

He turned away for the second time. Mackinson was all right—a good fellow. But he had a wife and some kids. And he couldn't do any good. Albright had known that; the police head was no friend of Greer's. Throw one in for good measure. But let the boys know about it, of course. It didn't do to cross up the Terminal gang.

Sanford Greer reached the parking place. His car was a manifestation of his wealth. It stood, gleaming, near the entrance. He slipped back of the wheel. A mark, of course—a target. But that didn't matter. One couldn't slink through days and nights, waiting. Marrinly, the South Side boss, had done that. Fear had made him a crawling creature before the *spot* was right.

The machine was sliding out into the street now. The parking man smiled at the attorney. As Greer swung the big sedan, he saw a white taxi pull out from the curbing. Mackinson was going to try, then. He was going to tag along.

"Dead men—" Greer observed in a monotone—"tell few tales."

He had told many—too many. "Little" Bateli, Dan Waster, "Red" Spanner—they had known that, before the juice had burned out their insides. But—that had been the job. He had known all this, certainly. A year and four months—a long term for a decent prosecuting attorney.

The car was winding through the traffic. He didn't glance behind. There was little chance of outdistancing a professional driver. But he would lose the cab beyond the terminal. There was less traffic through the North Side. Speed, there, would count. The cab couldn't keep up. Perhaps that would mean that Mackinson could get home to the kids in time for dinner. He hoped so.

Once, Sanford Greer turned his head and glanced up toward the southern sky. He failed to see a plane, but a thought hurt him. He wasn't so old—Gary wasn't so young. But flight— that was out of the question. He'd stick, in spite of everything. Persuasion hadn't meant much in his life. His lips moved again, as the car neared the terminal.

"It'll be soon. They don't want me on—the Rattner case."

He turned sharply near the freight station. This section of the city lay under a murk of smoke, dust and steam. It was a short cut to the suburb. The thought caused him a bitter smile.

"Very short!" he muttered, and pressed a foot down sharply on the accelerator.

The car responded. There were trucks, slow and lumbering, but they kept close to the curbing. He knew a narrow street, turned into it. The car held the turning arc well. He glanced into the mirror before him. The cab was not in sight. He was a block down the narrow street before it made the turn. Ahead were the freight tracks—a bell clanged sonorously, insistently.

A red light flashed an intermittent warning.

Sanford Greer stiffened a bit in the seat back of the wheel. He was doing forty as he approached the crossing. The engine loomed, on the left. Greer shoved down on the accelerator. He was over ten feet ahead of the engine. A glance showed him that it was a long freight haul. He relaxed, smiled slightly.

"It'll be soon," he muttered again. "Al's a damned fool."

He braked the car down, swung off the street that crossed the tracks. They might cut the train in two. He wanted to lose the white cab. The car turned up a rougher street. There were cobble stones surfacing it. Sanford Greer pulled up against a battered curbing line. He lighted a fresh cigar, placed his gun on the upholstering of the seat, close beside him. He got the car under way again.

He wasn't familiar with this street, but the direction was right. Perhaps he would be home in an hour, perhaps not. He thought about Gary again. Like Mackinson, the idea was to protect. With Gary it was love and instinct. With Mackinson it was duty. In either case the motivation did not count. It was useless.

Greer turned his head slightly. A flivver was pulling up. On the left. It had dilapidated curtains flapping. The driver did not glance toward Greer. He was bent low over the wheel. He rattled the flivver ahead of the powerful sedan.

The street suddenly narrowed. Lanterns rimmed some excavation work on the left. The flivver swung over to the right. It slowed down. Sanford Greer turned his head, not trusting the mirror's limited vision. There was no car behind. He used the brakes. The surface was very rough. The flivver was rattling badly, crawling.

A street cut across the one on which the two cars traveled. It was as bad as the one on which the cars moved. Coming up it, from the right, was an open car. It had a black top, and was black in color. It had a load of men.

The flivver rattled across the intersection. Greer followed the battered car. Then, suddenly, the flivver stopped. The brakes squealed as it came to a halt. The driver reached the cobbles— headed toward an alley on the right. He moved very swiftly. He didn't even glance back toward the halted sedan.

His action was enough. It told Sanford Greer that he had been right—it would be soon. The sedan was blocked ahead. It was just across the intersection of the streets. Already the man-loaded car was swinging into sight.

Greer opened the door on his left, slid to the cobbles. He held the gun in his right hand, held it low. The black car stopped. He could only see the hood of it—his own machine hid most of it from his sight.

It was fairly quiet—and then it was very noisy. Metal shot sound against Sanford Greer's ears. Glass in the sedan shattered. He felt a stinging pain in his right leg, another in his thigh. A machine-gun was clattering fiercely. He took a step forward; his right leg was half paralyzed. He crouched slightly, raised his right hand. This was a rotten way to go out—he couldn't see. He couldn't get around his own machine—

He went to his knees, started to crawl. A jagged pain streaked across his abdomen. His left shoulder thudded sound. Already his eyes held a mist. But he could see the men in the car now. He could see the sub-caliber machine-gun, the braced stand of it. He could see a face, grinning down at him. Mud danced up from the cobbles. The fingers of his left hand were all red.

He couldn't move them. Slowly he raised his right arm.

Laughter struck into a strange silence. Distorted, hideous laughter. The grinning face was a Benda mask in his failing sight. His gun wouldn't come up. The laughing head was rocking from side to side. A buzzing note was in Greer's ears.

A face turned. It laughed a word. Or perhaps it only seemed to laugh the word. But he heard it. Down on the cobbles, still trying to get his gun raised, he heard the one word. It was hoarse, amused, bitterly funny.

"Guns!"

This time there was no shattering of glass. Mud danced, close to Sanford Greer's knees. Cobbles chipped. The sub-caliber gun was jerking on its stand. Many guns flashed before his eyes for a brief second; many sounds reached his ears in a confused jumble.

Sanford Greer bowed to the guns. It was not a controlled, stately bow. He bowed to the sound. He crumpled to the guns and sound. Even before his head crashed heavily against the cobbles and the mud, he had ceased to remember earthly things. His body lay motionless. The trigger of his gun had not been squeezed.

The black car slid almost silently across the intersection. Two blocks away a police whistle shrilled. Four blocks away a white cab was turning; the passenger in the cab was staring tensely beyond an opened window. Forty blocks away an elevator was shooting upward in the City Hall. Gary Greer rode the elevator.

On North Ninth Street a flivver rested, blocking the path of a polished sedan. The flivver's engine was silent; the engine of the sedan was almost silent. But the switch had not been turned.

Warehouse buildings along the street spilled out flat faces, dull eyes. Figures moved slowly toward the body of Center City's prosecuting attorney. His gun rested in a pool of muddy water. Sanford Greer had died as others in Center City had died before him—*on the spot.*

IT WAS OVER now. He was calmer, steadier. He would never, he thought, be that way again. Rage had dominated, twisted every part of him. It was the ruthlessness, the brutality of the kill. Battered down on a mean street, fallen in mud—his body torn by gang bullets. There had been no chance. There never was a chance. And yet, before Sanford Greer the gangsters had always had their chance.

Gary walked mechanically. His eyes failed to see many things. He had been too late, but then, he had expected to be too late. Fingers touched the crumpled note in his pocket. The note S.G. had left for him. It was a short note. He knew every word in it. Three hours had passed since the phone call had come. For more than an hour now, he had been walking the streets of the city. Twice he had returned to the mean street on which S.G.'s body had been found.

He was a mile away from the spot now, moving steadily toward White River. It was dark—westward a storm was rolling up. Lightning flashed; there was the very distant rumble of thunder. It was hot, sultry. Gary's lips moved, muttering the words of the note.

"There was some good, Son—I haven't failed completely. No use in waiting for you—I am not afraid—"

Gary Greer smiled. It was a bitter smile. S.G. afraid? Of course he had not been. Only afraid for others. For Gary himself, and for Al Mackinson. Unselfish—he'd always been that way.

The pilot lighted a cigarette. His hands were very steady. He let the match drop to the sidewalk, stepped on it as though he were at the field. For a few seconds he stood motionless. Only his lips moved. His words were a promise to himself. They had no expression.

"I'll learn—if it takes weeks or months. I'll know. And when I *do* know, one by one—*they'll* know! For every gun in that car—"

He stopped muttering to himself. With an effort he moved along the street again. He paused near a low building, stepped into a narrow doorway. The cigarette, glowing redly, he held behind him, in his left hand. The fingers of his right hand touched metal.

Two shapes merged into the dull light of a street lamp, a hundred yards ahead. The section of the city was bad. The two shapes stood close together; they had had their backs turned in the direction of Gary's approach. Their attitudes were careless—too careless. No sound of voices had reached him. Perhaps they were waiting. In spite of his thoughts, his muttered words, he had seen the two men.

From the doorway he watched them. One of the men moved slowly away. He did not look back, but headed toward the Boulevard, three blocks distant. The other man lighted a cigarette. He was medium in size. A jagged flash of lightning, followed by a loud roll of thunder, seemed to startle him. He turned, moved up the street toward the doorway in which Gary was standing.

The pilot lifted the cloth of his coat pocket. The man moved slowly. He kept close to the low building. The place was some sort of a carpenter job-shop. It was deserted. And so was the street. Gary smiled faintly. His body was motionless, tense. The walking man stopped, directly opposite the doorway. He faced the street; his back was turned to Gary. He spoke in a half whisper:

"Rear of eight fourteen River Street. One flight up. Ask for Gus. Names for sale-price one grand. Coin—on the spot."

The man moved away. Gary's weapon moved slightly, under cover of his suiting material. The man had spotted him. Perhaps he had been followed. It was too easy, too simple. He was known to the gangsters. Here was one—

He checked himself. He lowered the gun. It was a Service Colt he had used in France, and had no silencer. It was bulky. He was beginning to understand what he was up against. He couldn't fight killers this carelessly.

Names for sale—for one grand. Eight Fourteen River Street. One flight up. Ask for Gus. The words rolled in his brain. The man who had uttered them was across the street now. A cool wind, preceding the coming storm, swept over the city. A trap?

He was known. "Coin—on the spot." The last three words of the sentence told him a lot. He had been foolish. Coming down into the section of the city where his father had been slain. Walking blindly about. It would have to stop. And yet, there were names for sale. Suppose it was not a trap? Men told many things—for money. And Gary Greer wanted information. He wanted names. One grand. He hadn't anything like that much on him, but Brandt would be in his office. He always had money in the safe. There would be no trouble getting the thousand dollars.

The man who had spoken, with his back turned to Gary Greer

was out of sight now. The lightning was sharper; the rain would start very soon. Thunder was rumbling, roaring almost steadily. It would be a sharp storm. The concussions in the sky sounded almost like France in Nineteen Eighteen. Big guns, little guns.

Gary moved out from the doorway, into the gusts of cool wind. He could feel the rain in the air. His Wasp was out on the Municipal Field; maybe the ground crew would get her into a hangar—most likely they would not. He wasn't liked at the Municipal Field. He was hated. S.G. had been hated.

Thunder roared again. Big guns—little guns. Something seemed to snap inside of Gary Greer's body. He threw back his head, laughed. It was a bitter, horrible laughter. The wind caught it, lost it immediately in a rush of other sound. Barrels going down, paper ripped loose, ash cans rolling in yards and streets.

The pilot was moving toward the Boulevard now. He wasn't laughing. His face was set grimly. Things would be changed— but first he must play in with fate. Or something more accurate, more precise than fate. He must get names. Names of guns. Names of killers. He must buy something that represented life. After that, there would be change. And after change there would come death. Death, he thought grimly as the first drops of rain pounded down from the clouds, *on the spot*.

EIGHT FOURTEEN RIVER Street was a gray, frame building almost lost in a jumble of other, gray, frame buildings. It was a cheap rivermen's boarding-house. In the rear, fifty feet from the cobbles of River Street, was a small and dirty speak-easy. Up above there were rooms. Downstairs, facing on the street, was a lunch counter.

The building gleamed wetly in the rain of a storm now abated, passed. At intervals lightning flared in the sky, but the rumble of thunder was distant and dying steadily. Water dripped down against rotted gutters. The building was almost dark—from the shutters of a room on the second floor yellow light streaked faintly. The speakeasy was noisy with boisterous voices, filled with hoarse and profane laughter.

Warped steps, uncarpeted, led up to the rooms on the second floor. On these steps was a man. He was a short, heavy-set man, and though his right hand hung limply at his side as he climbed the stairs, the arm was crooked, bent rigidly at the elbow. The man moved up the stairs very quietly. He seemed to know his destination.

At the top of the stairs he paused momentarily. Then he moved toward the rear of the boarding-house. He turned toward a door that faced a blank wall, and knocked. He knocked four times, very sharply. A voice came through the wood. The man outside made no move to turn the knob of the door, or to reach for it. He stepped to one side.

A key turned in the lock—the door opened slowly. The man outside heard footfalls within the room. He waited until they had ceased to sound. Then he entered the room, closed the door very quietly behind him. His eyes did not leave the face of the man seated on the edge of the cot.

The one on the cot was small, skinny. His hair was thin, yellowish in color. A sort of dirty yellow. It was hot in the room, and the man's skin had the appearance of being oiled. His face shone in the yellow-shaded light of a cheap table lamp. His hands gleamed oily for a second, then went toward the pockets of his baggy trousers. He had seen something in the eyes of the one who stood with his back to the closed door.

"Listen, Soapy—keep your paws in sight!"

The voice of the one who stood up was persuasive. It had a sharp edge, in spite of a slight huskiness. "Soapy" Tyler's hands flickered toward his knees, became motionless. His sallow, oily face became a shade whiter. His thick lips twitched; he wet them with his tongue. He had pale blue eyes, and they tried to smile into the dark eyes of the other man.

"How's things, Soapy?" The visitor smiled almost cheerfully. "It's wet as hell outside."

Soapy Tyler nodded his head. He started to say something, changed his mind. From below came the sound of shattering glass. Hoarse laughter drifted up.

The visitor stood with his left hand hidden from sight in the pocket of a striped, sporty coat. The coat was a different color from the trousers, which were white. Soapy stared toward the spot in which the hand was hidden; then his eyes met the visitor's eyes again.

"It was a hell of a storm," he muttered in a thick voice. "Had me scared, it did."

The man standing with his back to the door laughed. It was a nasty laugh. He had a thin face, a long nose. His teeth were very bad.

"Had *you* scared, Soapy?" he mocked. "Maybe there was somethin' besides the storm, eh?"

Soapy Tyler's eyes blinked. They were sort of watery. The fingers of his hands twitched. He shook his head.

"Nothin' else, Elbow," he stated. "Not a thing."

"Elbow" Gorringe nodded his head slowly. He moved away from the door, dropped down on a chair. The chair was battered; it once had a back. It wobbled beneath the man's weight.

"Not a thing, eh?" Gorringe mocked. "Well, now—ain't that funny?"

The man on the bed stiffened a little. He was watching Gorringe closely. He was thinking, and his thoughts were not pleasant. He made a motion as though to rise from the bed, but a slight movement of Elbow's body stopped him.

"It's hot as hell!" Soapy said weakly. "How about gettin' a window up?"

"Wait a while," the other man replied. "Maybe I'll open it— later."

It was his tone, more than the exclusion of Soapy's name, that drove fear into the heart of the one on the bed. He sucked in his breath sharply, started to speak, changed his mind again.

"I got a message for you," Elbow stated slowly. "From Sal."

The fear showed in Soapy's face now. He swallowed hard. He tried twice, and the second time got it out.

"Yeah?"

The man on the chair leaned forward slightly. He nodded. He showed his bad teeth in a wide smile.

"Yeah," he returned. "Sal says to tell you that was a bad idea. He tells me to give it back to you."

Soapy looked puzzled. Gorringe made a movement with his left hand—something dropped on the cot beside Soapy. He stared down at it. A gun—a Smith and Wesson thirty-eight. He started to reach for it, then stopped. Elbow grinned.

"Sure!" he stated. "Look it over, Soapy."

The man on the bed lifted the weapon with his right hand. He broke it, saw that the shells were in the chambers. He stared at Elbow Gorringe. And he tried to bluff.

"What was a bad idea?" he asked hoarsely.

"Not squeezin' lead at a certain gent," Gorringe stated. "Holdin' out on Sal."

Panic showed in Soapy's eyes. Then, in a second, he steadied.

"Bunk!" he stated. "Sal had the gat. He seen for himself. Three dead ones inside her, ain't there?"

The man on the chair nodded. "Sure," he agreed. "An' *then* some, Soapy!"

Tyler's body jerked. He stared at the weapon. His gun hand was shaking. Elbow was speaking again. He spoke in a monotone, as though he were reciting a piece.

"An' Sal says to tell you they jerked lead out of a certain party an hour ago. There wasn't any thirty-eights in him. How come?"

Soapy Tyler spoke in a thick tone. His voice rose.

"Maybe I missed him," he stated. "Maybe they made a mistake. Maybe Sal's guy is givin' him the wrong dope. An' maybe—"

"Maybe you shot at a cat!" Elbow cut in grimly. "Me—I wasn't ridin' along—I don't count. I'm just—" His teeth showed again in a mocking grin—"deliverin' Sal's message."

Panic gripped the man on the bed. His voice rose shrilly, high-pitched—

"I'd been drinkin', I tell you! Maybe my hand was shakin', Elbow. I got a look at him, down in the mud—"

"Shut up!"

Elbow's voice was sharp. His torso straightened on the chair. Soapy Tyler was stiff, staring at Gorringe. His eyes were wide, glassy.

"Sal says to tell you—" Elbow broke off abruptly. Soapy was squeezing the trigger of his Smith and Wesson. The room was filled with little clicks. The cylinder was rotating. The hammer was striking.

Elbow laughed. The weapon fell from the nerveless hands of Soapy Tyler. It struck the edge of the cot, slipped to the floor. Soapy, his face twisted, stared at the man on the chair. Elbow spoke again. His voice was husky, low.

"Sal says to tell you—this—"

Something jerked, inside his left side pocket. A popping cough filled the room. A champagne bottle's kick off. Only a bit more sharpness to it.

The man on the bed jerked his body. He sucked in his breath with a terrible effort. Elbow spoke again.

"An' this—"

His gun spoke again. And once more. He got up from the chair, turned toward the door. Soapy Tyler was rocking on the bed. His hands were pressed against his stomach. He bowed his head, fell heavily to the floor. Gorringe turned at the door, looked down at him. He was smiling with his eyes.

"I'll tell Sal, Soapy—" he stated in a hoarse voice—"that you got a little—stomach trouble!"

He went out, closing the door softly behind him.

THE CAB PULLED up to the curbing along River Street. Gary Greer nodded his head to the questioning look in the driver's eyes.

"Stick here," he ordered. "I won't be long."

He moved swiftly away from the cab. The first number he spotted was Six Forty-two. He smiled grimly. About two blocks from the address he was tracing. In the inside pocket of his coat were bills. Twenties. Fifty of them. One grand. If it were not a trap he would trade the bills for names. There was no way of telling how honest the man he had to deal with would be. It was a chance. It might be an honest squeal. The police were learning nothing. There was no clue to Sanford Greer's murderers.

City Hall was rotten to the foundation. A clue might not mean anything. He was taking the only way—his own way. Money meant little—one grand for a lie or a truth. It was a worthwhile gamble.

Seven Sixty. He was nearing the number. Figures moved along the sidewalk—men who walked drunkenly, brokenly. Men who walked furtively. Men whose faces were turned away from Gary Greer. River Street was a grim street. Odors from the black-watered stream reached his nostrils. His eyes were turned toward the stores, cheap, poorly lighted, that showed numerals. Few of them did.

Eight Fourteen. He moved into the entrance of the house. Voices reached him from the speakeasy in the rear. Stairs slanted ahead of him; he hesitated, then started up, From somewhere above he heard a man whistling. The whistle was off key. Footfalls sounded, on the steps. It was too late to turn. Gary lowered his head, kept climbing. He moved as though he were very tired, shuffling his feet.

The man coming down continued to whistle. He moved to the right, giving Gary room. Keeping his eyes low, the pilot noted only one thing. The right elbow of the man was rigid, crooked. The fingers dangled loosely from the right hand. The left hand was not in sight.

They passed each other—one climbing, the other descending, without speaking. Near the base of the carpetless steps the man with the crooked elbow started to hum. He hummed as badly as he whistled. His tone was guttural, hoarse. Gary reached the top of the stairs. He stopped, half turned. The man below was out in the street.

There was a very distant rumble of thunder. Gary Greer stood motionlessly, listening, waiting. Then he moved slowly toward the rear of the narrow hallway. Ten yards—and he stopped again. His ears picked up a faint sound, a groan. He got the direction from which it came. His right hand touched steel, inside a pocket. He moved on.

Another groan—a sharp hissing of breath. Then a pounding—a sound like the beating of fists on a floor. From below came a lilt of drunken song. A bottle crashed. Thunder rumbled again. There was the deep-toned note, distant and sustained, of a river boat. A big boat.

A door showed on Gary's right. He waited, standing still. A man was inside the room. There was heavy breathing, a dragging sound. Gary stepped close to the door. He knocked. Something was beating on the floor again; something was dragging.

Gary Greer drew his Colt from a pocket. He held it low, ready for instant use. He turned the knob slowly, shoved the door open. A hoarse groan reached him. He stared down toward the floor. A man's eyes were on his. They were wide, blue eyes. Glassy eyes. The man was dragging himself toward a pitcher in which was water. The man spoke.

"Greer!"

It was a low, throaty word. A hard word to get out. There was appeal in the man's eyes now. He wanted Gary. He wanted him close.

Gary shut the door behind him, moved to the other man's side. He dropped on his knees. The one in agony knew him, recognized him. His face twisted; his body jerked convulsively. He spoke hoarsely, biting out the words. He was dying, and he had something to say. He fought desperately to utter words.

"They got—Greer—laughed him—out of things! He—was my lawyer—good turn—years ago. Will tell you—who—"

His voice died. The fingers of his hands were twisting and untwisting. Once, he beat against the floor. Gary's face was set grimly. They had laughed at S.G.—as he had died! Bullets battering down from the death car—laughter on gangsters' lips—

Soapy Tyler straightened his body, rolled over on his back. His lips were as white as his face. But something had happened, inside of him. The terrible pains were dulling. He stared into Gary's gray eyes.

"—An' they—laughed—at me. Didn't work lead—on Greer. Sal got—wise. Had me—done—"

He sighed heavily. His eyes closed. For a second Gary thought the man was through. And then, with his eyes closed and his body relaxed, Soapy Tyler spoke again. He spoke very slowly, and thickly. He spoke names. And each one of the names he repeated twice. He spoke them like a child reading from a book. His eyes widened on Gary's gray ones.

"You—got 'em?" he muttered weakly. "You—wise to—"

Gary Greer nodded his head slowly. His gray eyes were narrow slits in the yellow light of the hot room's lamp. Names—that he would never forget! Not so long as he lived! Never!

Soapy Tyler was smiling. Gary kneeled beside him, staring into his white face. He thought of the one grand in his pocket. He reached for it. It might mean something to the man who was dying beside him.

The man on the floor cried out. He shouted fiercely a woman's name. His body twisted—became motionless. Gary stared at him for several seconds. He had seen death many times—now he was seeing it again.

He rose to his feet. Five names—and the sixth name was dead. Five killers of Sanford Greer, and one who had not killed. One with a faint spark of decency—who had paid a gang price for that spark. One who had thought something wouldn't count. It had counted.

Gary moved toward the door. He was soaked in perspiration. He thought of the man who had passed him on the steps, whistling. His lips pressed together tightly. Had he been one of the five names? Had he passed one of S.G.'s killers, on the battered steps?

"Steady!" he muttered grimly. "A name is only—a name!"

He turned back toward the body of the dead man. Instinctively he reached toward the man's wrist. He straightened again. This was different. He was seeking men. He was fighting men. And some friends of the men he was fighting would be in police uniform. Feeling a pulse meant a fingerprint. He had touched nothing but the knob of the door—the outside knob.

The man lay on his back. Over a wash-basin stand was a small mirror. It was cracked. And Gary wanted to be certain. He took a handkerchief from his pocket, got the mirror from the wall with the fabric protecting his finger skin. He set the mirror on the bed, wiped the glass clear. Then he moved back toward the dead man. When he lifted the mirror the glass was as clear as it had been after the polishing. He hung it on the bent nail again.

The inside knob he turned with his handkerchief. The outside one he wiped clear. His brain, as he moved down the steps, held names. Five of them. The names revolved like a circular disc. They were unfamiliar names—not one of them had he heard before. S.G. hadn't talked shop. Unfamiliar names—and now they had become important, bitter names. They twisted around within his brain.

His right foot slid over the edge of a step. Wood splintered off, gave way. He tried to catch himself, flung out a hand. His body twisted to one side. Arms crashed against the wall at the left of the stairs. He fell to his knees.

From somewhere below someone coughed. Some *thing* coughed. Once, twice—

Gary Greer heard the buzz-hum of a bullet. Wood spattered, above him. A splinter of the steps stung against the flesh of a hand. He threw his arms before his face, let himself pitch forward.

As he fell downward, forward—he heard more bullets pound into the wood of the steps. One thudded close to him. His arms struck heavily against wood. Pain stabbed through his body. He groaned heavily—let his body roll down a few steps. Then he was motionless.

He listened. There were footfalls, out in the street. But they were not coming toward him, toward the base of the steps. They were dying away. Faintly, above the river sounds, and drip of rain from the roof, he heard a whistle. Notes of a popular song, off key.

Gary Greer raised his head. His body ached from the fall. His arms and hands were skinned. He sat on the lower step, thinking. The whistling died away in the distance. A splinter of wood, giving away, had saved his life. A man had killed once, and had returned to kill again. He had failed—the second time. And because he *had* failed—

Gary got to his feet. He stood in the mean entrance of the River Street boarding-house, and started out toward the river. His lips moved slowly. The words he uttered were low, fierce.

"They know—and *I* know. Tomorrow the one who whistled—he'll know of his failure. They'll know I'm alive. That's wrong. It's got to be—changed."

He smiled grimly. There was a way—it came to him, standing in the narrow doorway of the River Street house. There was a way of giving himself a better chance of getting closer to five killers, five names. He limped out into the street, moved toward the waiting taxi. The rain struck his face. It was cool; it felt good. As he walked he grew calmer, steadier. Tomorrow he would make a beginning. A beginning—for more than one end!

2

Out of the Sky

THE EARLY MORNING open bus pulled over to the side of the road, a half mile south of the flying field. The driver twisted in his seat and stared back toward the wailing sound that was steadily increasing in tone. His lips moved.

"Bulls!" he muttered. "Riding the road fast!"

He had intended to use a stronger phrase; the sight of his one passenger stopped him. Clerical black—a white, high collar. And the minister's face was expressionless, almost a mask. He did not turn, stare toward the wailing siren. He looked straight ahead.

There was fog on the road. Out of it came a black shape. The siren wail diminished drearily, brakes squealed—rubber hissed on dirt. The open car came alongside of the halted bus. It had a red-lensed light at one side of the windshield. There were three men in the car—the one next to the driver leaned out. His black eyes searched the bus. He spoke in a husky voice, to the driver.

"Seen a yellow roadster on the road, Buddy?"

The driver shook his head. "Nothin' but trucks—I've seen," he returned. "What's up—bank bust?"

The man beside the driver turned his eyes toward the one in the clerical attire. He muttered something the driver of the bus failed to get. Then he jerked his head away. He spoke to the car driver in a low tone. The black machine moved forward, picked up speed rapidly.

The bus driver smiled toward the minister. He shook his head slowly.

"Tough crowd—the road dicks!" he stated. "Ain't very sociable."

The clerical man did not speak. His gray eyes flickered slightly. The bus driver shifted—the bus rattled into motion. The other car had vanished with a low hum into the fog ahead. Its siren wail came back on the wind, rapidly growing distant.

The bus driver was ahead of schedule. He always was, in this early run. No traffic to hold him up. He drove slowly. Sometimes passengers complained, but the minister said nothing. The holy men were like the bulls, the bus driver thought—not very sociable.

It had been a big night—and the driver was weary. He dozed a bit at the wheel. He didn't exactly doze, but he wasn't as alert as he might have been. The curve of the road that marked the approach to the South Side flying field snapped him out of it. It was a sharp turn—a fellow had to be on the job.

The wail of the police car's siren had ceased to sound. The bus driver suddenly wondered how far the minister was going. It was muddy along the edge of the road near the Field; if the clerical one was getting off he could find a dry spot. He turned slowly in the seat. Then he swore. The bus was empty. His passenger had departed.

The driver stopped the bus. He climbed down from the seat, stared back along the road. Wisps of early morning fog prevented him from seeing more than a hundred yards. The minister was not in sight. The bus driver swore again. A cheap sport, the minister was. Fares were collected as the passengers departed. A dead beat.

The driver climbed slowly back into the driver's seat. He twisted around, stared back at the seat the minister had occupied. Something caught his eyes. Something slightly crumpled, greenish in color. A bill—a crumpled bill.

Ten seconds later the bus driver stood staring down at a five dollar bill. His eyes held an expression of awe. The minister had left a five dollar bill—and had vanished while the bus was in motion.

The bus driver returned to his seat. He suddenly remembered the bulls in the black car. They had been looking for somebody. But, the minister—

"It's all wrong!" the driver muttered grimly. "The church guys don't hand out coin—not that way. That bird—he wasn't no pulpit spieler! He had a frozen face—"

The bus driver shook his head slowly. But he shoved the bill in his pocket—and drove on. The bulls' loss had been his gain.

O'LEARY HAD THE south gate of the Field. He stood up when he saw the dark-frocked figure coming along, close to the wire fence that enclosed the Field. South Side had thousands of dollars' worth of ships in the hangars. It was an organized field—and it was well guarded. O'Leary moved toward the gate. His eyes widened—he stepped to one side.

"Mr. Greer!" he muttered. "I didn't recognize you in—"

"Call the main gate, O'Leary." Gary Greer's voice was hard, almost monotonous in tone. "Tell them no one is to get into the Field—until I give the word. And that includes—the police."

O'Leary nodded. He stepped into the small house just inside the gate. He called Mardigan, and repeated Gary's words. When he stepped outside again Gary was moving toward the A hangar. He was moving swiftly, his lean body erect.

"God!" O'Leary muttered thickly. "He's taking it hard. What a face!"

O'Leary was right. And O'Leary was wrong. Gary Greer had suffered—his face showed that. But the watchman missed out on his tense. Gary Greer wasn't "taking" it hard. It was over, finished. Arrangements had been made. Funeral arrangements. Civic affairs he didn't care about. That would be, in Center

City, a mockery. His father had been rubbed out by desperate men, rotten politics. Now let them praise the dead man. He would not be present to hear them, to read what they said—in a rotten press.

Inside the A hangar Gary Greer did several things swiftly. He got rid of the clerical collar, got into a suit of overalls—flying overalls. Crew men came toward him. He read it in their faces—sympathy. And he didn't want that. He spoke quietly, without expression.

"I want the Wasp—want to get off in thirty minutes. Load her all the way. I'm flying—westward."

He turned away. The crew men moved toward the little ship that Gary had always flown. Only one of them remained behind. Jess Condon, who had been at the Field since the first dead-line had been chalked out. He spoke haltingly.

"I'm—sorry, Gary. You know how I feel. If you ever need—"

Gary Greer interrupted. He spoke in a very low tone.

"It's all right, Jess. I'm going away. It's all right."

Jess Condon turned away from Gary. He moved toward the little ship at one end of the hangar. Gary watched him go. If he needed help—Jess Condon would see him through to the limit. And there was Pete Ranning, and Vance Edger. And yet, numbers could only hurt. Sanford Greer had been put on the spot, rubbed out. Numbers had only made certain a death. Many bullets of different caliber made for confusion.

Sanford Greer had died alone. And one gangster had not spilled lead at Gary's father. For that—the gangster had died. The other killer had seen to that. But his lips had uttered names, before death had taken the red from them. And Gary Greer would never forget those names—killer names. He didn't need help. That would only expose his friends. It was a double battle—from now until the time when five names would cease to have any importance. A battle against gangsters—and a fight against those who enforced Center City laws. Laws that were often bitter, twisted things that served the gangsters' employers' interests.

Gary moved toward the small room at one end of the hangar. The door was locked—this was his room. He used a key, entered. From the 'chute closet he took a Russel lobe-type. It was the smallest 'chute made. A minimum of safety. He placed it carefully inside of a brown leather suit-case. He selected helmet and goggles. At a small desk he wrote a note. It was addressed to a name he loved. A woman's name.

His face was twisted as he wrote the words. They would hurt, punish. But they would count. They would mean things. Because of them it might be that he could hurt, punish. Law wrote that he should not. Instinct told him that he should. He thought of the war. He had been given guns—two prop-synchronized, battering machine-guns. He had been told to kill, *ordered* to kill. Why? He had never been quite sure. There was a medal—he got it from the desk drawer, placed it on top of the envelope in which he had put the note to the woman's name.

The medal had been praise. Honor. It had been given him because he had killed. He had won—the others had lost. And now five men had murdered one man. Center City law was rotten. Gangster law ruled. Sanford Greer had been honest, fair. He had died in the mud of a street gutter. For that— five names would be washed out. The law said that this was not right. But the Center City law enforcers decreed that those other violators of the law should not be hunted out and punished. And Gary would try alone.

The telephone bell rang. He lifted the receiver, listened.

It was Pete Ranning, at the main gate. Police were there; they wanted to see Gary Greer. They had important news. But Pete had not known that Gary was at the Field. What was he to do?

"I'm *not* here," Gary stated in a steady voice. "Tell them that. Don't let them in. They haven't a warrant—they can't get in. That is, not according to the law. If they *do* get in—call me. Clear?"

There were things in the office to be put in order. Pete would have charge of the Field. Five minutes passed—the phone bell rang again. It was Pete; the officers were insistent. They were sure Gary was inside. He would be interested in the news. It was important.

"I'm not here," Gary stated quietly. "Have them kept out—then come over to the A. hangar. I'm flying out, Pete. That's all."

He worked on. He had thought, leaving the house an hour earlier, of driving to the Field in his yellow roadster. He had started out in it. But that had been foolishness. Soapy Tyler had died at Eight Fourteen River Street. Soapy had given him names. And only a crashing fall on the battered stairs had saved Gary from bullet death. A man with a crooked elbow had hummed off key, after that fall. But no body had been found—Gary had not been riddled by bullets as his father had been. And now—the gangsters knew that.

These things Gary had thought about, driving a few blocks in the yellow roadster. And he had changed his plans. A cleric's collar was not enough. He had abandoned the roadster.

Killers—riding in the car with the red light and the wailing siren—a police car. Killers—stopping a bus—and making a mistake. A natural mistake, perhaps—he was not as well known as his father had been. But, in another three hours—

Gary Greer's lean face was turned toward the door. There was a light tap. He called—Pete Ranning came in.

"They're outside," he stated. "Sore as the devil. But the gate's closed. They only half believe you aren't here. And they swear it's important."

"Death—" Gary said in a dull tone "—is always important."

He saw Pete's eyes widen. Ranning started to talk, started to sympathize. Gary cut in, speaking very quietly.

"I'm flying westward, Pete. You have the Field on your hands—until I return. Run it as it's always been run. Walter Garon is handling money matters. If you need money—see him. What you don't need—bank. You have a free hand."

He was conscious of the fear in Pete's eyes. He knew what Pete was thinking. Another who must be hurt. He spoke again.

"A note," he said, and gestured toward it and the medal. "It's for Miss Rawlings. When she calls—tell her it's here. Don't mail it. I think—she'll come for it."

He saw the twisted expression on Pete's face. He smiled, shook his head.

"Don't figure it wrong, Pete. I'm taking a trip. The trip hasn't an address. I want to rest—my nerves."

He stopped. Pete Ranning was watching him closely. For the first time since Sanford Greer had been battered down into the gutter of a mean Center City street—Gary jested. It was a terrible jest.

"I've been given the names of some friends, Pete—I want to look them up. It may be the sort of medicine I need."

Pete Ranning's blue eyes were narrowed on Gary's gray ones.

"You have plenty of friends *here*, Gary," he reminded quietly. "Why not put off the trip for a while?"

Gary shook his head. "It's important," he stated quietly, and saw Pete start at his reiteration of the word used by those outside in the black car. "Let's go out to the ship. She must be ready."

They went out. Gary sensed that Pete was watching him closely. Pete and the girl—this would hurt them most. Walter Garon was a business man. He would feel it, but he wouldn't be hurt deeply.

The Wasp, her rotary engine humming, was on the dead-line near the hangar. The ground crew were working around her. Gary fixed his suitcase in the special compartment built just back of the cockpit. Pete spoke in a grim tone.

"You'll want a 'chute, Gary."

Gary nodded. He smiled at Pete. One of the ground-crew men went back into the hangar.

"Almost forgot it, Pete," Gary stated. "Of course—I want a 'chute."

He stared up at the sky to the west of the Field. It was gray— there were dark clouds high in the air. He spoke to Pete again.

"I'm heading for Pittsburgh, Pete," he said slowly. "Any weather out that way?"

Ranning spoke in a low tone. "It'll be bad over the mountains, Gary. Cut the trip. Stick with us here. You'll pull out of this. We all know how you must feel. It's getting late in the season—you may run into sleet or snow. Pass it up and—"

"She's a good ship—" Gary interrupted. "Weather doesn't mean much to a good ship, Pete."

But he knew that Ranning was seeing through his words. He knew he was hurting. Breiting came out from the hangar with an Irving 'chute pack. He gave it to Pete Ranning.

"You packed her yourself," he stated.

Pete nodded. He turned toward Gary, helped him get into the 'chute harness. The throttled down nimble of the Wasp's rotary engine was a steady beat in Gary's ears. He smiled at Pete—it was a grim smile.

"All right, Pete—keep things moving. Pretty soon—I'll drop down out of the sky."

Pete stared at him. "Out of the sky!" he muttered. "Better wing down at Dale Field, Gary, before you get altitude over the mountains. They'll have the latest weather reports there—"

Gary Greer gripped Pete's right hand. His face was almost expressionless.

"A good idea, Pete—and when I get off—let the police in, if they still insist. Maybe they're right—maybe it is important!"

He climbed into the tiny cockpit of the little ship. He waved to the ground-crew men as the wheel blocks were pulled out. But he didn't turn his head toward Pete Ranning again, as he shoved the throttle forward. The little ship started to roll. A gust of wind tilted a wing, but Gary corrected for it instantly. He zoomed her off the earth, then leveled, picked up speed. Slowly he climbed the Wasp toward the west.

Gary Greer didn't look over the side toward the main gate. A faint smile played about his tight-pressed lips. A killer car was at the gate—a borrowed police car. But the killers had slipped up. They had made a mistake. He had seen only one of them. A face without a name. And he was after names. He relaxed in the cockpit, held the little ship in a steady climb. Her engine roar was steady; she was tuned for a long flight. But there would be no long flight. Never again—for this particular ship. She had a mission to perform. She had a task. A name was to be dropped—*out of the sky.*

IT WAS ALMOST noon. The weather was bad, and rapidly growing worse. Clouds were moving swiftly at ten thousand, but ahead, westward, they were much lower. The mountains were coming into sight—some of them were tinged with white. The first snow of the coming winter season. A lightning storm, back in Center City, not many hours ago. Snow on the mountains. A nasty, gusty wind.

Gary Greer wiped a splatter of oil from his goggle-glass. His arms were tired—and not from gripping the stick. For the last hour he had been working with the 'chutes—and it was cramped, one-armed work. There had been no chance to fly the little plane with the stick between his knees. The air was too tough for that. And it had been hard work, changing 'chutes in the air.

But he was sky-riding now with the small lobe 'chute attached to his body. The suitcase he had tossed over the side, while winging over a desolate spot. For the last half hour he had been doing things with the Irving 'chute that Pete Ranning had helped strap about his body. He had ripped several of the shroud lines loose—he had twisted the belt, torn several buckles loose. It had not been an easy job. And it was not yet completed. The Wasp would have her part to do.

Nosing the ship down slightly, he stared at the country below. It was rugged country; the first slopes of the Allegheny mountains were running toward the plane. A town lay over to the southward, gray and sprawled along a slope. Mining town, he decided. Beyond the town the country was desolate, pine covered, rough.

The air washed back by the propeller was becoming colder. Fuel was getting low—he had roared her at high speed all of the distance. And she was a small ship. The time for action was approaching. At seven thousand feet he leveled her off again. He banked her slightly to the northward.

The mountains ahead—the peaks of them—were spotted with snow. There was heavy pine covering them. Gary shook his head slowly. It mattered a lot—and yet it did not matter. He had cared so much for S.G. that there was only a dull edge to danger. But he would try—would try hard enough to make it. It was his only chance. The plans were carefully made—he could guess how the thing would be taken.

For fifteen minutes he roared the ship onward. Then he picked out the town. It was a tiny town, and he mapped it as Larnville. A coal miners' town, on the west slope of a fairly high mountain. There was a valley, fairly wide, running northward for many miles. In the valley was a stream. The silver color wound from the town, northward. To the west of the stream there were no other towns that he could see. The country was bad—thickly pined, very rugged.

Bad—and yet good. He banked the little ship away from the town, to the north of it. He roared her over the stream. Gray clouds seemed lower to the southward. The town was obscured by a squall of rain now. Cold rain. The air was bad, bumpy. A peak ahead was snow covered.

Gary nodded his head slowly. The wind was from the west. He had almost seven thousand feet of altitude. He didn't need that much. Slowly he moved the stick forward, wiped from his goggle-glass another splattering of oil. Then he snapped the safety-belt buckle loose. And he let the ship glide with her engine throttled down until she had dropped to three thousand feet.

At that altitude he circled the sky perhaps a half dozen times. His keen gray eyes searched the slopes below. Rock and pine—no mountain shacks, no houses. And perhaps two miles to the eastward was the valley with the stream in it. Slowly he nodded his head.

"This is—the spot!" he muttered. "Good as—any!"

He nosed the ship out of the bank, held her for several seconds in a mild glide. Then he straightened in the cockpit. With his right hand he jerked the rip cord of the Irving 'chute, now held inside the cockpit. The canvas snapped open—Gary released his grip on the stick. With both hands he flung the loosely folded 'chute at the whirling prop.

For a split second he thought the back wash would stop the half opened 'chute from hitting the prop. It almost did—but he had put strength in the toss. There was a crackling as the duralumin prop battered the 'chute fabric back.

The material twisted about the struts of the left wing tip. The ship was shrilling downward now. Gary swayed in the cockpit—then flung himself outward, to the left side. His right leg struck the fuselage sharply. He plunged downward, his right hand fumbling for the rip-cord of the lobe 'chute, over his left thigh. His fingers touched it.

He was somersaulting now—he got a glimpse of the plane, plunging downward perhaps fifty feet distant. There was very little sensation. He closed his eyes—jerked the rip-cord ring.

The silk of the 'chute crackled as it spread above him. The

harness tightened over his flying suit. He was drifting now—the silk spread swaying in the wind, above his body. He sucked in a great gulp of air, stared downward.

He saw the Wasp, curving slightly, battering down against the green of pines. The trees were very thick where the ship was plunging. There was a booming crash. And almost instantly a great red ball of fire danced upward. The ship had struck—her gas tank had exploded.

Gary twisted around in the harness. He was drifting perhaps a thousand feet above the slope of a mountain, but already the strong wind was pulling the silk spread back toward the valley—and the silver stream of water.

He let the 'chute drift without making any attempt to work with the shroud lines. Too much altitude yet—to begin worrying about the landing. That was the great danger now. Seventeen feet a second—that would be the approximate speed of his drop. If he were battered into a pine, slashed down across the jagged boulders below—

He twisted in the harness again, stared downward and westward. The ball of fire was not in evidence, but he could see red flames licking up from the pines. They wouldn't last long—everything was green and wet. And the ship would burn to a skeleton quickly enough. But there would be enough left; there was little chance that the plane would not be found—in the air search that would follow soon enough.

A thousand feet above the earth a strong cross current ripped at the silk-spread above. It slanted the silk sharply; Gary swung back and forth like a pendulum in the harness. He twisted his head—stared toward the spot where he would drop. The valley was a good mile distant—he guessed that he'd strike earth a half mile from it, and on the down slope of the mountain into which the Wasp had crashed.

There was heavy pine growing below, and in the path of the drifting 'chute. But there were occasional clearings, and spots covered by jagged rock. The latter would be the most dangerous—with a bad drag to be fought, after the drop to earth.

Five hundred feet above the slope Gary Greer spotted a clearing in the pine. There was a fairly steep cliff—below it a stretch covered by smaller growth and huge boulders. Below the stretch, so far as Gary could see, was thick pine.

The stretch was his best chance. Reaching up, he pulled down on the shroud lines slanting toward the harness from the 'chute silk—at the curve that was the leading edge of the 'chute.

Instantly he was slipping sharply toward the cleared stretch—and losing altitude rapidly. The rocky sides of the cliff seemed to shoot up at him. He released his grip on the shrouds as his body slanted down past the cliff's edge. The slope with the small growth was less than fifty feet below him now. But the wind was strong. He was forced to slip the 'chute again.

Ten feet above the ground—he released his grip on the shroud lines for the second time. The pulled-down silk filled with air—his rapid drop was checked. He swung his body outward, kicking his feet.

A jagged boulder flashed beneath him. And then he struck!

Almost instantly he was jerked over on his face—there was a battering blow on the side of his head. He fought off a wave of blackness—pulled desperately down on the shroud lines. As the silk collapsed he was dragged down the slope. Branches of shrubbery tore across the skin of his face—he closed his eyes, kept pulling down on the shroud lines.

And then there was no more drag. The fabric of the silk had ripped, collapsed—in the shrubbery, on the rock of the small stretch. He was down—and he was alive!

For several minutes he lay motionless. Then, slowly, he got to his feet, got loose from the 'chute harness. He limped around a bit. He lighted a cigarette. Far in the distance he heard the whistle of a locomotive. It came to him very faintly. His left side ached; his face was a mass of red. But he was down—*out of the sky*.

And he was dead. The skeleton of the Wasp. Something would be left of the 'chute—the Irving 'chute. The buckles would not burn. And the 'chute was ripped by the propeller—the harness was twisted, torn. They would not find his body.

They would reason as he wanted them to reason. That is, unless somewhere along the line he had slipped up. He did not see where. The burned wreckage of a plane—a twisted, broken 'chute—no body. Something had gone wrong in the air. The engine had failed. He had jumped. The 'chute had tangled with some part of the falling plane. His body had ripped from the harness—crashed down into the thick growth of towering pine. Virgin growth, probably. What chances of finding what remained?

Very little. They would search, of course. Those he had been forced to hurt would see to that. Pete Ranning. Joyce Rawlings. But they would find nothing more than he had planted—planted from the sky.

There was work to be done yet. He would pack the 'chute silk, bury it. He would make sure that no torn pieces remained in the growth, on rocks. He would work over his footprints. Searchers might come this way. Down in the valley he would bury his flying suit. For the present he would keep his helmet and goggles. When it grew dark he should be near the town he had seen. It was only a matter of following the stream.

He would take the train for some other town. There he would buy clothes—and wait. In his money belt was sufficient funds for a long time. But he did not plan to stay away from Center City a long time. The headlines would come first. Headlines in the Center City papers. If for no other reason than the murder of his father, the crash of Gary Greer's plane would be first class news. Many people would see the headlines. Many names would learn of another name—*out of the sky.*

Five of the names would count big. Five killers would laugh or sneer. Five men would believe that the son of the man they had murdered was dead. Gary Greer smiled, raised a red-streaked hand to a red-streaked face. This was the real beginning. Now he could fight back—because he had ceased to exist.

CENTER CITY LAY dripping under a gray fog. There was the fog—and there was the smoke slowly spreading under the moisture weight, slowly moving across the black water of White River. Up in the editorial room of the *Gazette* a red-headed chap was writing "sticks." Unimportant, five-line paragraphs—under a small-type "head." The red-headed one smoked a cigarette as he wrote. He looked bored. A copy-reader called over to him from the raised platform on which was the copy-readers' long desk. It was nearing dead-line time.

"What you got, Ed? Anything?"

The red-headed one shook his head. He didn't raise his eyes from the battered typewriter.

"Nothing much. Follow up on the Greer plane crash—searchers called off after a week of it. No find. And a stick for 'Babe' Lewis. The police released him today. His alibi for the East End Trust stick-up was good enough. That's all."

The copy-reader yawned. The Babe always had good alibis—and the Greer stuff was dead. Both items could go over the dead-line. One was cheap stuff, the other was old stuff. They'd make the second morning edition, be on the streets by one o'clock. Not important enough for the "bull-dog," eleven-thirty paper. They'd go as fillers, back on page ten, at that. The copy-reader yawned again. He wished he'd taken that job doing a column out in Kansas City. At this time of night everything was slow—and he always wished the same wish.

The red-headed reporter got slowly to his feet and moved toward a dirty window. On his way he tossed the two sticks on the copy-readers' desk. He lighted another pill from the stub of the one between his lips. He looked out into the night.

"She's thick!" he muttered. "A hell of a good night for a murder—over on River Street."

The copy-reader grunted, glancing down at the name—Gary Greer. He was trying to get something on the red-headed one, but there wasn't an "a" in the last name, at that. So he just yawned and wrote out a head—*Plane Search Off.* Then he remembered what the one at the window had said.

"The *night's* all right for a kill," he muttered toward the dirty window, "but they don't mean anything—around River Street. Cheap stuff."

The red-headed one nodded his head, grunted. Nothing meant much to him. He'd been a reporter for three years. Everything was old.

RIVER STREET WAS a gray canyon, the walls of which were not tall. Warehouses, terminals, docks—on one side. Cheap, ill-smelling rooming-houses on the other. A cobbled street, with heavy trucking in the day. Not so much at night. It was one-thirty.

"Sailor" Gleason polished glasses back of the small bar in his speakeasy opposite the Mallard dock. The Sailor had never been on a boat except the time he'd gotten drunk and fallen asleep in a pile of rope on the tug-boat *Hattie H.* A brother had been a sailor, and from him Gleason had acquired many wild tales. He had also picked up a swagger that was often mistaken for sea-legs. Around River Street Gleason was considered a tough character. He was big, and there was strength in his arms. And hair on his chest. Actually he was a coward. So now he polished glasses and fawned on one he feared.

"The bulls can't hang on to you, Babe," he mouthed. "No, sir! They ain't got the brains to do *that* little thing!"

"Babe" Lewis sat at a small, dirty table in a corner of the room. It was a dark corner, and Babe liked it dark. He was small, dark-eyed. His right hand he kept in the right-hand pocket of a soiled trench-coat. Several glasses were on the table—the Babe had had companions. Now he sat alone. His reaction to the Sailor's compliment was not a cheerful one. The Babe scowled.

A battered clock at one end of the room attracted his attention. He swore harshly, got to his feet. The Sailor grinned at him. Gleason was dumb—he went right on talking.

"Charlie's frail was around earlier," he stated. "She'd said you was goin' to be in the clear pretty quick."

Babe Lewis stiffened. He turned his body toward the Sailor.

There was an expression on his face that Gleason didn't expect. The Babe spoke.

"You talk too much, Sailor!" he muttered. "Lay off that stuff about Charlie's moll, see?"

The Sailor nodded his head. There was a blank expression in his eyes.

"I didn't mean nothin', Babe," he stated. "I didn't know you was—" He checked himself. The door of the speakeasy opened slowly. A man entered. The Babe was standing near a wall; he leaned against it now—watched the newcomer closely. The Sailor watched him, too. The man was lean, his face was very pale. He wore rough clothing, walked with a slight stoop. Almost immediately his back was turned to Babe Lewis; he moved toward the bar.

"Beer!" he muttered in a hoarse voice.

Sailor Gleason stopped polishing the glasses. He smiled slightly.

"It takes coin, Mac," he stated.

The newcomer tossed a dime down on the bar. Gleason reached for a beer glass. The glass was the real thing—a relic of better days. The beer was not. He slid it across the wet board toward his customer.

Babe Lewis moved toward the door. Sailor Gleason called out to him.

"Pleasant dreams, Babe!"

Lewis failed to reply. He went out into the fog. The customer downed the beer in one drink. It was sickening stuff. He spoke in a husky voice to the man back of the bar.

"That Babe Lewis?"

Sailor Gleason grinned. "You ain't a dick, are you?" he asked.

"The Babe's just out of the jail house. It ain't tight enough to hold him."

The one at the bar smiled faintly. He turned away from the bar. The Sailor swore with feeling.

"The devil help the dick that runs into Babe Lewis tonight!" he muttered.

The customer was moving toward the door of the speakeasy. Sailor Gleason watched him go out. It was a new face, and new faces didn't appear often in his place. Only when they transferred the dicks around. And somehow, it was a face Sailor Gleason couldn't forget. The customer had almost a mask. He smiled—yet there was little expression. He smiled with his lips. And his lips were white, thin.

The door of the speakeasy closed back of Gary Greer. He stood for a few seconds, looking to his left, listening. The figure of Babe Lewis had vanished into the fog. But Gary could hear the muffled footfalls. He followed along the broken paving of the street by the river.

He was very calm. A small item in a paper, very near another small item that concerned him—and he had traced a name. It hadn't been luck. For over an hour he had been along River Street. He had never seen Lewis before. He had been tracing a name. Now he was following a name. A killer name.

Ahead was a street lamp. The fog almost smothered a weak light. A figure stood near the lamp, bent over. A match scraped; there was a faint flare. Smoke mingled with the fog as Babe Lewis exhaled. Gary Greer walked up close to the other man. He was within five feet of him when the Babe swung around. A corner of his coat bulged out toward Gary. His eyes were narrowed on Gary's.

Gary Greer smiled faintly. He spoke in a low, shaky tone. "Got a smoke, Babe?"

Lewis straightened. His eyes were little slits, searching Gary's lean, white face—searching his gray eyes.

"I don't get you," he muttered slowly. "An' I ain't got a smoke."

Gary Greer nodded his head. Both his hands were in sight—he dropped one into the left pocket of his coat now. He saw the Babe's right arm become tense. He withdrew his hand; in his right fingers was the stub of a cigarette. He put it between his lips.

"Got a light, Babe?" he muttered.

Lewis used his left-hand fingers to take the newly lighted cigarette from between his thick lips. He kept his right hand buried in a pocket of his trench coat. Gary touched an end of his stub to the other man's cigarette. He stepped back a little.

"Thanks, Babe," he breathed softly. "Where's Sal these days?"

He saw the Babe's eyes widen. The man drew in his breath sharply.

"Who in hell—" he muttered—"are you?"

Gary smiled with his lips. "I'm Greer!" he said slowly, clearly. "Gary Greer!"

Babe Lewis stared at him. Then he grinned. It was a slow-spreading grin. It made the gangster's face hideous. He chuckled.

"Sure! Sure you are, Mac!" he muttered. "An' *me*—I'm Sal the Dude! Say—the sniff stuff ain't so good in—"

He checked himself. The white faced one who stood before him had ceased to smile. His body was rocking from side to side, swaying. The Babe stared at him.

"Hell!" he muttered. "Get a grip on yourself, Mac—you're

wobblin' all over—"

He checked his words again. The white-faced one had dropped to his knees. He was directly in front of Babe Lewis now. His right hand was fumbling at his throat; he seemed to be having trouble breathing. The Babe swore again. A coker—passing out right beside him. Not so good.

"Lay off, Mac!" he muttered. "Pull yourself up and go find a flop. Get on your dogs—"

He stopped. The white-faced one was pitching forward. The Babe took a step forward. He reached out with both hands. But they never touched the swaying body. The white-faced one suddenly stiffened. His right hand moved downward, into a pocket. Cloth came up—there was a blunt point to it.

Babe Lewis cried out fiercely. His own right hand dropped. And then his body jerked—he swore hoarsely, chokingly. The white-faced one's right arm was jerking, too. Sound cut through the deadening blanket of the fog. Gun sound. Maxim-silencer sound. The Babe's right hand never got a grip on his gun. He slumped to his knees, swayed. His eyes were wide, staring up at the eyes of Gary Greer. He saw something, cried out—

"Greer—for God's sake—stop that—"

Gary Greer turned away. He walked shakily several feet. Mechanically he slipped his Maxim-silenced gun back into a coat pocket. His eyes held a tortured expression. He turned.

Babe Lewis had recognized him. He had smiled—smiled as Lewis was dying. But they had laughed. Had Lewis, in those last seconds, before his body had slumped down into the wet gutter beneath the street light, recognized him? Had the gangster caught a flashing resemblance. Gary thought so.

Voices came to him—perhaps a block away. He heard the

patter of running feet. Police. The gangster's police. People. Enemies—one way or the other. He stared down at the motionless form of Babe Lewis. Then he moved swiftly away from the voices, the sound of running footfalls. The fog obliterated him.

A chance? No, he had given Lewis little chance. But he had looked into the gangster's eyes. He had seen the eyes of one of his father's killers. One. There were four others. It had been hard—that smile. It had been hard—that kill. But Lewis had killed more than once. And he had killed honest men, decent men. He had murdered for gain.

Gary Greer paused. He listened. Back of him a police whistle shrilled. The fog gave it a strange detached sound. Gary moved on again, turning away from the river, toward the town. He remembered three words Lewis had uttered—"Sal *the Dude.*" That would help. It clarified a name. And now—he was a killer.

An owl taxi rounded a corner, two blocks from the river. Gary hailed the driver, slipped inside. He gave the address of a cheap rooming-house, across the town. He relaxed in the seat. Each night he had heard the mail ships—winging over the roof of the cheap house, from his own field. From a dead man's field!

He lighted a cigarette. The streets were wet, glistening. On such a night—only there had been greater fury—Sanford Greer had been battered out of things. And now one name was done, scrawled off the list. One name—out of five. And Lewis had known—had known before he had died. He had seen the eyes of a dead man—looking from the eyes of one he thought dead. He had cried for mercy—as S.G. had never done.

Gary Greer closed his eyes. His body rocked with the cab.

His face was expressionless. The cab turned a corner—an electric light sign conquered the fog, ahead. *Gazette.* Up in the editorial room a red-headed reporter had a phone receiver to his head. He listened, then hung up.

"Hell!" he muttered. "I got my River Street murder, at that. The Babe's out, Joe. Can you beat it?"

The copy-reader grunted. He'd been on the desk fourteen years. Babe Lewis finished off. Good for half a column—but not big news. Too cheap.

"Yeah?" he called back to the reporter. "About time. Dig his past out of the morgue, Ed. And you might mention that it was suspected he was in on the Greer spotting. He probably wasn't—but what the hell!"

3

The Pay-Off

"FIFTY MILE" LISEMAN stood a few feet away from Pete Ranning and smiled cheerfully with his cherub-like face. Jack Liseman was short and rather insignificant in appearance. He had wide, round eyes, blue in color. His prefaced title had been derived from the fact that Liseman's alibis varied little. Whenever the police brought him in as a suspect he always proved that he had been fifty miles or more distant, at the time the crime had been committed. His thin lips moved; he spoke in a rather high-pitched tone.

"Someone told me you had hangar space for rent at this field, Mr. Ranning. I got a ship I'd like to keep here. Don't use it much—it's an old Standard, built over. My name's Liseman."

Liseman stopped. There was a questioning expression in his wide eyes. Pete Ranning smiled faintly. He marked the man as one unfamiliar with planes. The use of the word "it" betrayed unfamiliarity. And the ship wasn't to be used much.

"Guess we can park her, Mr. Liseman," Ranning said slowly. "How's she powered?"

The little man stared blankly at Pete. Then he laughed a sort of nervous laugh.

"How's she powered?" he muttered. "You mean—oh, there's a Curtiss engine—"

Pete nodded. "I'll turn you over to the hangar superintendent," he stated. "You can look over what we've got. At the north end—the space is. Anything that goes wrong—any complaints—look me up, Mr. Liseman."

The little man smiled. He was very much amused, and trying a little not to show that fact. He was renting ship space at the South Side airport. The Greer airport. That is, it *had* been Gary Greer's.

"Everything'll be all right, sure," Fifty Mile stated. "This used to be run by Greer, didn't it?"

Pete Ranning's face showed no expression. A week ago it would have twitched nervously at such a question. But he had steeled himself, was forcing himself to accept things as they were.

"Yes," he replied slowly, and turned toward his desk. He picked up a phone, called the hangar superintendent. The drone of ships in the sky came into the room. Fifty Mile lighted a cigarette.

"Too bad about Greer—the younger one," he said slowly. "Took his old man's death pretty hard, I guess. He was—"

"What sort of a license have you got for the Standard?" Pete cut in sharply.

Liseman grinned. "None," he replied. "I've got a friend who is a pilot—I just ride up for my"—he hesitated, grinned more broadly—"health. Steadies my nerves. I'm in the shipping business."

Pete Ranning dropped his eyes to some papers on his desk. There was something about the little man that bothered him. His tone of voice. The way he said things. And he seemed amused.

Jansen came in, Pete introduced the two men, told the hangar superintendent what Liseman wanted. The two went out. Pete made a note on a slip of paper. He'd keep his eyes on the Standard that Liseman had flown in, if the hangar space was rented. There was something about the man he didn't like.

He worked over plane details for several minutes, and then the door of his office opened slowly. A man entered; the door was closed back of him. Pete Ranning sat up straight in his chair. It was unusual for those he didn't know to get past the office boy. The man moved toward him with a slight limp. His head was held low; he raised it suddenly.

Pete Ranning stared at the man. The face was a pasty white—the corners of the lips, also colorless, were turned downward. There was no expression in the eyes, which were gray. And yet, there was something familiar—

"Steady, Pete—keep your voice low. It's—Gary."

Pete Ranning sucked in his breath sharply. He got to his feet. Gary Greer was smiling, but the smile was mocking, hideous. The make-up of his lips, his whitened face—made it that way. It wasn't intended to be hideous. Pete stood back of the desk, trying to speak.

"Gary!" he muttered, finally. "You didn't go down—"

He broke off, dropped into the chair. Gary Greer stood motionless, spoke in a low tone.

"My name's Jones, Pete. I deal in junk, scrap—get it? I'm here to see if you've got stuff at the field I can use in my yard. That clear?"

Ranning was getting control of himself. He nodded his head, still staring at Gary Greer. He got to his feet, came around the desk. They shook hands. Pete swore softly.

"God—what a jolt!" He was breathing heavily. "A damn fine one, Gary! It's great—"

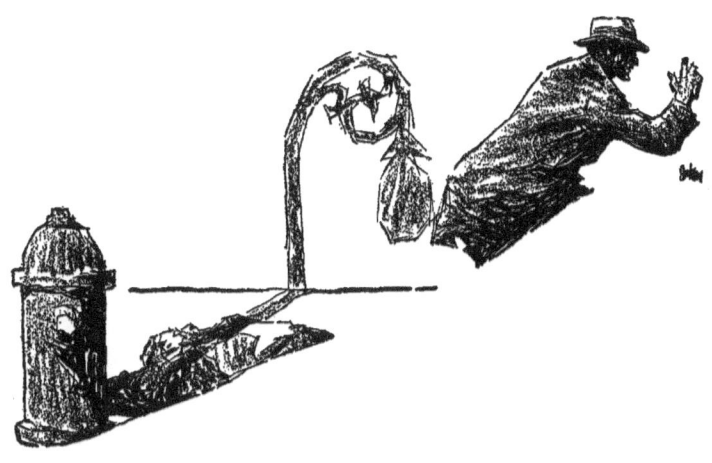

"Forget that name!" Gary's voice was low, sharp. "I'm Jones—
dealer in junk, scrap! Don't miss that—"

"Right." Pete smiled faintly. "But how the devil did you—"

"Extra 'chute in my luggage. Let the ship crash—and got
loose. And Pete—you're the only soul alive that knows—*I'm*
alive. And you must *forget* it!"

Pete Ranning was calmer now. He looked Gary in the eyes.
"All right, Jones," he said slowly. "But—why?"

"You know this thing"—Gary spoke quietly—"because I
need you. I need a ship—and money. The reason? You don't get
that, Pete. Just stick with me—and don't make a slip. How's
Joyce—taking it?"

Pete shook his head. "Pretty hard—now," he said slowly. "At
first—she didn't believe. She wouldn't give up. Said they hadn't
found your body. But in the last few days—"

Pete shrugged his shoulders. Gary's face twisted; he turned
away from his friend. When he faced him again there was no
expression in his eyes. He spoke in a low tone.

"I've got things to do, Pete. They *may* not take long. They may take long. I'd give a lot to let Joyce know. You know that. But—it can't be. Not until—"

He broke off abruptly. Pete Ranning nodded his head. His blue eyes were on the gray ones of the man he had failed to recognize, until he had heard a voice. But he had sensed the familiarity with the man he had thought dead. He spoke quietly.

"Anything I can do, Gary—*anything*. I guess you know that."

Gary smiled again. He spoke in almost a whisper.

"I've seen it in a mirror, Pete—this smile. But you know it isn't meant that way—not for you."

He reached into a pocket of his cheap suit. It was dark in color, stained. The cuffs of the trousers were frayed. He lighted a cigarette. Pete filled his pipe, his hands shaking a little. Gary said:

"I want a Ryan engine mounted in that Greer Special we worked on a few months ago, Pete. I'll need the plane in twelve hours. You can take her off, and set her down at the place I designate. And I'll need more money. You can draw it—"

The phone bell rang. Pete lifted the receiver. He stiffened, his eyes narrowed on Gary's face. And Gary's body jerked as he distinguished the voice, distorted as it was in the transmission. Joyce Rawlings' voice!

Pete Ranning's eyes were on Gary's. The owner of the South Side Field shook his head slowly. His lips were pressed tightly together. The voice coming through the wire died.

"I'm sorry, Joyce"—Pete was trying to keep his voice level— "but there isn't anything new. Not a thing."

Gary Greer smiled. It would have been a grim smile, except for the cleverly penciled lip lines. Joyce Rawlings—the one girl in the world that he loved, talking over the phone about him!

"I guess—we've *got* to believe it, Joyce." Pete's voice was husky. "But if anything turns up—"

Pete broke off. The girl spoke for several seconds more. Gary turned away, moved toward a window of the Administration Building that faced out upon the Field. But he did not go up to the window. He watched a plane take off gracefully, curve up toward the sky. Then Pete spoke again.

"It was hard to do that, Gary—can't you tell her—some way?"

Gary's fingers were clenched at his sides. He shook his head. His voice was very steady.

"My name's Jones, Pete. Try and get that clear. Do you think this is—fun—for me? It isn't. It's just a job, Pete—a nasty job. But it's got—*to be done!*"

Pete Ranning smiled faintly. "All right, Jones—" His voice was changed—"and if you want to look around—"

Gary faced his friend. He listened for several seconds, listened to dying footfalls in the corridor beyond the office.

"A man came out of here—with Jansen—as I came in," he said in a very low voice. "What was—his name?"

"Liseman," Pete said slowly. "It seems a little familiar—think I've seen it in print. But I can't place it."

Gary Greer stood very still. His gray eyes were narrowed. Pete saw for the first time that the goggle scar over his left eye—a thin red line—had been carefully lined out with white color.

"What did this Liseman want?" Gary asked.

"Wants to rent hangar space, for an old Standard, rebuilt. Powered by an O.X.5. Doesn't fly it himself, but has a pilot. Doesn't expect to use it much. Jansen's showing him the hangar space."

Gary nodded his head slightly. His gray eyes were little slits. He spoke slowly.

"Get me five thousand—in hundreds, Pete," he said steadily. "I'll be in for it tomorrow. I'll send my name in as Jones. The kid was away from the gate, so I walked in this time. Don't keep me waiting—any time you get the name—I. Jones. And have the boys work on the Special."

Pete nodded. He stared at Gary, still shaken by the sight of him.

"If there's anything else I can do, Jones—"

Gary smiled. "That's better. You can't do anything else, Pete. You'll be doing a lot if you follow instructions to the dot, Pete. Forget me as one man—remember me as another."

Pete Ranning's face twisted, but he managed a smile.

"About Liseman—" he asked—"do we rent him hangar space?"

Gary Greer's face was expressionless. He nodded his head.

"It's very important, Pete—that we *do* rent him hangar space," he replied. "Any junk at the north end? Think I'll look around up there."

Pete Ranning watched Gary's eyes. But he saw no expression in them—nothing that told him what the owner of the South Side airport was thinking. "Some old fuselage material piled up back of the empty hangars," he stated. "Haven't made any changes since—"

He stopped. Gary was moving toward the door. Footfalls sounded outside—there was a knock. The office boy came in. Gary turned slightly away. He bent his shoulders a bit. The eyes of youth were sharp, keen. The boy left some papers, went out. Gary spoke with his back to Pete.

"I'll see you tomorrow, Mr. Ranning. Don't forget me." His voice was louder now, husky. It had a curious, flat note that was unnatural. "I'm always looking for—junk."

He went out, closing the door back of him. The office boy glanced in his direction, then went on sorting mail on his desk. Back in the office, Pete Ranning sank down into his desk chair. He sucked in his breath sharply. He was shaking—his heart was pounding. Pete had had a few jolts in his life—but this was the greatest. A dead man—coming back. The man he loved—walking in—walking out.

Suppression—that thing Gary Greer was hiding from him. What was it? Pete Ranning shook his head slowly. He thought of the girl—he knew how much Gary loved her. And yet—even she was not to know. She was to suffer. Why? And Liseman—the name was familiar. Gary had seen him. He had recognized him. Who was the man?

Pete Ranning refilled his pipe. He tried to relax, but when the phone buzzed unexpectedly his whole body jerked. As he reached for the receiver he swore softly. It might have been a celebration—Gary's return. Instead, it was something else. He groped for the word, mentally—found it. It had been a *preparation*. A sinister preparation. It almost took away the wonderful feeling caused by his finding life—where he had expected death.

He spoke into the mouthpiece of the phone, waited. There was a buzz on the wire; Central's voice cut through it, telling him the call was long distance. Then another voice came through the wire noise. It was distant, distorted. But Pete got the words.

"Hello—Ranning? Pete Ranning?"

Pete tried to answer—the voice at the other end kept questioning. Finally it ceased, then came again, clearer.

"This is—Gary, Pete! Gary Greer! I'm alive—get that? I'm all right—"

The wire buzz was too great—it drowned out words, then they came again. Pete was stiff in the chair.

"I'll be in—tomorrow. I'm at—Dunning—forced landing—was hurt—"

The voice broke off. The wire buzz died abruptly. Pete started to call Central back. The voice sounded again, very faint.

"That you—Ranning? This is Gary Greer—"

Pete Ranning spoke into the mouthpiece of the phone. His brain was clear—he tried to make his words clear.

"Gary Greer is—dead." He spoke slowly, his voice steadying. "There's a mistake—Gary Greer's dead. Who is this—"

The wire buzz died again. Pete Ranning was facing the window that looked out on the field. He could see the deadline, down toward the north end. And along it walked the figure of Gary Greer. It wasn't Gary's old walk. This man's figure was bent forward; the walk was slow, not decisive. The clothing was shabby, not pressed well. But it was the figure of the man who had talked to Pete Ranning only a few minutes ago. And that man was Gary Greer.

Pete straightened. He hung up the receiver. His blue eyes were narrowed. He spoke slowly.

"Gary's fighting something. Maybe he's fighting the ones who killed his father. That voice wasn't Gary's. And I played it right. It's the thing I've *got* to learn—Gary Greer is dead!"

FIFTY MILE LISEMAN sat with a thin-faced individual

on the bed of a cheap room. Both men were nervous—twice the thin-faced one reached for cigarettes, and each time Liseman swore softly. There was no smoking.

The room held an odor. It was cheap perfume. On the dressing table—a gilded, cheap affair in a corner of the room—was a picture. Liseman had difficulty in keeping his eyes from the picture. It was the likeness of one who had departed. The man's name had been Lewis—"Babe" Lewis. Three bullets had been shot into his body, not long ago, over on River Street. There had been a heavy fog.

Liseman smiled grimly. He didn't regret the Babe's passing. He'd never had much use for Lewis. The man had been a braggart—too strong physically. Once he had twisted Fifty Mile's right arm almost out of its socket. But the Babe had been no fool. He had talked to his moll—and there was something Liseman had that the kid wanted.

Steps sounded on the thinly carpeted stairs of the rooming-house. The thin-faced one got to his feet, moved close to the closed door. When it opened he would be behind it. Liseman sat on the bed—he faked a broad smile. But his cherub-like face was pale.

The footfalls sounded nearer the door, ceased abruptly. The room was fairly dark; Fifty Mile sat without moving. There was the click of the key in a lock, the door opened inward. The figure of a girl slipped inside. The door was closed again—the lock snapped.

The figure took a step away from the door. Breath was drawn in sharply—the girl's body stiffened. A hand went to her mouth, stifling a cry. Liseman spoke in a low tone.

"It's all right, Doll—just Jimmy an' me!"

For several seconds there was silence. Then the girl moved a few feet and snapped on an electric light. It gave rose color to the room. She faced the man on the bed. Her name was Doll Reiner; she had a doll-like face, but she wasn't so young. Even the rose-colored light showed the lines about her mouth, under her dark eyes.

Jimmy Frett coughed. The girl turned slowly, swore—faced Fifty Mile again. Her lips twitched.

"What's the game, Fifty?" she asked in a hoarse voice.

Liseman sat with a hand in the pocket of his light coat. The right hand—in the right pocket. He continued to smile.

"The grape-vine says you say I got something that belongs to you. I figured maybe there was a wrong in it, Doll."

The girl stood with her hands on her hips. She was dressed plainly, cheaply. She shook her head slowly.

"The Babe never got his coin," she stated. "I was his girl—you knew that. I've been hard up, Fifty—an' I need the five grand."

Fifty Mile chuckled. It was a brutal chuckle. Jimmy Frett, over by the door, swore softly.

"Who said you was the Babe's moll, Doll?" he muttered. "The Babe wasn't so particular, an' you know it."

Rage struck at the girl. She whirled on the thin-faced one.

"You shut up, sky pilot!" she cried shrilly. "I *was* the Babe's—"

"Keep your voice low!" Fifty Mile spoke sharply. "An' you stay out of this, Jimmy! *I'm* running this gab meeting."

The girl faced Liseman again. Her eyes were narrowed. She was trying to control herself.

"You got a nerve—you two! Bustin' in here—gettin' inside this room—"

She broke off as she saw the expression in Liseman's eyes. A little stab of fear caught her. She went back to the old argument.

"Didn't I go around with the Babe? Didn't he tell you—all of you—that if anything happened to him—"

Fifty Mile chuckled again. He spoke in a genial tone. But there was an undernote in his voice.

"What did you make him cold for, Doll? Breakin' with you, was he? Gettin' set for the walk-out?"

The girl stared at the man on the bed. Her eyes were wide.

"*Me*—rub the Babe out? Me? For God's sake, Fifty—you don't think *I* done—"

Liseman swore softly. There was a hard expression on his face now.

"It don't work, Doll!" he snapped. "The Babe was off you. You were on River Street—Jenny seen you ten minutes before the bulls started blowin' whistles, two blocks from where the Babe went down. He was quittin' you—for that blonde kid—an' you got clever—"

"You're lyin'!" The girl's voice rose again. Her eyes were on Fifty Mile's. She didn't see Jimmy Frett move in toward her from his place by the door. "You got the Babe's coin—from that—"

"Shut up!" Liseman's voice was fierce. "How much you want, Doll?"

The girl's eyes widened. There was eagerness in her tone.

"He had five grand comin' to him. I'll play fair with you, Fifty. You can keep a grand for—"

Her words were smothered by the cloth pressed into her mouth. She struggled. In a flash Fifty Mile was up from the bed. He got her arms down; held her squirming body. The sickening odor of chloroform filled the room. The girl wasn't strong—life had battered her around a lot. But she fought— and tried not to breathe. And the strong fingers of the thin-faced man held the saturated rag over her lips, her nostrils. Slowly she relaxed. Frett picked her up, carried her to the bed. He laid her down.

Liseman drew a deep breath. His cherub-like face was very white. He spoke in a whisper.

"Turn that rag over—let her get a good dose, Jimmy. She ain't got much of a pumper inside her."

The thin-faced man turned the rag over. He wore soiled gloves—they were saturated with the anaesthetic. He straightened. Both men faced the door. The sound of footfalls came into the room.

They waited, tense, motionless. The steps were outside the door now—now they were moving along the hall of the rooming-house. Someone was ascending the stairs to the floor above. Fifty Mile made a face, coughed. The muscles of his mouth twitched.

"Can't take—a chance!" he whispered. "Wind that cord!"

The thin-faced man smiled faintly. He was very calm. He spoke steadily.

"Two grand, Fifty—an' I'll take it now!"

Liseman reached into a hip pocket. He produced a thin roll, but the bills were large ones. He counted out the two thousand. The chloroform was making him sick. He wanted to get away. It might be noticed. He tried to remember if he'd touched Doll's flesh. It didn't matter much—he'd never been fingerprinted. But he *might* be, in the future.

The thin-faced one was moving back toward the bed; he

had slipped the bills in his pocket. In his right hand fingers he held a small piece of cord. It was strong cord. He bent over the girl's figure.

Fifty Mile shuddered. "Make it fast," he muttered hoarsely. "I'm gettin' sick."

The thin-faced one failed to reply. He straightened, got his gloves off. He turned toward Liseman.

"How's she sound—clear going down?" There was a tight-lipped smile on his face. Fifty Mile drew a deep breath.

"Sounds all right," he muttered. "Is the Doll—"

Jimmy Frett was a grim humorist. He had nerves of iron. Unlike Liseman, he stayed away from the white flakes. And anyway, he'd never liked the Babe, nor his moll.

"She's done—*her* dance!" he stated grimly. "Get going—let's do ours!"

THE MAN BACK of the wheel of the flivver laundry truck straightened up a little. He got the engine going, started the truck. It was a small truck, and the name painted on the side was not in the Center City telephone directory.

Gary Greer backed around in the narrow street. He'd tagged Liseman since that individual had rented hangar space at the South Side Field, hours ago. It hadn't been difficult. Liseman hadn't moved about much. He'd met a thin-faced man at the corner of River and Third Street—and the two had taken a cab. The truck had followed the cab, but Gary had been very sure they hadn't seen it. He had parked the truck when the two men had left the taxi. He had tagged them to the house from which they now departed. When they had gone in he had gone back for the truck. It was a chance he had to take.

Two persons had entered the cheap rooming-house near the spot where he had parked the laundry truck. One was an elderly man. The other was a girl. Now Liseman and the thin-faced man were moving back toward the spot where they had left the cab.

They were a half block ahead—and knowing which way the taxi was headed, Gary Greer let them get further ahead. Then he drove toward the next street at an average city speed. The truck cut in behind the cab as it headed toward First Street. It was dark; early evening.

Three blocks along, and the cab slid up the curb before a drug store. The thin-faced man got out, went into the store. The cab moved on, heading toward the North Side. Gary settled down back of the wheel. His gray eyes were narrowed. And then, very suddenly, the cab turned back toward one of Center City's busy streets. It pulled up before a cigar store, located on the corner. There was no room for Gary to get the truck in behind it. He made a turn, came back on the other side. The cab was near the entrance of the cigar store. The door was opened. Gary stopped the truck—waited. Several minutes passed. The driver was smoking a cigarette. He leaned out and closed the door of the cab. Then he drove off.

Gary Greer smiled grimly. He knew by the driver's actions that Liseman was gone. He'd lost the trail. The cab driver hadn't looked into the store for his man. He'd simply waited a few minutes, with the door opened. Then he'd closed it and driven off. Gary got down from the truck. He crossed the street, went into the store. There was an entrance on the other street. Liseman had used it for an exit.

Gary used the telephone. He called Pete Ranning. He wanted to know if there was anything new. It was I. Jones talking. Pete's tone told him there was something new. Gary said he'd be out at the Field in thirty minutes.

Back in the truck, he headed toward the South Side Field. There was a grim expression in his eyes. He'd lost track of a face, a name. That was the disadvantage of working alone. And yet— there was no chance of him having aid. He wouldn't involve Ranning. There would be suspicions, perhaps.

He left the truck some distance from the Field. It seemed strange—seeing faces he knew, men he knew—and not speaking to them. He was changed—very changed. The office boy sent in his name—Pete had him admitted immediately. He closed the door back of Gary, locked it. He phoned out that he was not to be disturbed.

"Just after you left this morning, Gary," he said in a low tone, "I had a phone call. Seemed to be long distance. Central said it was. Someone called—said it was you. I couldn't get to you, while you were on the field. Could have, I suppose—but I was worried about it. This Liseman was out there—and you were sticking pretty close."

Gary Greer stared at Pete. He nodded his head slowly.

"That's right—keep away from me as much as possible," he said. "Someone called—and said it was Gary Greer, eh? Give any reason, Pete—for turning up just now?"

Pete frowned. "Said he was alive—was at Dunning—would be in tomorrow. Said he had a forced landing, but that he was all right. Used your name, several times."

Gary was not smiling now. His eyes met Pete's squarely.

"What did you say?" he asked.

"I said you were dead," Pete replied. "I said there must be some mistake. But it gave me a jolt, Gary."

The pilot nodded his head. "It gives *me* one," he muttered. "It can't be that anyone knows—"

He broke off. Pete Ranning's eyes were on his. He spoke pleadingly.

"What's it all mean, Gary? Let me in on the thing. I can't fight for you half so well—in the dark."

Gary smiled faintly. "Perhaps you can fight better—in the dark," he contradicted. "You gave that fellow the right answer, Pete—and you were working in the dark there. You told him Gary Greer was dead. He is. It might have been a joke of some kind. Dunning—that's about thirty miles southwest of Center City. It seems to me—"

He stopped again, shrugged his shoulders. He was worried, but he didn't want Pete to see it.

"Any other news?" he asked.

Pete nodded. "Liseman's ship came in this afternoon—an old Standard. But her engine is sweet. New—about fifty hours running, I'd say. And most of that on the block."

Gary spoke quietly. "How soon after Liseman left the Field—did the ship come in?" he asked.

"About two hours," Pete replied.

"Who flew her in?" Gary shot back.

"Fellow named Green—Eddie Green. Set her down prettily. I talked with him. He says that Liseman's an importer—got a lot of money. Likes to sky-ride once in a while. This Green's a fairly tall, slim chap. Very thin face. Acts calm—and seems to be sort of amused about Liseman."

Pete nodded. His eyes held a peculiar expression.

"Didn't stay on the Field long, did he?" he asked.

"Said he was going to leave in a half hour," Ranning replied.

"Turned the ship over to our crew."

Gary lighted a cigarette. He closed his eyes, spoke again.

"Did you look at the ship closely, Pete?"

The field manager nodded. "Got plenty of modern equipment on her," he stated. "Including all the latest instruments inside. And wing lights, flare releases."

"Good job for night flying, eh?" Gary asked slowly. "Right for it?"

"All set," Pete replied. "That was the first thought that came to me. I asked the thin-faced fellow about it. He grinned—said that business often made Liseman take a night hop. After he'd gone I gave the ship a close look-over. Nothing concealed inside. No fuselage room. Looks like a clean cut job. A pleasure ship, I'd say. The sort of job these gentlemen fliers like. But the night stuff bothers me a little."

Gary smoked quietly for several seconds. As he was about to speak, the telephone bell rang. Pete lifted the receiver. The one at the other end did most of the talking. From time to time Gary could catch a word, most of it was not distinguishable. Ranning spoke finally.

"That's part of our service, Mr. Green. We'll have the ship on the dead-line within a half hour. The ground-crew's on all night—it won't matter when you go up or how long you stay up with your passenger. Fuel is charged on the monthly bill."

The one at the other end spoke again. Gary Greer was sitting back in his chair—his eyes on Pete Ranning. His face was expressionless.

"Publicity?" There was amusement in Pete's voice. "There's no publicity on a night flight, Mr. Green. Too common. That's all right. 'Bye!"

He hung up. Gary was smiling cheerfully. Pete Ranning swore softly.

"Green thought there might be some publicity because his passenger wants to take a sky-ride—at nine o'clock. Can you beat that! Said Liseman wouldn't want it. Funny, though—he sort of rushed that ship in. After he'd said he wouldn't use her much."

Gary Greer got to his feet. He was still smiling.

"Forget about Green and Liseman, Pete," he instructed in a low voice. "Treat them just as you treat the others. I'm staying at a downtown hotel—and after I poke around the Field a bit I'm going back for some sleep. By the way, you might let the ground-crew men think, indirectly, that I'm sort of interested in flying, besides buying up old ship material. That'll give me more freedom around the Field."

Pete nodded. His blue eyes were on the white, lined face of Gary Greer. There was a puzzled expression in them. He looked at the stooped shoulders as Gary rose; The owner of the Field had been so straight, so clear-eyed, brown-faced. He looked old now—old and sick. And yet, there was something within the depths of Gary's gray eyes—something that was not old. Something Ranning did not understand.

"See you again, Mr. Jones," he said in a normal tone. "And say—that Special job is ready for you."

Gary showed surprise, "You got the engine mounted in a hurry," he said softly. "Is she tested out yet?"

Pete nodded. "Ready for the air—a half hour ago," he stated. "I had a big crew on her all day, since this morning. And I've got that other stuff—"

He moved toward the desk. Gary Greer listened to the whining of the Field siren. His face twisted. The mail plane was due in. He thought of his father—of the gangster car. He thought of the body in the mud. Half closing his eyes, he saw the slumping figure of Babe Lewis. He had been the first. The first to pay. It had been a crude kill—that one. But the fog had obliterated the killer. The press had figured it was a squeal kill. The police had kept off, as much as possible. Rage had gripped Gary, that night on River Street. But now—now he was calmer. Now he would move slowly.

And the game was becoming a tighter one. There were the police to be reckoned with. There were the other gang members. When the second name was wiped out—there would be suspicion.

It would be hard, a fight—to go on. But—an honest name had been rubbed out. These other names, they counted for nothing good, decent. If he could see the spark of decency—

Pete was moving toward him; he handed him an envelope. Gary slipped it into his pocket.

"Thanks, Pete," he said in a low voice. "Now, here's a change. I may want to test out the Special tonight. Have her on the dead-line. It's"—he glanced at a wrist-watch on his left hand— "six-thirty now. I'll *want* to test that ship out, come to think of it. Have her loaded with fuel—*loaded*, Pete. I'll go up at seven-thirty. Put a new crew on her—a crew of men who never saw me much, when I was around here. Got any new men?"

Pete Ranning nodded. His eyes were narrowed on Gary's. He said nothing.

"You can take me out. I'm Jones—but I fly some. I'll go for a rather long hop—several hours, probably. Can't tell exactly. Want you to check me off—and meet all incoming planes. Clear?"

Pete nodded his head. Five minutes later Gary Greer was driving a laundry truck back toward town. In a cheap hotel he bought the evening paper. He read it carefully. There wasn't much in it. But on the first page there was a flash—it was in the late news column, and it had been squeezed in. A landlady of a rooming-house had broken into a room occupied by one Doll Jacobs. The landlady had smelled chloroform. Doll Jacobs, about whom she knew little, was dead. A tight-drawn cord had been found about her neck. She had been strangled to death. The police were investigating.

Gary lowered the paper. His face was expressionless. He repeated the address given in the paper slowly. His truck had been parked across the street from the address given. He had seen two persons enter the rooming-house, after Liseman and the thin-faced man had entered. The elderly man would walk out again. But the girl—

Gary reached for a cigarette. His fingers were steady. He thought of Soapy Tyler, dying. Giving him names. Names of killers of an honest man—his father. Gangster names. He lighted the cigarette. Then he moved toward the door. There was work to be done.

IT WAS TWENTY minutes of eight when Gary Greer took off the Greer Special. She was a two-place, radial-engined ship, painted a gray color. The take-off was sloppy. Several of the ground-crew men commented on it. Pete Ranning swore harshly.

"This fellow Jones may be a good dealer in plane material"—he stated loudly—"but he's not much of a pilot! I'm sorry I let him take that crate—" He broke off, turned away. In the light above the Field the ground-crew men could see the Greer Special banking sloppily. But she got altitude. Her winglights showed for a while—then the roar of her engine died as she faded from sight in the western darkness.

Over by the north hangar a thin-faced pilot was inspecting a Standard, two-place ship. There was a faint smile on his face as he went about the job. Jimmy Frett—whom Pete Ranning knew as Green—had money in his pocket—big money. The man he was about to wing away from Center City had more money. Frett suspected that Liseman was a coward. The game wasn't up yet.

There had been an important kill—but Frett hadn't been in on it. He knew what had happened, and sometimes knowledge paid. Liseman was a quitter—he was flying out. He had the payoff coin, but he wasn't paying off. Not in *that* way. And Liseman had something on Frett. He had seen him fasten a cord around a woman's neck. A weakling was always dangerous. But the coin—that came first.

At twenty minutes after nine the thin-faced pilot was getting restless. The Standard's engine was revving up, on the deadline. Fifty Mile was not present. Frett walked away from the ship, and smoked. From time to time he looked down the deadline of the lighted airport, toward the distant main entrance. There was no sign of Liseman. But Jimmy Frett wasn't worried.

"He'll show!" he muttered. "This is *one* time he won't be fifty miles away!"

AT THE PRECISE second that the thin-faced one uttered words about Fifty Mile's sure appearance, that individual was riding toward the main entrance of the South Side airport in a cab. He sat up straight as the cab jerked to a halt. A voice came to him, husky, indistinct. He caught several of the words.

"—ship crashed—over that way—get in through—north end gate."

The cab driver turned his head, spoke to Liseman.

"Fellow says a plane's crashed in the road. Got to detour here, go around to the north side gate."

Liseman swore softly, then remembered. He nodded his head.

"All right—my ship's at the north end of the Field, anyway. Save a walk—can't get in with the cab."

The taxi swerved to the left. Liseman got a glimpse of a man with a flashlight, turning away. It seemed to him that the cab moved for a long time, making the detour. The road was rough. The cab was going a long way out of the regular approach to the Field. Finally, the driver braked it down. He turned, opened the door.

"Looks like the gate's closed," he muttered, pointing toward a concrete wall and a steel gate.

Fifty Mile grunted. "I'll make 'em open it!" he stated. "How much?"

The driver told him—he tossed the man a five-dollar bill. He didn't want the change. Slowly he moved toward the gate. There were no planes in the air, but he could hear the steady beat of a ship's engine, beyond the gate. The cab backed around, rattled back over the muddy road.

Liseman reached the gate. He could see lights on the Field, through a slot in the steel at one side of the gate. He tried the heavy latch—the gate was locked. He swore hoarsely. A voice sounded; back of him.

"Anything wrong?"

Fifty Mile whirled, his right hand dropping toward a pocket. He was nervous. This was the break-away—he didn't want a slip. Before him stood a very pale man. He was stooped, and in the light that came through from the Field, Liseman saw that the man's clothes were cheap, ragged.

"Want to get inside," he stated. "A ship crashed in the main road—had to detour."

The report of the ship-crash had unnerved him, too. He stared at the white-faced man. The fellow was smiling.

"No ship crashed, Fifty Mile!" The voice was very hard. "Going away, Killer?"

Liseman stiffened. His right hand fumbled for the pocket of his coat. He couldn't see the white-faced man's hands, either of them. But a narrow stream of light came through the gate opening, from the Field floodlights. It struck on the stranger's face. It accentuated the pallor. The man was smiling. It was a hideous smile.

Fifty Mile got a grip on his gun. And then, above the rumble of the plane's engine, within the field, he heard a staccato, low cough. His body jerked—his own gun cracked. There was another cough. Pain tore at his lungs. He went to his knees. He tried to squeeze the trigger of his gun again, failed. The last thing he saw, before he pitched forward into the mud beyond the gate, was a face, white and smiling, that was half familiar. But *as* he pitched forward—he remembered something. He remembered a death car—and his gun streaming lead down at a prosecuting attorney. One word bubbled with his life, from red lips—

"Greer—"

And then he died. Died in the mud beyond the Field, with the steady beat of the engine of the plane, he had intended to use for escape, gone from his ears. And Jimmy Frett had been right. This time Liseman's alibi had failed. He hadn't been fifty miles away from the kill.

AT ten-thirty the Greer Special came down out of the west. All the time that it had been landed on the wood-enclosed field less than ten miles from the South Side airport, Gary Greer had been busy.

He set the ship down in a rough landing. The ground-crew men groaned. Pete Ranning, out on the dead-line, swore out loud. Gary taxied in. He cut the engine, climbed down.

Pete Ranning grunted. "About time!" he muttered. "We were getting worried—it's ten-thirty. Just cruising around, Jones?"

Gary Greer smiled faintly. He wiped a smear of oil from his face, jerked off his helmet and goggles.

"The air's great," he said slowly, almost tonelessly. "Just cruising." He moved slowly from the field, with Ranning at his side. His eyes went toward the north end.

"Looks like a ship over there," he said, pointing. "Private—or Field ship?" Pete Ranning spoke very slowly. His blue eyes were narrowed on the Standard at the north end.

"That's Liseman's ship," he said. "His pilot's waiting. Liseman hasn't come yet. Must be held up somewhere. Business—maybe."

He looked at Gary narrowly. But the pilot only nodded his head.

"Maybe," he said quietly.

4

High Odds

PETE RANNING WIDENED his blue eyes, stared at the girl who stood before him. There were sounds drifting into the manager's office, the usual South Side Airport sounds. Drone of ship engines in the sky, the sudden rumbling of engines being tested, revved up on the dead-line. Pete heard the sounds and yet was hardly aware of them. The girl's words had shaken him.

"Must be—a mistake, Miss Rawlings," he said slowly. "Though I'd be mighty glad to believe—"

The girl's expression checked his words. Joyce Rawlings was tall, dark-haired. She had clear brown eyes—and they seemed to be looking through Pete Ranning now. They seemed to be penetrating, boring into the thoughts that were flashing through his head.

"No mistake, Mr. Ranning," she said in a husky voice. "You know that. Gary Greer is alive. Oh, why can't you tell me the things I want to know, *must* know?"

Pete Ranning noted that the girl had lowered her voice. He hated to lie. But he was loyal to Gary—and in the past three days of police investigation he had lied more than once. The game was a fighting game—and Gary's enemies were not fighting cleanly. It was a game the girl should not play.

"Gary Greer is dead," he said slowly, but his eyes did not meet the girl's. "The death of this man Liseman—"

He saw the girl's eyes flicker; there was a faint smile playing about her firm lips now. She spoke very quietly.

"The *murder* of this man Liseman, Mr. Ranning—that is in the chain of my evidence that Gary is alive."

Pete Ranning tried to smile in an amused, superior manner. It was not easy. He admired the girl that Gary loved. She was a clever girl. And Gary had many things to think of, too many tracks to cover, perhaps. If he had made a slip—

"And the chain is strong Miss Rawlings?" he asked slowly, moving closer to her.

"Stronger than—*death*," she said simply. "It is all quite clear, Pete. Let's stop being formal. You called me Joyce—before this terrible thing began. I'm not a child, Pete. I used to sit and listen to Gary's father talk, by the hour. I, too, know something about criminals. And the ways of politicians—and the police—Center City police."

Pete Ranning managed a smile. It was a grim smile. He spoke slowly.

"What makes you think Gary is—alive?" he asked.

"I know Gary. He went through a war. There isn't anything he's afraid of—with one possible exception. I'm not sure about *that*. He loved his father. Two underworld characters have died since Gary's father was shot down. One of them was important; he counted. He was killed just outside the field."

The girl stopped; her eyes met Pete Ranning's again. He spoke slowly.

"That's almost always the case—in Center City crime. One big killing—several smaller ones—"

The girl shook her head. "I've had three men searching the mountains where the plane crashed—since the day after the wreckage was found." She smiled faintly as Pete stiffened. "Gary tried to do a good job of it, Pete—but he failed. He's alive!"

Pete Ranning groaned. The girl was silent for several seconds. Then she spoke quietly.

"Two crooks have died—since that plane's wreckage was found, Pete. The police haven't a clue. But—*I* have."

Pete Ranning stared at the girl. Her voice was very low.

"Gary didn't want me to know—to know what he intended to do, Pete—and he didn't want the members of the gang to think he was alive. So he crashed that plane. He came to this field, later. He came to *you*. He needed your help—if Liseman was to die."

Pete Ranning found courage then—courage to act. He laughed bitterly. The girl was right, of course. But he would bluff—bluff just so long as he could.

"Joyce—" he said in a shaken tone—"this thing has hit you hard, naturally. Of course, we have no proof—"

The girl smiled faintly. "Haven't *we?*" she asked. "All right, Pete. But I want to tell you something. You had a phone call from a man—long distance, some time ago. You were told that Gary was alive. That was a trick, Pete—I was responsible for the man calling. You were shaken up by that call—but you didn't betray Gary. Just wanted you to know that I sent the message through."

Pete Ranning stared at the girl. She was still smiling. He could think of nothing to say.

"One thing more—I said that Gary was afraid of only one thing. That is I, Pete. He wouldn't go on, perhaps, if he thought it would involve me."

Pete's eyes were narrowed on the girl's. She was determined, he knew that. She was fighting.

"It won't involve you if—"

He turned away. The girl whistled softly. When he faced her again, knowing that he had made a bad break, the smile was gone from her face.

"It *will* involve me, Pete. I'll *make* it involve me! Other murders don't right a first murder. I've *got* to stop Gary."

The field manager managed a twisted smile.

"Gary Greer—is dead, Joyce," he said slowly.

The girl looked him squarely in the eyes. She spoke in a very low voice.

"Dead men have white faces—lips without blood, Pete. The expression of their eyes changes. But—*dead men don't walk the streets of Center City!*"

She turned abruptly, moved from the flying field office. Pete made a movement as if to stop her, to call out. But he didn't speak. She had seen Gary. She knew. And from this point on—she, too, was in the game. Pete Ranning dropped down into his desk chair. Gangsters, police—and now the girl—for

Gary Greer to fight. He shook his head slowly.

"Three to one!" he muttered harshly. "High odds!"

"FRENCHY" LAMONTE SAT across the table from the man with the bull-like neck, and twisted the ends of his waxed mustache nervously. Frenchy was short, slender in build. For years he had carried the "front" for the Terminal crowd. Frenchy was no fool—no stupid "gun" to be used carelessly by a gang leader. He knew his New Orleans, and he was nervous now because he had taken a hand in a game outside of that city. The man opposite him spoke in a strangely thin voice for his bulk.

"Fifty Mile Liseman knew a lot of things bad for a guy to know, Frenchy," he stated. "Somebody wanted him to forget 'em. They *almost* rubbed him out down here, a year ago."

Frenchy nodded. The dull tone of an auto horn sounded in the narrow street of New Orleans *Vieux Carré*. It was around ten in the evening, and pretty warm outside. In the small room of the *Blue Bottom* café, a ceiling fan revolved, stirring warm air. Frenchy twisted the sharp ends of his dark mustache, spoke in a cold, toneless voice.

"That bird was due to wing this way, Squeak. He had coin—I was slated to get a hunk of it. He's the second of certain gents I know—to dig his face into dirt. It begins to look funny."

"Squeak" Rosen shifted his two hundred pounds, spat toward a receptacle provided for that purpose.

"Maybe you an' me'd better sort of hang close for a few days, Frenchy," he suggested in his high-pitched voice.

The one with the waxed mustache nodded.

"Charlie's doing some work for me, Squeak," he stated. "Got him looking around a little. He knows the flying birds."

The big man swore softly, his eyes on Frenchy's.

"Lookin' for a 'gun' to fly down here?" he muttered. "You must have made yourself right prominent, Frenchy."

The little man swore. "Me—I was just up there fixing for some truck stuff, Squeak," he stated. "But somebody may get me wrong, see?"

Squeak grinned brutally. The grin showed considerable gold work. Footfall sound drifted into the room. Frenchy and the big man shifted their positions slightly. Their right hands drifted toward pockets. But the movements were leisurely, and their faces expressionless.

Outside the closed door someone coughed. Coughed twice. Frenchy grinned, gestured toward the door. The big man went over and snapped a key. He opened the door. Frenchy called out cheerfully:

"Hello, Charlie!"

The newcomer was middle-aged, blond-haired, blue-eyed. His last name was Elvey. But he hadn't any idea how he'd come by the name. Not that it mattered any. He tossed an envelope down on the table before Frenchy.

"God—but it's hot!" he muttered.

Frenchy extracted an envelope from the opened envelope. The second one, smaller than the one in which it had been mailed, had not been opened. It was addressed to Frenchy, while the other had been addressed to Charlie. The one with the waxed mustache played safe, when it came to mail.

He read the contents of the second envelope. Then he whistled off key for several seconds. He looked at the postmark—Center City. His eyes went to Charlie's blue ones.

"All right, Charlie," he muttered. "Shoot."

"Guy named Jones—I. Jones—sets a ship down at Rice Field just at dusk. Buys hangar room for a week, and says he may want the ship any time, so the boys are to keep her filled with gas and oil. Paid cash, but seemed to have trouble finding enough to foot the bill. Radial engined ship—monoplane single-seater. Special job, they say at the field. This Jones says they needn't keep the ship on the dead-line, that he don't *figure* on using it for a week or so."

Frenchy's face held a twisted smile. He nodded.

"But when he *does* use it—wants it in a hurry, eh?" he muttered. "What's he look like?"

Charlie shook his head. "No one out at the field seems to be sure," he replied, "They say he looked a bit pasty. Came in from the eastward—said he'd winged over from Florida. Only strange ship to come in today, Frenchy—and likely doesn't mean a thing."

The one with the pointed mustache continued to smile his twisted smile. He read the letter again, then tore it into little pieces. The little pieces he dropped in an empty glass—and let a lighted match drop on top of them. Charlie and Squeak watched them burn in silence. Then Frenchy spoke.

"The scribble's from Frett," he said slowly. "He tells me to watch out for any guy flying a radial engined, special job crate. He's been doing a little poking around, after the bulls let him off in Center City. He was Liseman's pilot. He says a guy named Jones got into the air while he was waiting for Fifty Mile to show. This guy came down after a few hours—but Frett thinks he may have come down *before* that time. The bulls up there are looking for Jones—and they're not finding him. So maybe this ship's coming in *does* mean something, Charlie."

Charlie swore softly. His eyes met Frenchy's.

"Yeah," he muttered. "Maybe if does, at that!"

Squeak Rosen dropped his two hundred pounds into a battered chair. He grunted heavily. His eyes were little slits looking into the eyes of the man who twisted his mustache nervously.

"Sure!" he shrilled. "Maybe it does, Frenchy!"

GARY GREER TURNED off St. Charles, moved toward the French Quarter of the city. He was tired; he'd been in the air a long time—but there were several things to be done. They *could* be done tomorrow—but tonight would be better. Gary had no knowledge of the man he was looking for—no knowledge beyond a name and a fact. The name was clear in his brain—the fact was that Frenchy Lamonte only left New Orleans on short visits.

Gary walked slowly, a faint smile playing about his thin-lined lips. He looked years older than he was. A pasty-white make-up, carefully applied, subdued the brown color of his face. His lips, too, were bloodless. It made his smile a strange one—a bitter, lifeless smile.

In the right-hand pocket of his light suit was a wire that he had got from the Western Union office ten minutes ago. It had come through in code—and was from Pete Ranning. Gary thought of it as he moved into the French Quarter. Joyce had seen him, knew that he was alive! She had had the mountains searched; he might have guessed that she would make every effort. But then, all he had wanted was time. And he was working fast.

He had sent a coded wire back to Pete. It consisted of two

words only—two words that counted. "Continue denials." He wanted Pete to stick to that. He was dead. But what would Joyce do?

He smiled. What *could* she do? *He* had names—and the names could lead him to cities, states. But Joyce Rawlings had nothing like that. She had seen him—she believed he was alive. But he would give her no proof. He couldn't do that. She would risk much for him—and he could not have her risking anything. He loved her too much.

He stopped, lighted a cigarette, got away from his thoughts. Going on again, he turned into a street that was almost an alley. Iron-worked balconies were above the street—the houses were old, many of them crumbling. A dimly lighted café was across the narrow street, he headed toward it. This was chance work—but he might gain something.

Inside there were empty chairs, two tables, a short bar. Gary leaned against the bar, waited. A thick-set individual came out from behind some faded red curtains. He smiled broadly. He questioned Gary with small, squinted eyes. Gary spoke.

"Seen Frenchy around?" he asked casually. "The Babe said he might be over this way."

It was a miss. Gary knew that right away. He knew it by the flicker in the depths of the tiny eyes. He knew it by the way the bartender's lips parted.

"*Which* Babe," the man questioned slowly, "said *which* Frenchy might be around here?"

Gary swore. "Babe Schaefer said Frenchy Lamonte might be around," he muttered. "Gimme a beer, will you?"

The bartender fizzed out a beer. Gary dropped a quarter. He didn't look at the thick-set one's face. He wondered if he'd hit blindly—on the Babe Schaefer guess. Every city had a Babe something-or-other. And this city had a Frenchy Lamonte. Schaefer wasn't such an uncommon name. He lifted the beer, drank. As he drank he watched the bartender. The man was smiling at him. It was an amused smile. But he was trying to make it a genial one.

"Schaefer sent you here, eh?" he muttered. "Guess it's all right, then. Sofie's in back—guess she knows where Frenchy is right now. Most always does. I'll ask her—stick around."

He vanished through the curtain at the rear of the speakeasy. The beer wasn't much good. It was the wrong brand. That told Gary a little story. He'd mentioned two names, before he'd asked for the beer. If the names had meant anything the bartender wouldn't have handed out the wishy-washy stuff. He'd have set up the grade drinkers paid coin to get.

No distant hum of conversation came into the café from behind the curtains. A long-drawn boat whistle reached the place, from the Mississippi. Gary finished off the beer. He did a little thinking. If he'd blundered to some spot close to Frenchy's hang-out, it was ten to one that the bartender was sending for Lamonte. He'd get a look-over, at least. He didn't want anything of the sort.

Then he heard voices—the bartender calling the name of the woman—a second voice, pitched higher, answering. Gary's eyes narrowed. The woman had a peculiar voice—it might almost have been the man's, disguised. The voices became a murmur. Gary hesitated.

And then the bartender came through the curtains again. He was smiling broadly. He took Gary's empty glass, filled it again.

"Sofie's gone over to ask a pal of hers about Frenchy," he

stated. "You look sort of hot and tired—drink up!"

Gary forced a grin. He sipped the beer. It was a different brand this time. He could taste the alcohol in it. It was strong stuff. The bartender chuckled.

"Better, eh?" he muttered. "Guess if you know Frenchy and the Babe—you rate the best poison."

Again there was that flicker in his beady eyes. Gary chuckled, too.

"Sure is better," he agreed. "Yeah, it'll be good to see Frenchy again."

The bartender nodded. He started to speak, then appeared to hear something that Gary *didn't* hear. And there was nothing the matter with the pilot's ears.

"Sounds like Sofie," he stated to Gary. "Be right back."

He vanished through the curtains. Gary spilled three-quarters of his glass of beer into the trough close to the bar. He spilled it quietly, then raised the glass to his lips. He held it there—and did some quick thinking. This man with the beady eyes was tricking him. Why? Had there been a slip-up? Or was it part of the system? And if it were part of the system—could he sit in the game, and beat it?

Subdued voices came to him again. The bartender's voice sounded above another voice. There *was* someone else this time. But it didn't sound like a woman's tone.

Gary dropped his right hand into the pocket of his coat. He felt the effects of the quarter glass of beer. The voices back of the faded red curtain died. The bartender came back into the café room. He walked behind the bar, passed in front of Gary, moved toward the door. Gary turned slowly, faced him. He heard someone cough, back of the red curtains.

Slowly he backed toward the wall opposite the bar. He set the empty glass on a table, as he moved away. But he didn't take his eyes from the thick-set one.

That individual was opening the door that led out to the narrow French Quarter street. He looked in one direction, then the other. He made a clicking noise with his lips, then stepped back inside. But he left the door opened.

"Here's Frenchy now!" he stated cheerfully, and turned toward Gary.

A form showed in the door space. An arm moved—the door was shoved wide. A slight, carefully dressed individual entered. He had a dark smear of a mustache, rather long sideburns. He moved his head like a bird. His eyes met Gary's.

"Bon soir, Monsieur!" he greeted. His hands were at his sides, his eyes met Gary's smilingly.

Gary spoke hoarsely. "You are Lamonte?" he asked. " 'Frenchy' Lamonte?"

A puzzled expression showed in the eyes of the slight man who had addressed Gary in French. He half turned, as though to question the bartender. Gary's eyes followed the slight one's gaze. The bartender was back of the heavy wood. He was bent forward slightly—his eyes were on Gary. But not on Gary's face—on the pocket into which the pilot had dropped his right hand.

And then, in a flash, Gary Greer saw through the game. They had worked fast—the bartender and his aide back of the curtains. But this man who had come in through the front door—he was not Frenchy Lamonte. He was a man, perhaps, that others wanted out of the way. He had come in unsuspecting, with hands at his sides.

"He's Lamonte!" the bartender snapped. "But he don't speak our language—"

The slight man turned toward Gary. His face was white now, twisted. *He* saw through the game, too. He tried to speak—but the words were only a whisper. Gary's voice, pitched low, cut through the other man's weak effort.

"He's not Frenchy—"

Then he saw the bartender dropping out of sight back of the wood. He saw the slight man stiffen—his eyes go wide. Fear showed clearly in them, terribly. He was staring toward the faded red curtains.

"No!" He cried shrilly, finding his voice. "For God's sake—don't—"

The first shot crashed, and the body of the slight man jerked convulsively. The second shot clipped splinters of wood from the facing of the bar. The third seemed to spin the slight man in a half circle—his body hunched forward, dropped heavily.

Gary Greer was down on his knees. There was a table between his body and the faded, red curtains. He got a glimpse of a hand—a wrist. It wasn't a large hand, or wrist. He raised his gun, was about to squeeze the trigger—and didn't.

There was a play on—and he figured in it. It wasn't just chance. Someone had figured that he would squeeze lead at a certain human who had been called in through the front door. He'd hesitated, and the bartender had tried to lead him on. Then, when he hadn't squeezed lead, some other human had.

There was no sound or movement from the man on the floor. No sound from back of the red curtains. The shots had not come from a Maxim silenced gun—surely they would be heard outside the tiny café. There would be the police—

Gary straightened. He called out in a low tone.

"You—behind the bar! Show yourself—"

A siren wailed dismally in the distance. Gary swore fiercely. Police—and this wasn't chance, either. The whole thing had been a plant—and he wasn't out of it yet.

He held the cloth of his coat pocket high—a few steps brought him close to the man on the floor. Pie faced the faded curtains. There was no movement of their material. The siren of an ambulance or a police car sounded closer. Gary bent down.

One, glance at the wide eyes was enough. Fear was still mirrored in them. The one who had last come in from the front door was dead.

Gary moved toward the bar. He reached out with his left hand, raised his empty beer glass. With a swift movement he hurled it down toward the left end of the bar. Then he slipped around the right end. His eyes narrowed on the floor back of the bar. No human crouched there! The bartender had vanished! A tightly closed trapdoor pointed the way of his going.

Three strides brought him to the trap. He bent down, tried to move it. But it didn't budge. Fixed from below. Voices sounded, raised, outside the door. Gary groaned. He took a step toward the curtains, stopped. That would mean certain death. They had trapped him, baited him. He was alone with a dead man. True, his own gun was probably of a different caliber than that used on the man who curled beyond the bar. No shells were gone from his gun. They couldn't get him for the kill—but once in the hands of the police, questioned, pawed over—

No—the curtains were not the way out. There would either be death or no escape back of them. And the trap was securely fastened. It was the front door—his only chance. He would go out the way he came in.

Once again the siren cut through the heat of the night. It was within a block or so of the place now. And the voices beyond the half-opened door were louder. There were more of them. And there was no wild rush to get into the place. That told Gary something. It told him that the place—the unnamed café—had a reputation.

He moved from behind the bar, went out through the door. He closed it back of him. Beyond the glare of the light over the entrance, he saw faces. He smiled. Instead of turning away from the group of men—he moved toward it. An arm shot out, gripped his left arm just above the wrist. He was unprepared for it—his gun was useless. He was swung partially off balance.

"Who—went out?" a voice questioned him in a hoarse whisper.

Gary continued to smile. But he didn't look at the one who questioned. His eyes were on the red spotlight of the car that rounded the intersection—was rolling toward the café entrance. Not an ambulance—but a detectives' car.

"Frenchy!" he muttered grimly. "The moll got him!"

The grip relaxed. A voice muttered a harsh oath. He took a step forward—was through the group. A figure on the running-board of the car dropped off—headed toward him. The car rolled on past him, brakes squealed.

Gary turned toward the street. The one who had dropped from the car was heavy. He had a stomach. But he could move swiftly enough. *He* was in the street, too. A big hand closed over Gary's right arm, above the elbow. For the second time he was jerked off balance.

"What's the rush?" a voice muttered. "Stick around—something may come up!"

Gary brought up his left arm. It had everything he possessed in the way of arm muscle back of it. His body was in close to the bull's—his clenched fist cleared his own face by only an inch. The other man was taller—six inches taller. The blow caught him just under the right jaw bone. His teeth clicked together noisily, his body stiffened, then sagged. He groaned as he collapsed forward.

But even before the bulk of his body hit the surface of the narrow street, Gary was moving. He didn't run. He didn't look back. Close to the curbing he moved, his body bent forward.

Pain was stabbing up through his wrist and left arm. The hand felt numb, useless. But the pain was above it. He turned a corner. A uniformed officer was running toward the narrow street. His breath was coming in great gulps. He was a half block away, and Gary slowed down to almost a stroll.

The officer jerked his head toward him. He seemed about to stop—when the siren of the police car wailed. The officer swore pantingly, and pounded on. As he turned the corner, Gary Greer broke into a run. He turned off the street, to the left. It was his guess that the driver of the police car had spotted the form of the big bull he had dropped.

There were people on the street into which he had turned. Black people. He was in the negro section. He slowed down again. There were children playing in the street—many of them. Glancing at the knuckles of his left hand, he saw that they were badly skinned. He had hit hard—it had been necessary. A slip there—and the bull would have used lead.

There was the wail of another siren. It had a lower tone. Gary halted. He was almost directly in front of a boot-black stand. The eyes of the negro who ran it gave him the idea. The negro was staring at him curiously. His white make-up would attract instant suspicion. The bull he had knocked out had seen his face, even though the street had been dark. The bartender had seen it. The men outside—

"Gimme a tin of polish, George!" he muttered, and produced a quarter.

The black proprietor stared at him dumbly. The low-toned police siren sounded nearer. Then the black one grinned, handed him the polish. Gary crossed the street. A dimly lighted entrance had a sign on it—"Hotel." He went in. There was a dingy desk—no one at it. He guessed that the clerk was out in the street, curious about the racket the police were making. His eyes sought a second sign, found it. Down the flight of stairs he went, into a mean room. There was a cracked mirror.

Gary Greer shut the door. There was no key. He got his hat off—went to work. Several times a siren wail came down to him. In three minutes he'd done a fair job. He didn't have to worry about his hands—they'd have to be black, too. His lips were the hardest to get right. And his left hand was almost useless. Thoughts stabbed through his head as he worked with the black polish.

He had a hunch that the kill had been important. Perhaps *he* hadn't counted—had been the break the killers were awaiting. It had been a close go. The one who had greeted him in French hadn't been killed blunderingly. It hadn't been a street knifing, a shot from behind. The man had counted. And he had been surprised. Even so, before the lead had torn through his clothes, into his body—he had realized. He had begged for mercy in one tortured plea.

And the first siren had sounded too soon. There had been a phone call. The bartender and his accomplice or accomplices—they had worked rapidly and smoothly. Perhaps they had not thought that the man they planned on trapping would use the front door. Perhaps they had thought that the police car would arrive sooner.

Gary slipped the black polish tin under a dirty newspaper in a corner of the room. He moved out through the doorway, up the stairs. There was a shine to the polish—but there was a shine to the faces of the negroes in the section, too. The heat caused that.

The desk was still vacated. Outside there was excitement. A negro police officer was moving along the pavement. He was looking at faces and hands. Gary grinned. He cut across the street, moving very slowly. There was a pool-room opposite the hotel. He decided not to mix with the crowd in there. The police, if the kill was worth it, would search such places as poolrooms. The negro section bordered on the French quarter, was practically a portion of it. There would be many negroes in the round-up. The black polish was an asset now. But if he were taken to the station—it would be a serious liability. It was a job to pass in the night—not in the day.

Gary Greer checked his speed. He had been unconsciously walking fast. Southern negroes didn't do that. He walked flat-footed, slowly. He tried to remember the direction of St. Charles Street, headed that way. There was no longer the wail of police whistles.

The plane was at Rice Field. He'd given the name of I. Jones when he'd rented hangar space. He hadn't liked the idea, but it was a safe play. He had a limited commercial license under that name. And sometimes inspectors around the fields liked to look at the papers a pilot held. He didn't want the plane tied up. The ship was important.

He was on a well lighted street now. And he reached a decision. The name of Frenchy Lamonte had figured in the killing. He'd used it, the bartender had used it. Others—at least one other, back of the faded, red curtains, had heard it used. A man was dead. The police were making the usual racket. It would be wise to get into the air, wing clear of New Orleans. It was a defeat—and the first tough one he had met. He could fly the ship with his right hand; he would only need the left for throttle work. And night flying wouldn't bother him—he had done considerable dark winging.

A cab was cruising along the curb. Gary figured that he was six or seven squares from the café in which the slight man had been battered out of one life. He hailed the cab. The driver grinned at him. He was a negro driver.

"I sure craves a good hotel, boy!" Gary stated huskily. "An' I mean—the best!"

The driver grinned widely. "Tha's the Booker House, you all wants!" he stated, and closed the cab door after Gary.

The cab jerked into motion. Gary relaxed in the seat. Red showed through the black on his left hand. But he was smiling faintly. He'd tried to get close to one Frenchy Lamonte. A name on his list. Instead, it was his idea that Frenchy had got close to him—too close. There were a lot of things he didn't know. In the hotel he'd get liquid to remove the blacking. He'd phone the field, have them get the plane on the dead-line. He'd get the papers—the killing had occurred close to the normal dead-line of first editions, but there might be a printed "flash." He'd be able to learn who had crashed down on the floor of the café on the narrow street.

His body stiffened as he heard the staccato clatter of an engine—a motorcycle engine. The driver looked out the left side, back. Then he pulled over toward the curb. He used squeaky brakes.

A motorcycle mounted by an officer in khaki curved in front of the cab. The officer dismounted, kicked the stand beneath the rear wheel. Gary forced his body to relax on the seat. He grinned faintly. The interior of the cab was fairly dark, but the officer jerked a flashlight from his pocket as he came to the door. He opened it, used the light on Gary's face.

He scowled, then chuckled. "You sure are shinin', Black Boy!" he muttered. "Sort of sweatin', eh?"

Gary chuckled. The officer swore cheerfully.

"Well—we're lookin' for a pasty faced gent just now, George," he stated. "So you're all right!"

He slammed the door, extinguished the flashlight. He waved the driver on. Gary swore softly as the cab jerked into motion again. The black polish was working. And in the shelter of a *good* colored hotel, when he had removed it, he could pass out unnoticed. Many negroes who were almost white in color frequented the better class colored hotels.

One thing was certain—the detective he had battered down had recovered, and had remembered a face. The man-hunt was on. The police would rate the one who had battered the bull down as the killer of the slight man who had talked French. The trap had failed—if it *had* been a trap—so far as Gary was concerned. But it had been a narrow escape.

Gary Greer ran the tips of his right hand fingers over the torn knuckles of his left hand. He remembered Pete Ranning's coded wire. Joyce Rawlings had seen him—knew he was alive. He could fool others, perhaps—but not Joyce. She would try to stop him, of course. And if her eyes met his, pleaded with him—

"They won't!" he muttered fiercely. "Not until—I've finished. Not until the names are no longer names. They killed—these names. They killed something of mine, a part of me—"

He broke off abruptly. The cab was slowing down. There was an ornate entrance, to the right of the cab. It marked the Booker House. Gary paid the driver. As he moved slowly into the hotel, he smiled grimly. The quarter he had paid the boot-black had been a sweet investment. He couldn't remember any time he'd made a better one.

GARY GREER WORKED over his face, and read the "flash" item in the paper the boy had brought to Room 504. The last minute news sentences were brief. One Gaston Dégonne had been murdered in a Vieux Carré speakeasy. The man was important for one very definite reason. He was a stool-pigeon. He had been shot twice—through the stomach, and just over the heart. Plains-clothes man Jim Burke had been knocked down by the murderer, after a desperate fight. The other bulls had been inside the café at the time. The dragnet was out, and the police had a good description. That was all.

Gary smiled grimly. The "desperate fight" amused him, and he doubted the "good description" part of the item. But he had been right about the kill. Stool-pigeons were always important, to the police. He got the last of the black color from around his lips. And then he heard it—the distant drone of a plane in the sky.

He stood stiffly, listening. The drone increased in tone. It wasn't a mail ship engine-beat. He knew that. Wasn't heavy enough. The plane wasn't carrying a load. She was a little ship. And little ships didn't fly so often at night.

Gary snapped out the lights. He moved toward the open window. The room was on the fifth floor—the top floor. There was a three-quarter moon. The plane was getting altitude, he guessed. She was winging over the hotel, but he couldn't see her yet. He swore softly.

"Sounds like—*my* job!" he muttered.

His little ship had a peculiar song in the air. He'd heard the engine roar through the curved exhausts many times—from the ground. Others had tested it—back at the South Side Field. There weren't many ships with such a sky drone.

He stared up—and the ship came into sight. Gary's body stiffened. The moon gave light to the gray wings—he could see the round fuselage. The wing lights were not on; the ship was flying at about fifteen hundred feet, and climbing. He could see the tail assembly clearly as she winged eastward. It looked very much like the tail assembly of the ship he had left at Rice Field hours ago!

Gary fumbled for the card given him at the field. He found the card—but his fingers failed to find something else—something that he had placed in the inner pocket of his light suit. His limited commercial license was gone!

Turning away from the window, he snapped on the room lights. He searched his clothes. The paper was gone. He got the Rice Field number, steadied his voice. He was fighting for calmness now. The ship in the air—it looked like *his* ship. And if the police had found the license in the café and it must have dropped from his pocket when he had leaned over the dead man, or over the trap door back of the bar—

The field was answering him. He spoke in a low tone, as clearly as he could.

"This is Jones—I. Jones. Took hangar space with you late this afternoon. A special job—single-seater. Want the plane on the dead-line, please. Think I'll beat the heat, and make Miami—"

He stopped—his words died. The voice at the other end of the wire had cut him off. It came clearly.

"Night manager speaking. You say you want Mr. Jones. He took off five minutes ago in his plane. I can still hear his exhaust beat—"

Gary Greer stood very straight. Slowly he hung up the receiver. There was no use in more talk. The police hadn't got his license card—but someone else *had*. And someone knew his plane, knew he had winged to Rice Field. Someone had replaced him in the cockpit—was winging eastward now. *He* could hear the drone of the engine, too. He had not seen the night manager at the field. And the one who had stolen the ship probably had presented his license, or had shown it in some way, to convince that official. A different crew was on— but the keys were in the ship's ignition switch. They had to be—Gary had wanted the chance of getting the plane warmed up, on the line.

He was fighting the gang, the police—and the girl he loved. Perhaps there was suspicion, now, that the son of Sanford Greer had *not* died in the plunge from a plane. One thing was very certain. He turned slowly toward the open window and the faint exhaust drone of a ship. Whatever he did—it must be done alone. He smiled twistedly, thinking of the girl he loved—and then of his father's body, lying in the mud, riddled with gangster lead. He spoke in a low, hard tone.

"High odds—with Frenchy dealing, and maybe *flying* now! But I'm still sitting in, Killers! Maybe *I* can stack the deck, too!"

5

Within the Circle

THE BLUE EYES of Pete Ranning went toward the door that led from the Field Office corridor into the room he occupied. He leaned toward the surface of the desk, slipped open a drawer. The friction of wood against wood created no sound; several days ago Pete had greased the drawer carefully. His right hand moved forward—a voice came to him, cool, steady.

"You'll have to move that mirror, Pete—the angle's perfect for me. Bad—for you."

Pete turned his head toward the small mirror. He muttered several words that the girl did not catch. She was inside the room now, with the door closed back of her. She smiled faintly.

"Alone?" she questioned. "Down here late, aren't you?"

Pete Ranning smiled back at her. His eyes went toward the mirror—came back to hers.

"I'm alone—or *was*, until you came in, Joyce," he said slowly. "Or *thought* I was."

She stood looking down at him. Her eyes were narrowed slightly; her face was pale. Slowly she turned her head toward the mirror.

"Why'd you move it, Pete?" Her voice was steady. "You *did* move it, didn't you?"

For several seconds he was silent. Then he shrugged his shoulders.

"You're mixing in, Joyce. It's foolish of you. But you deserve the truth. I *didn't* move that mirror. It was hanging at least four feet to the right of its present spot. At ten o'clock Benson, pilot of the night mail, shoved open that door. I didn't spot him until he came in. It's now almost one. The mirror's been shifted in the last three hours."

He rose. The girl was at his side as they moved toward the mirror. It was a small oblong glass. It hung alone on the wall. The hole made by the nail of its old position had been plugged with something that looked like chewing gum. The walls were almost that color—brown-gray.

Pete Ranning turned, walked back to his desk. He sat in the chair and stared toward the door.

"I was out of here from ten-thirty to eleven, or a little after," he breathed half aloud. "Then I was out again for about fifteen minutes, just after midnight."

The girl walked toward a chair at the right of his desk. Her lips were set firmly. She moved the chair slightly, her brown eyes going to the office door. She sank into the chair; her eyes met Pete's. She laughed in a low, half bitter tone.

"Queer, isn't it, Pete? This fighting—something you can't quite see?"

Pete stiffened a little. His blue eyes flickered.

"Why don't you get away, Joyce?" he asked. "Why don't you—"

Her expression stopped him. The drone of a ship engine reached his ears. Yellow light suddenly flooded the field beyond the windows of the Operations Office. A siren wailed. It had a strange sound in the quiet of the night.

"Transport—from Chicago," Pete stated slowly. "New service—night flight. Doing well."

The girl nodded. "Pete—" she said slowly—"why would Gary want to change that mirror?"

He was sitting straight now, staring at her. She was smiling; but it was a grim, tight-lipped smile. She wore a tailored suit—rather shabby. A small, dark turban allowed wisps of her black hair to contrast the color of her skin. Her voice had a husky note.

Pete Ranning shook his head slowly.

"Gary's dead," he stated softly. "I wish—"

"That I wouldn't insist he isn't?" She laughed lightly. "Still lying to me, Pete? Still bluffing? Well, he isn't. And Pete—" her smile faded suddenly— "here's something you don't know. He's left New Orleans."

The man back of the desk fought for a blank expression. But his eyes showed that the city's name had registered. The girl smiled faintly again.

"A stool-pigeon named Dégonne was killed, before he left. But, Pete—Gary didn't kill him."

Pete Ranning forced a smile. "That's *something*, Joyce," he stated. "Several humans have been killed lately—it's good to know Gary isn't the one responsible—"

"Stop sparring!" The girl's voice was suddenly sharp, cold. "Money can do a lot of things, Pete. I've got money. I'm spending money, and I'm getting results. Gary's back—he's in Center City!"

Pete Ranning turned the jerk of his body into a movement toward some papers on his desk. The girl was smiling again, smiling coldly. She half turned, looked toward the mirror that hung in the new position.

"Why would Gary—move it?" she murmured to herself.

Pete Ranning rose from the desk. He moved close to the girl who had been engaged to Gary Greer, looked down at her. His face was expressionless. He spoke quietly.

"Gary's father knew too much for the big crooks. They put him on the spot, murdered him. A car-load of them shot him down. During a storm. Gary loved his father. But revenge was futile. The Center City police were too crooked to help. So the next morning he took a plane off from this field. He wanted to get away. We gave him a 'chute. The ship crashed in the mountains—the 'chute was found, ripped loose from the body harness. He had tried to jump, after the plane's engine had failed with no landing spot in sight. His body had torn loose—"

He stopped, turned away. The girl laughed.

"That thought almost broke my heart," she agreed. "Until I had the search made. Until my men didn't find the body. I know Gary, Pete. So do you. He wouldn't go out—that way. He'd go out fighting. I've seen him. Once before he left for New Orleans—"

"Why New Orleans?" Pete was facing the girl again.

She was not smiling. "You sent him a wire there, Pete," she stated quietly. "You warned him that I was trying to spoil things."

The muscles of Pete's face were twitching. He tried to laugh, as though it were ridiculous. But it wasn't much of a success. He turned his eyes from those of the girl.

"What—nonsense!" he managed.

"That's what the wire was, Pete," she replied quietly. "You used a very simple code. Not for me—but for a man my money is hiring. You've been watched for days, Pete. Every move you make. I've a man working right at the field. You're careless,

Pete—because you're not expert. You phoned that message in—the one to Gary. I've tapped in on three of your calls, Pete—and this one counted."

Ranning moved back to his desk chair. He dropped into it. His face was older, his eyes had a more strained look. The girl went on.

"I'll finish the story you were telling me, Pete. The plane was found, crashed in the mountains. A ripped 'chute was found. The plane was burned—but metal doesn't always burn. It does not always melt. Gary had a bag with him. There were buckles on it. They weren't found—not a trace of them. No trace of the bag. Why not?"

Pete said nothing. His eyes were half closed.

"I'll tell you why. That bag held a *second* 'chute. Gary used it—and tossed that bag away, long before he reached the spot where he dived the ship—and jumped. You know all this, Pete. So do I. And I know other things. The police are commencing to get suspicious. *Others* are beginning to get suspicious. I've studied the thing, Pete—*how* I've studied it! The ones working for me have studied it. We're going to stop Gary from going on.

We're going to stop him before the police stop him, or before the gangsters—" her voice was a little shaken—"stop him."

Pete Ranning spoke in a low voice. "If you *were* right, Joyce—what good would it do—this interfering? He'd hate you for it."

She smiled twistedly. "He can hate me—if I can stop him from going on, Pete. A gangster named Liseman is dead. He was killed just outside of this field. A gangster named Babe Lewis was shot to death, down on River Street—"

"A gangster named Steve Brady was murdered, out in San Francisco—" Pete's voice was mocking.

The girl shuddered. Here eyes held an expression of fear. She was silent for several seconds.

"You used a word then, Pete," she said in a low tone, "that I've never used. It's what I must stop Gary from doing. I want to save him—from himself. Everywhere he goes—there's a death. And the names connect, Pete—they connect with the shooting of his father in some way. Yes—in every case!"

She rose suddenly from the chair. Her eyes were boring into the blue, tired eyes of Pete Ranning.

"I will stop him—from going on!" she said fiercely. "He's come back to Center City, Pete. I know that. He's come back into the circle. It's a vicious one. The police and the gangsters—they both suspect that Gary's not dead. He's fighting them both. And he's fighting me. I don't care if you tell him that, Pete—when he comes here to you. He's fighting me—only I want to *help*. The others—they want to *hurt*. Pete—" her voice broke, then steadied— "when he comes here—"

Pete Ranning laughed. It was a harsh, hurting laugh.

"You've seen a face that looked like another face, Joyce," he stated grimly. "Your operatives are out for the money you have.

They make simple wires appear coded ones. They make you think I'm fighting you—so that it will be more difficult for them to give you results. Because a body isn't found, buckles aren't found—that doesn't mean that Gary isn't dead. Because gangsters die—that doesn't mean—"

He stopped. The girl was turning. She was facing the mirror on the wall. Her eyes were wide. Pete's hand moved toward the greased wood of the drawer. He did not look toward the wall mirror. His eyes were on the door that led to the corridor. Slowly, very slowly—it was opening!

Pete Ranning sucked in his breath sharply. He saw the girl's right hand go toward her throat—his own fingers tightened over the grip of the gun in the drawer. Beyond the building a ship engine roared, then died. The floodlights on the field were abruptly extinguished.

Pete lifted the gun above the level of the desk. He aimed it toward the opening door. The crevice was great enough now to allow a body to slip through. The girl's body was tense, rigid.

A figure stepped into the room—the door did not close. Pete cried out, rose from the chair. The girl cried out, too. Her voice was a half sob.

"Gary! Gary!"

Pete Ranning was staring at the figure. The man turned toward the girl—he smiled faintly. It was a twisted smile. The corners of the lips were pulled down. He walked toward the desk. The girl cried out again. "Gary!"

And then the shot sounded. It was a crashing, tearing sound. The corridor flung it into the small office. Pete Ranning stiffened. The girl did not scream—the back of a hand went to her lips.

The man who had come in pivoted. He choked a little, went to his knees. He did not throw out his hands. His body curled downward. He sucked in one deep, tortured breath—then his figure shuddered, relaxed. He was motionless.

The girl was at his side. But Pete Ranning had swung around. He was facing the screen of the window behind and to the right of his desk. He stared at it—there was a hole in the sheen of copper. A small, neat hole!

And his keen ears, despite the crashing of the gun in the corridor, had picked up the cough-rasp of a gun outside. Gary had been shot down as he faced the window—the gun fired in the corridor had been a blind crash—

"Pete!" The girl had risen. She was standing staring down at the figure on the carpet of the office. "Pete—it isn't—Gary!"

Ranning moved from the window. He heard a voice calling, out in the corridor, as he knelt beside the man on the floor. He stared into the face of the dead man. The eyes were open—wide open. They were gray eyes. But they were not the eyes of Gary Greer. The hair was sandy in color, rumpled. The lips were narrow. There was a goggle cut over the left eye—a reddish scar. But the eyes—they were not the eyes of Gary Greer. Pete Ranning felt it, sensed it—even as the girl had sensed it.

The voice of Jansen, the hangar superintendent, sounded clearly.

"Ranning—Pete! What happened—"

He was in the room now, staring down at the figure on the floor. He muttered the word hoarsely.

"Gary—Greer!"

Pete Ranning was calmer now. He spoke sharply.

"Call the watchmen at the gates. Tell 'em no one leaves the

field until I give the word. Tell 'em there's been a murder. No one leaves. Hurry!"

Jansen moved toward the phone. Pete spoke to the girl. Her face was very pale; her hands were clenched at her sides. But she met his look bravely.

"Wet a towel—in that wash-room, Joyce. You know where—"

She turned, moved steadily toward the wash-room. Jansen was talking to the watchman at the Number One gate. Pete opened the dead man's vest. He had been shot just under the heart. He had been facing the window with the hole-drilled screen.

Joyce was back. She handed him a wet towel.

"He's—alive?" she whispered.

Pete shook his head. "Dead," he said quietly.

He lowered the towel, rubbed it briskly over the skin above the dead man's left eye. Then he raised the damp towel. He heard Jansen, who had come over from his desk, mutter surprisedly.

"It's *not*—Greer!"

Pete Ranning rose to his feet. The white of the towel was streaked with dull red from the painted skin of the dead man. The scar had vanished. Pete was trying to get control of himself, to think clearly. He moved toward his desk.

"I'll call—the police," he said slowly. "It's not—Greer, of course. Gary is—" his eyes met the girl's squarely—"dead. Weeks have passed—"

He knew what she was thinking. He knew what he wanted her to think. *This* was the man she had seen—this was the man her operatives had traced—but this was not the man who had come to him days ago, in this same office.

"God!" Jansen's voice held a note of awe. "They look alike!"

The girl was watching Pete with narrowed eyes. There was a tremulous smile playing about her colorless lips. Pete called the police, reported. He hung up the receiver. His eyes went toward the moved mirror.

"The one that killed him—" he muttered half aloud—"stood outside, shot through the screen with a Maxim silenced gun. He shot right on top of the other crash. He had light in here—and he could look toward that mirror through the screen. He could see the man in the corridor, knew when he was in position—at least I think he could. I'll check up on that in a few minutes."

He stopped. His eyes met the dark brown eyes of Joyce Rawlings again. Jansen was muttering.

"He's so close to Gary—his face, his build—"

The girl spoke. "Gary Greer is dead," she said slowly. But her lips still moved. She was talking aloud because of Jansen. She was fighting Gary—but she was protecting him. Protecting him from the police. *Trying* to protect him from killers.

Pete spoke slowly. "Go out and see how things are coming at the main gate, Jansen," he ordered. "Don't let those guards allow anyone to slip through." Jansen nodded, moved out. Pete Ranning looked down at the dead man, then at the girl.

"You see—" he said slowly. "You thought this man—"

She was shaking her head. His words died. There was a clear light in her eyes. Her voice was firm.

"If Gary Greer is dead—why did *he* come?" she demanded. "Why was he *killed*—if Gary is dead?"

Pete Ranning's face was expressionless, But he shook his head slowly. The girl was looking down at the face of the dead man. She was calm—very calm.

"I believe you, Pete," she said quietly. "This is *one* thing—you don't know. But this man has a *name*—"

She saw Pete Ranning start. Her eyes were narrowed. But she spoke very calmly, very slowly.

"And it might be—" she was looking beyond him, toward the bullet-torn screen now—"a very important name, Pete. A name that—counted!"

PETE RANNING STOOD five feet from the copper screen of the office window, and looked toward his desk. Green turf was beneath his feet. There was no moon; it was a very dark night. He could see clearly the spot where the nameless man had stood. He could see the mirror. The corridor beyond the room was dimly lighted, but in the glass he caught the reflection of Jansen's body movement. He swore softly. The door was only half opened. It was the way the one who had resembled Gary Greer had left it when he had come into the room.

Pete Ranning turned away from the window. There were men in the office—many men. Headquarters' men. The girl had been questioned, had been released. She had answered questions stupidly. Callahan came toward Pete now. The detective was smiling grimly.

"Toby knows the corpse," he stated. "He's a guy named Franey—sniffs the white stuff and hangs around the South Side poolrooms. Petty thief—served two sentences. But why in hell was he rigged up—"

He checked himself. Pete looked blank. But he was thinking. Gary Greer had been using a pasty make-up. The dead man's face had been chalky in color, when he had come into the room.

But only the scar had been painted over his left eye—the color of his face had been natural. A dope user.

Callahan was speaking again. He was short and thick-set, and he had a black mustache. His straw was slanted back from his forehead.

"Guards at the gates say no one's left," he stated. "You say no plane has taken off the field since this bird went down. Pretty hard to get over the concrete and wire you've got around the circle. Greer had this stuff set up to keep crooks out, eh? They were stealing ships, weren't they?"

Pete nodded. "We keep a lot of ships on the dead-line, material in the hangars. Valuable stuff. And we're pretty close in to the city. We lost a plane and some material—and Greer fenced the place in. Good job."

The detective nodded. "The boys are lining up your men," he stated. "Killer must be inside, unless one of the gate men is fixed. Must be somewhere—within the circle."

Pete stiffened a little at the words. The girl had used the same ones. His eyes went across the grass of the circular field. It wasn't such a big stretch, but it was big enough for anything taking off without a trans-Atlantic load of fuel.

Callahan was moving toward the dead-line and Hangar A. The flood-lights were on. Several other detectives came around from the entrance of the Operations Office. The room was almost empty now. Down the dead-line men were gathering in groups.

Pete Ranning stood staring toward the office. The mirror had been moved—the one who had shot the dead man had wanted to see the one in the corridor, the man who had fired the crashing shot. But why? Why had he not simply waited—

waited for the one who had been killed to come in? Certainly he had known that the man would come.

The telephone was ringing in Pete's office. He moved around the building, entered the corridor. A detective was speaking over the phone. He nodded toward Ranning.

"Hold on a second—here he is now." He spoke to Pete. "Call for you—long distance, I guess. Coming through bad."

Pete took the receiver. "Ranning!" he said loudly. "South Side Field—Ranning talking!"

There was a click or two, then a voice came to his ears very faintly.

"Alone, Ranning?"

Pete stared toward the door leading out to the corridor. Two words—but his heart was pounding. The detective was outside, but Pete heard no footfalls. Outside—but listening.

"All right, Harry," he said loudly into the mouthpiece of the phone. "Ship's down all right, eh? No fog?"

There was more clicking, Pete heard the detective moving along the corridor. Then the voice came again, very faintly.

"Let me know—when it's clear, Ranning. Need—perfect work—to get out of this."

Pete's eyes were narrowed now. He was calmer. He spoke very low.

"Go ahead, Harry—let's have it!"

And then the voice of Gary Greer was speaking slowly and steadily, at the other end of the wire. It was only faintly disguised in tone.

"I want another ship, Pete—and a chance for a getaway. Couldn't make the gate—after the kill. Figured you'd use the phone. There's a Ryan on the dead-line—at the north end.

Keep the detectives away from her—and have one of the boys crank her and rev up the engine. Leave the switch keys inside. Clear? Gas for a long flight. Clear?"

Pete's face was twisted. "Right," he muttered. "Where are you?"

The voice was almost a whisper. "On the Field line—booth in Hangar Six. Hangar's dark—get me the chance to climb in that warmed-up ship. Pete. Don't fail!"

Pete spoke slowly. "You'll make it. Listen, Harry—" he glanced toward the corridor— "Franey's dead. Bullet below the heart—"

Gary Greer cut in sharply. "Came back to see you, Pete—I was followed. Franey's finish was planned cleverly—damn cleverly. They'll search the Field right. I've got to have a ship, Pete—they got mine in New Orleans. The docs had given Franey two weeks to live—I'm taking care of his wife—"

Pete swore softly. "Joyce was here—when he came in—" he interrupted. "But why was Franey—"

"Joyce!" There was surprise in Gary's tone. "Did she—"

"She knew it wasn't you," Pete spoke in a low voice. "Who got him, Harry? He was shot from outside—"

"He was shot—inside!" Gary's voice was low, steady. "They got him in their car—after they'd made him up Pete. Have to quit now—detectives poking around here. Get me the ship, Pete—have her warmed up. And watch— Callahan!"

There was a sharp clicking sound—the receiver had been hung up. Pete stared toward the window. He moved toward the screen with the hole in it. The hole was low—he had not examined it close before. Now he caught sight of a splinter of wood. A hole dug near the sash of the window. And inside the hole—lead!

"Never—came through!" he muttered. "Got him—in the corridor!"

His eyes went to the mirror. He thought of Franey coming in. The way his body had jerked at the crashing sound in the corridor. But they had heard no sound, until he had shoved open the door. No cough-rasp of Maxim. That had come *after* the crashing shot, and from the outside. But the bullet was embedded in the window sash.

Pete pulled himself away from his conflicting thoughts. He moved from the room. Hangar Six—Gary had phoned from the booth. A Field wire—no chance of anyone listening in. That was why he had talked. Gary wanted a ship—a Ryan.

He had been followed to the field; he had not come in through the gates. There was one other way of getting into the place, and Gary would know of it. Few did. He had seemed surprised at Joyce being there. That meant that he had not stood outside the window of the office. But then, how had he known about Franey? And he *had* known, because the bullet fired from outside had struck into the wood of the window sash.

Pete moved along the dead-line. He called to Barrenor, a veteran mechanic.

"Go up to the north end and warm up the Ryan near Number Six," he ordered. "Leave the keys in the ignition switch—and leave her prop turning. I may want her in a half hour or so. Come back this way as soon as she gets revving up nicely—for the investigation."

Barrenor nodded, moved toward the north end of the Field. Pete walked toward the group of men gathering half way down the dead-line. He saw Toby and Callahan talking together, and remembered Gary's final words. "Watch out for Callahan." He smiled faintly. He'd watch out for *everyone*. And the girl had said that Gary had returned to Center City. He swore softly as he neared the two detectives. Callahan had a peculiar smile on his face.

"Where's that bird going?" he snapped at Pete, pointing toward Barrenor.

"Going to warm up the Ryan—relief ship for the north-south mail plane. Pilot just called up he was down in the emergency field near Barley Flats—conked engine. Got to get him another ship. Barrenor's warming her up—but as soon as she gets turning over he'll come down."

The detective nodded his head slowly. His eyes were narrowed on Pete Ranning's.

"I'll look her over before she takes off," he stated. "Anyone hear you answer that phone?"

"One of your men was in there," Pete answered.

Callahan nodded again. "You can point him out later," he stated. "Just wanted to know." He smiled faintly.

Pete grinned. He reached for a cigarette. The lines of the circle were tightening. They were being drawn in. And Gary Greer was on the inside.

GARY GREER STOOD near the wall of Number Six hangar. There was only a faint light creeping in between the cracks of the end doors; he had entered by the small door at the rear of the hangar. On the dead-line, perhaps fifty feet from the hangar, the Ryan's engine was purring steadily. Seconds ago it had roared—now the beat was low.

He guessed that the mechanic had left the ship. There would

be the blocks under the wheels to be removed—and then she would be set for the take-off. He smiled faintly.

There was sound running along the wall now. He turned swiftly toward the door. The small door through which he had entered. It opened, then closed. He could hear quick breathing. His right hand was gripping his Maxim-silenced weapon. He faced toward the door. There was silence, and then a voice.

"Gary—Gary!"

It was low, clear. It was the voice of Joyce Rawlings!

He held his breath. But fear gripped him. The girl knew the Field—she knew the hangars. There was too much she knew. If her hand ran along the wall—

It didn't. Flashlight glare cut through the darkness—the beam shot toward the fuselage of a ship, the tail-assembly of another. And then it swung toward him. He stiffened—then smiled. There was no escape. The white light held him in full glare.

"Gary!" The girl's voice was weaker now. "It *is*—you!"

"Steady—drop the beam, Joyce." He spoke calmly, quietly. The light from the flashlight was suddenly dimmed. "You win—Joyce. I can't fight you—all."

She moved toward him, speaking no word. And then she was in his arms—and he was holding her tightly. Finally, he spoke.

"How did you—come here?" he asked quietly. "You're alone?"

She nodded. There were tears in her eyes; she smiled through them.

"I went out—after they finished questioning me. They let me go. But I came back through the other gate. No orders to stop anyone coming in. I felt you were here somewhere, Gary. I heard the mechanic start to rev up the ship's engine—and when he climbed down I asked him why it was being warmed up. He said Pete had told him to do it. I was suspicious. I looked in Number Five hangar—then came here. Oh, Gary— you've hurt me—"

"Steady!" He held her away from him. "I've *had* to, Joyce. It's been hard. And you've—beaten me."

She was calmer now. Only a faint light from the flash struck their faces. They spoke above the rumble of the Ryan's engine.

"When that man—came in—" Her voice shook a little, then steadied— "and the shot sounded—"

Gary Greer smiled faintly. "You thought it was I—you never believed I'd crashed in the ship, did you, Joyce?"

She shook her head. "Gary—" she said slowly, fiercely— "you've *got* to stop! We'll go away. It's terrible—this killing—"

"All killing is terrible!" he cut in bitterly. "I never forget that, Joyce." Her eyes were meeting his gray ones. He looked older, more tired. His face was pasty in color; his lips were made up a little. His face seemed to hold a peculiar half smile. Half laugh.

"Gary"—her voice was very calm— "you sent that man here tonight, because I suspected you were alive. You knew I believed it. You wanted to convince me I was wrong—"

He shook his head. "I was trying to get a plane, Joyce—to reach Pete. I was afraid to use the phone or a messenger. And I was followed. I didn't know you were here, until I reached the corridor near Pete's office. Heard your voice. And then Franey came along. He was the only man I had working with me—in Center City. He only had a few weeks to live—bad heart. I got one look at him—he was made up, rigged to look like me. But he was sick—very sick. He nearly went down once, in that corridor. Another man was holding him up—I couldn't see his face. I got into the office next to Pete's—heard the shot crash. Heard another gun let go, outside. Then I broke for it—and made this hangar. I called Pete—and he had the ship warmed up."

Joyce Rawlings was meeting his eyes squarely.

"You didn't—kill Franey, Gary? He isn't one of—the names on—"

His eyes flickered. He shook his head slowly.

"I wanted Franey with me—we looked like twins. I don't know what happened in the office, Joyce—but I didn't kill Franey," he said. "What *did* happen?"

She told him. His face was expressionless as he listened. When she had finished he spoke quietly.

"Franey was almost dead when he went through the door," he stated. "That final crash might have finished him—his heart was bad. The man outside—he never got Franey. Not through that screen. The mirror was shifted so that the one who shoved Franey into the room could know when to squeeze the trigger of his gun. He wanted to see into the room from the corridor, without being seen. Maybe he wanted to get Pete's reaction to Franey's entrance. Maybe he wanted to see—how Pete would take *my* coming in. Understand. Pete might betray the fact that I was alive—by *not* being surprised."

The girl's eyes were wide. "He didn't," she replied. "We both showed surprise."

Gary nodded. He was holding the girl at arm's length, smiling faintly.

"Then Franey went down—after the gun crash—after the one outside had fired a gun with a silencer. But that man didn't fire at *Franey*, Joyce. He was already finished—it was only a matter of seconds. The gun crash in the corridor was to get Pete Ranning's back to the window. The man outside was trying to kill—*Pete!*"

Joyce stared at Gary Greer. He spoke grimly.

"I'm talking this way to you—because I've done the one thing I tried *not* to do—I've exposed you and Pete to danger. You must tell him, Joyce—and you must go away. Pete can take care of himself. They're closing in on me now. The police, the others. But I'm going through—"

Joyce spoke softly, steadily. "Gary—you mustn't! You've got to stop—"

His expression prevented her from going on. She knew Gary Greer. She knew that he would never stop—not until the killers of his father had been brought to justice.

"Tell Pete that the man outside—the one who fired at him—"

Gary's voice died. A hoarse shout sounded, above the rumble of the Ryan's engine. The girl's body was tense in his arms. For a brief second his lips met hers.

"I'm fighting—through!" he muttered fiercely. "Tell Pete— that man was—*Callahan!*"

Then he was moving toward the end doors of the hanger. He did not turn. Joyce Rawlings was leaning against the wall, sobbing softly. Another voice sounded. Gary Greer slipped through the doors that were opened several feet.

He moved toward the ship slowly, his head held low. But his eyes were working. Two men were running toward the Ryan— one of them was shouting. It was Pete Ranning—the one who called. He was calling the name of a mechanic, but Gary knew that the shouts were meant as a warning for him.

He was beside the wheels now—pulling out the blocks. The

Ryan was a two-place open job. He swung into the cockpit. His hand shoved the throttle forward. The ship started to roll.

His right hand was on the stick—he moved it forward, pulling the tail skid off the earth. Wind rushed around the cowling—he had goggles in his pocket. But there was no time to use them, not until he got off.

The flood-lights helped—but the takeoff was cross-wind. He fought the ship out of a ground skid by using the foot pedals. His head was turned to the right. Pete Ranning was standing motionlessly, shaking a fist. The figure of another man was fifty feet from Pete. He held his left arm high, as though to ward off a blow. But the short muzzle of a weapon rested on that arm. And the fingers of his right hand were squeezing the trigger of that weapon.

The Ryan was lifting. A duralumin strut crackled sharply. The fabric of the fuselage back of Gary Greer was suddenly ripped. And then the two-place ship was zooming up into the night. And Gary Greer was jambing his helmet over his head, pulling down the goggles over his gray eyes. The prop wash wind sang fiercely against the beat of the engine. He muttered words.

"Got to work fast—now. Out in the open. They can hurt Joyce—Pete. Got to work—fast!"

He stared down over the side of the fuselage, as he banked the ship westward. The South Side Field was a circle of white flood-light. He could see Pete's figure—and the figure of Callahan. The detective had lowered his weapon.

Gary Greer leveled off the plane. His face was twisted into a grim smile, a half laugh.

"They got—Franey. He knew too much. They tried for—Pete. And—Joyce is down there, back there—"

He laughed. It was a terrible, bitter laugh. The rush of wind swept it away, into the night air. Gary was staring at the dark horizon blur ahead. He had almost lost, again. Beaten in New Orleans. Almost trapped here, in Center City. He had a plane. He had warned Joyce to tell Pete of the danger. He had seen Callahan use a gun—a silenced gun. Another name? He was not sure of that. But Joyce *knew* that he lived now. And because of that fact, she would be constantly in danger.

Gary Greer climbed the ship up into the darkness. Once, miles away, he twisted his head, looked backward and downward. The Field was only a little circle of light in a great mass of darkness. And he had the feeling that he had lost more than he had gained—within that circle.

6

The Carnival Kill

GARY GREER, HIS body tense, his stubble-bearded face turned toward the opening of the tent flap, stood motionless and listened to the whistle. It reached his ears above the distant murmur of the carnival crowd, above the shrill sounds from the merry-go-round and other Midway amusement devices. It was a whistle that he had heard before. There were certain sounds that the son of Sanford Greer would never forget. They had been stabbed into his ears, his head. Certain sounds—and sights.

The whistle was low, tuneless. It had a peculiar quality. It was not the whistle of a man who liked to purse his lips and make sound. It was not the whistle of a human who made such a sound carelessly, unthinkingly. It was deliberate, desperate. It had a forced, unreal note.

Gary Greer muttered the name in low, grim words. His eyes were narrowed, staring toward the closed flap of the tent.

"Elbow—Gorringe!"

He was sure of it. Back at the cheap house on River Street, in Center City, Gorringe had whistled in just such a manner. Off key, inhumanly. Seconds before, he had spilled lead at Gary— the pilot's lucky fall had been the only thing that had saved him. And lying at the foot of the stairs, he had heard Gorringe move away, whistling. Whistling off key, strangely. Covering up. Fighting his own nerves.

Gary Greer strained his ears. The whistling had died now—carnival sounds had drowned it. But he had not been mistaken, he was sure of that. Gary's ears were keen. Few men whistled as one man did. And that one man was Elbow Gorringe.

Footfalls sounded beyond the tent. Gary turned away from the flap, moved toward the rough table in one corner. On the table were several envelopes. They were addressed to Larry Connors, care of the Johnny Barnes' Show. Gary lifted them, dropped them into a pocket of his brightly checkered suit. It was important that he get mail addressed to Larry Connors—it was more important that no one saw him addressing letters to himself.

A voice sounded. "Connors—oh, Larry!"

Gary Greer turned his head toward the flap of the tent. He spoke in a flat tone.

"Yeah, Eddie—come on in!"

The one who entered was short and thick-set. There was a grin on his browned face. He spoke cheerfully, dropping on Gary's cot.

"You're a lucky guy, Larry," he stated. "Join up with this show—and within a week we go into a big town."

Gary managed a faint smile. "Where's that, Eddie?" he asked. "Carsonville?"

Eddie Lee swore softly. "Hell, no! Ten days, Larry, in a real burg. Center City!"

Gary Greer felt his muscles twitch. But he managed a faint chuckle.

"Great!" he stated. "Ever been there, Eddie?"

The mechanic shook his head. He was a boy Gary had picked up three hundred miles from Center City, more than a week ago.

"Burke just told me—he's Allenday's right-hand man, you know. There'll be crowds watching those fifty loops of yours, five hundred feet off the ground, Larry. And watching my double 'chute cut."

Gary nodded. Center City. The carnival outfit going in there—just after he'd got a trace of—

His train of thought was broken by the wail of a siren. He glanced at his wrist watch. It wasn't within an hour of the time for his plane stunting. And this siren wail was a different one from that of the siren on the small field to the west of the carnival lot.

Eddie Lee was staring through the half-opened tent flap.

"Bull wagon!" he muttered. "Say, it's pulling in near the freaks' line of tents! Something wrong—"

"Go over—and see, Eddie." Gary spoke calmly, but he had to fight for that calm. He was thinking of the off key whistle again. "Come back and tell me—"

The mechanic and 'chute jumper was gone. He was running toward the lineup of freaks' tents. Gary Greer dropped down on the cot. His lips were smiling faintly—but his eyes held a grim expression.

"Elbow Gorringe!" he muttered. "I've got to—make sure—"

He went from the tent, moved toward the Midway. It was almost three o'clock. The day was gray, cloudy, but a good crowd had turned out.

His eyes moved constantly, searching the crowd, as he walked the Midway. His thoughts were racing. Babe Lewis was dead. "Fifty Mile" Liseman was dead. Both had been murderers of his father. "Soapy" Tyler was dead, and the man who had whistled, ten minutes ago, was the one who had shot down Tyler, who with his last breath had given Gary Greer names. Five names. Three of the killers of Sanford Greer were still alive. And now—they were fighting back. They knew that he had not died in the plane crash—his scheme had failed. Perhaps, he thought, correcting his reasoning, they did not *know* he had not died. But they were suspicious. They were fighting back— and the police were fighting with them. Center City police were corrupt. Perhaps they were fighting to save themselves. Sanford Greer had been destroyed to save big names, officials of the police department. His son would be destroyed in the same way—on the spot—

Gary pulled up suddenly. His eyes went across the Midway, toward Dan Cullen's shooting gallery.

"Gorringe!" he muttered. "But why's he hanging—"

His muttering stopped. A man was running down the Midway, his face twisted and white. His lips were moving, but no words came from them. He zigzagged, dodging the humans who stared at him. Charlie Beggs, handling a wheel game, called to the running man.

"Bert—what's wrong?"

The man with the twisted face didn't seem to hear. He was breathing heavily as he passed Gary. A second man came hurrying through the crowd now. It was Burke, assistant to the manager of the Johnny Barnes' Show. He stopped near Gary to light a cigarette; his hands were shaking. Gary turned his back to the shooting gallery, across the Midway. He spoke in a low voice.

"What's wrong, Mr. Burke?"

The lean man snapped out the words. He was excited, but his voice was steady enough.

"It's that kid Walling—some one murdered him!"

Gary Greer stiffened. Burke was moving on now. From the distance came the clang of the show's ambulance. Walling—done in. Walling, the boy with the baby face, who was not a boy at all. The one from whom Gary Greer had been learning things. Not things of importance—he hadn't dared that, not yet. But little things—names and places. Past events. Things that might give him a clue to the owner of one name. One name that Soapy Tyler hadn't been able to clear up for him, dying up in the mean room at 814 River Street. Walling had known his Center City—and now he was dead!

Slowly Gary Greer swung around. Elbow Gorringe—he had to be positive. The man had his back to him—he couldn't see the right arm. He worked around to that side. The crowd was scattering now—a show up the Midway was beating tom-toms to attract attention. The man at the shooting gallery was turning away. Old Dan Cullen was appealing to him, kidding him. Gary crossed to the shooting gallery side of the Midway. He kept his head down, watched the one he suspected with narrowed eyes.

The man half turned—Gary saw the crooked right elbow. He saw the body of Gorringe stiffen—then the man was turning toward the gallery again. For a second Gary thought Gorringe had recognized him, but immediately that idea vanished. Joe Kelly, one of the show dicks, was strolling along the Midway. His eyes were moving from side to side. They rested on Elbow now.

And as they rested on him, Gorringe took the gallery gun that Dan Cullen was offering. He stood awkwardly. Cullen was strolling toward the targets; Gorringe lifted the gun to his shoulder. He held the rifle against his right shoulder—the fingers of his right hand were on the trigger. There was a sharp crack—nothing broke in the line of clay figures. Again and again the gun snapped—there wasn't a hit.

Gary Greer smiled grimly. Kelly was a new man—he'd been picked up from a small town local force, two weeks ago. Walling had told him that. Kelly wouldn't know Gorringe. He'd know what he saw—a man shooting as the normal human shoots—and missing every target he tried to hit.

The show dick was turning away now. He moved toward Gary. He nodded.

"Hello, Connors!" His voice dropped. "Someone filled Walling up with lead—four bullets. Drop in the yellow tent after a while, will you?"

Gary nodded. "Sure," he agreed.

The dick moved on. Gorringe was playing safe. He was trying a second gun. Still he was missing. He swore suddenly, set the gun on the counter. Then he grinned at Dan Cullen.

"I'm rotten!" he muttered hoarsely. "Cripes—I'm rotten!"

Gary Greer kept his body turned to one side. Gorringe was moving away now. He was whistling! That same, flat, off-key whistle. Gary's heart was pounding. The man was a fool. He didn't even know that he whistled this way. Covering up his nervousness, fear. Playing that he was a rotten shot—squeezing the trigger with his right hand.

Gary watched the man move away. He didn't follow. He could see the crooked elbow—the right one. Gorringe hadn't sprayed lead with his *right* hand—not when he'd fired at him. Not that night back in Center City's River Street—the night Soapy Tyler had been rubbed out.

Walling was dead. Why? Because they had located him in the carnival? Because they had been looking for him? There were things that Gary knew. Walling had felt fairly safe—he had talked.

Elbow Gorringe was almost out of sight now. Gary hesitated. The man was the killer of Walling, he was sure of that. It was a chance. He could squeal—he could call Kelly back—point Gorringe out. But the killer was clever. Already he had an alibi. Dan Cullen would remember him. He had failed to hit a target. He had shot with his right hand. And Gary did not yet know the circumstances of Walling's death.

It might be a trap. Gorringe might know that he was with the outfit, had been with it. It would pull Gary out in the open. He would be recognized. Gorringe might not be alone. And there were the police.

Gary Greer turned his back on the figure of Elbow Gorringe. Walling was dead. He would go down to the yellow tent—the manager's tent—and get the details. There were questions for him to answer. He wasn't worried about them. The carnival was going into Center City. That meant he'd have to drop out. Another thought pulled his body tense.

Could he drop out? Was it a frame-up? Fear struck at him as he realized the significance of the thought. Walling was dead—he had been one of the Center City gang. Had Gorringe known that it was Gary Greer who was flying the carnival stunt ship? Was it a trap?

His eyes were on the faces in the crowd ahead. Suddenly his body stiffened. He turned abruptly. Callahan!

The police officer from Center City, the man who had fired at him as he had taken off a week ago from the South Side Field, coming down the Midway!

Escape. That was the only thought in his head now. Callahan coming one way. Gorringe going the other. Gary was almost beside the shooting gallery—an idea came to him.

"Got a drink back there, Dan?" he questioned, trying to keep his voice steady.

Cullen smiled at him. "Sure thing! Swing over the counter, Stunt Man!"

Gary vaulted the counter. Cullen was bending over a bucket of water, placed in a cool spot. Gary squatted down. His head was below the counter as he reached for the dipper. He was out of sight of the Midway. Cullen was barking.

"Step up, Gents! Step up, Ladies! Knock the ducks all over the place! Hit the bell an' get a *real* cigar! Even the children can do this—"

His voice trailed off. He chuckled, looked down at Gary.

"Kelly looks right busy," he stated. "Got a guy with him—"

"Walling's dead!" Gary cut in sharply. He didn't want Cullen talking this way. Callahan was no fool. He might get wise to the fact that someone was back of the counter, beside the shooting gallery boss. "He was shot to death."

Cullen swore softly. Looking up as he drank, Gary could see his eyes following Kelly and the man with him. He guessed that the man was Callahan. They were heading back toward the yellow tent.

"The kid—dead!" Cullen swore again. "Who done it?"

Gary drank another dipper of water, shook his head. Callahan in the carnival grounds! Why? He straightened slowly. Kelly and Callahan were lost in the crowd.

"You been training any gunmen here?" Gary asked grimly. "They don't know who got Walling?"

Dan Cullen shook his head. A faint smile played about his lips.

"Had a guy here a few minutes ago—sure thing *he* didn't do it!" he breathed. "Couldn't hit a thing!"

Gary Greer wiped his mouth with the back of a hand. He swore thickly.

"Guess the show'll still go on!" he muttered. "Thanks, Dan!"

The shooting gallery proprietor nodded his head.

"All right, Stunt Man!" he came back. "Don't fall out of that plane this afternoon!"

Gary grinned. He vaulted the counter. Cullen was barking again as he moved off, away from the yellow tent's direction. There was a bitter smile playing about his lips. He needed details—but one thing was certain, they were closing in. Away from Center City, he had thought he was outside the circle. Foolish idea. Callahan was here. Elbow Gorringe was here.

Irony. Dan Cullen thinking that Gorringe couldn't shoot! Gary Greer moved along the Midway. He was due to fly in about an hour. The ship was less than an eighth of a mile from the Midway. He could take her—get in the clear.

But—*could* he? If it were a trap—this carnival kill—if Callahan and Gorringe were working against him—could he get away?

Gary Greer reached into a pocket of his brightly-checked suit, found a loose cigarette. He got it between his lips, lighted it. The thin voice of Madame LaFrance came to him.

"I look into the future, *ladees* and gentlemen—I can read the stars—"

Gary Greer drew a deep breath. He exhaled a thin stream of smoke. Madame LaFrance's real name was Nellie Blotz. Last week she had been with the Rodeo Show, taking tickets. She was launching out on her own. And she was reading futures.

He was walking slowly now, his eyes searching the crowd. Walling dead. Gorringe and Callahan on the lot. He thought of Joyce Rawlings, of Pete Ranning. How about *his* future? The net was tightening—had been tightening since he had shot down, "Fifty Mile" Liseman. But the show was still on. Three killer names remained on his list. And he had made a promise.

"I'll—go through with it—stick!" he muttered grimly. "Sky stunts—at four. Business as usual!"

GARY GREER SAW Eddie Lee running toward him, as he approached the yellow-colored tent occupied by the show manager. Eddie was waving him off, gesturing wildly. Gary hesitated, then turned off the lane between tents, toward the one he shared with the mechanic and 'chute hopper. Eddie was at his side now. He spoke in a low, excited voice.

"Don't go back—to our tent, Larry!" he muttered. "They've framed you!"

Gary stared at the brown-faced youngster. Eddie's eyes were

wide; he was staring along the tents used by the carnival folk. He pulled Gary toward one.

"In here!" he muttered. "This is Cy Murphy's cover—he'll be busy on the Midway for hours."

Gary allowed his mechanic to shove him into the tent. Eddie drew the flap tight back of them. He spoke in a low voice.

"Listen, Larry—they've framed you. Walling's dead! You know—you were pretty thick, and I told you I didn't like that guy. He acted sneaky. He had a lot of enemies. Anyway, he's dead—with three bullets in his head. Someone got him twenty minutes ago, over near the gasoline pumping engine. They found some letters in his pocket, Larry—signed by you. Supposed to be signed by you. I know they weren't—you wouldn't do—"

"Steady!" Gary's voice was calm. "I didn't write him any letters, Eddie. Did you see 'em—talk low!"

Eddie Lee nodded. "Kelly got a look at them—then made a break. Said he was after you. Two letters—looked a lot like your handwriting, Larry—but it isn't. Signed by you. Stuff about Walling paying you what he owed you, or you'd get him—and get him right."

Eddie's eyes were on Gary's. He swore softly. Gary was thinking back. Kelly had said that he would get hold of him, and that was after he had read the letters. And yet, the show dick had *met* him on the Midway. He had told him about Walling being murdered. He *hadn't* got him. Why not?

"I told them you were in the tent," Eddie was saying. "They laughed at me. Kelly and that come-on bird, Mattox. Even Burke was suspicious. I tell you someone bumped him off—and framed you. They knew you hung around with Walling—"

"Easy!" Gary's voice had a warning note as Eddie Lee became excited. He was thinking about the letters. The mechanic had seen them. The boy was right, of course. He was being framed. But Eddie Lee didn't know *why* he was being framed.

Gary Greer smiled faintly. Kelly hadn't taken him to Burke, to the manager's tent, for a good reason. What was the reason? He was framed—Mattox had been a fancy writer, a petty forger. Walling had told him that. Mattox had probably scrawled the notes. There were specimens of Gary's writing at the headquarters tent. He had signed for fuel for the plane.

The shrill music from the Midway drifted into the tent. Gary drew a deep breath. Kelly was no fool. But he hadn't had brains enough to do this alone. Gorringe was the man back of it. Gorringe or Callahan. His body was suddenly tense. That was it—Kelly hadn't brought him in, hadn't grabbed him on the Midway, for just one reason—a sweet one. They had *wanted* Gary to attempt escape. They knew who he was. They wanted to be sure this time. Attempted escape from the frame-up would put him in a tough spot. An admission of guilt.

Gary Greer stood just inside the tent, his face expressionless. Eddie Lee was talking in a low voice. He was saying things that were not half so important as the things Gary was *thinking*. Walling was a cheap crook. Police had driven him into a carnival, as police had driven many crooks into the free and easy life of a traveling rube fooler. He had died near the gasoline pumping engine—and Gary could guess *how* he had died.

Walling had been lured there—shot down. Gorringe had done that trick. Seconds before Gary had heard him whistling in the manner peculiar to him, he had done in "Baby Face" Walling.

And they had framed the man who was fighting them. For the second time within a week he was in a nasty trap.

He cut in on Eddie's words in a hard, low tone.

"How were those threat letters signed, Eddie?"

The mechanic spoke in a harsh tone.

" 'Larry Connors'—damn 'em! You've got to get—away, Larry. They've got you fixed—"

Gary Greer was nodding his head slowly. He spoke in a low, level voice.

"Listen, Eddie—you're right about that. I didn't shoot down Walling, of course. He didn't owe me any money. Someone's out to get me. I don't know, why."

He smiled grimly. But it was part of the game. He'd have to play it with the mechanic as he was playing it with the others.

"I've got to get away. They'll have a guard at the ship. You get out there—try to keep him away so that I can get aboard. I've got a hunch they'd like to grab me trying to get away—that's evidence for them, see. For that reason, even though the guard out there may suspect that you're revving up the ship so that I can get in the clear, he'll let you go through with it. Then, at the last second, they'll try to grab me. Maybe we can beat it, Eddie—maybe we can't. But I don't want you to do a thing—only what I tell you. That clear?"

The mechanic smiled faintly. "Don't be afraid of getting me in a jam, Larry," he muttered. "But I'll do—just as you say. No more—no less."

"Good!" Gary nodded his head. "I want your 'chute—and I want to take off alone. My 'chute's in the ship. I want you to be sure the plane's right for the air—no watered gas, no filed feed line copper. Bring me your 'chute—your helmet and goggles.

I'll stick here. Be careful, and don't come in if you're spotted. If anyone stops you—tell them you think I've ducked out. Act as though you believe I'm guilty. Got it?"

Eddie Lee nodded. His face was twisted.

"You'll get away, Larry!" he stated fiercely. "I'd like to go with you."

"I'll send for you—when this thing is cleared up. Someone will squeal sooner or later, Eddie. I'll hide out somewhere."

Eddie Lee stuck out a hand—Gary gripped it. The mechanic smiled faintly.

"I don't figure on getting back in this tent again, Larry," he stated. "I'll work around to the back—from our tent. I'll shove the 'chute pack under the canvas. Then I'll head for the field. Give me fifteen minutes—from the time you get the 'chute silk."

Gary nodded, smiling. "Luck, Eddie!" he whispered. "See you again!"

The mechanic managed a grin. "Maybe, by sticking with the carnival, I can find out who was after you, Larry," he stated grimly. "I can get some kind of a job—and that'll help."

Gary Greer turned his body away from the partially opened flap. Eddie Lee was cautiously staring outside. Even as Gary started to wish the mechanic luck—he was gone. His short, thick-set body vanished from sight. Gary closed the tent flap tightly.

"Needed—Eddie Lee!" he muttered. "He's sticking. This is—a tight corner."

Music from the merry-go-round came to his ears. He reached for a pill, lighted it. Elbow Gorringe, picking up his trail after the take-off from Center City. Working with Callahan. Out to get him—but out to get him right.

Gorringe had finished Walling, Gary was sure of that. Gorringe knew that Gary Greer was the stunt man with the Johnny Barnes Show. Why hadn't Gorringe shot down Gary?

The answer wasn't so hard. The frame-up was safer. It was one thing to *attempt* murder—another thing to *succeed*. They had succeeded, in Walling's case. But even had they failed—the consequences would not have been great. And if Gorringe had failed to get Gary, it might have been different. The crooks, the killers of Gary's father, were fighting with a desperateness born of fear. They knew that he was destroying, revenging. But they were still fighting him with cunning. The frame-up proved that. This was the second one, and executed with more skill than the time they had almost trapped him at the café in the French Quarter of New Orleans. One Gaston Dégonne had died in that speakeasy. This time it had been Walling.

Gary Greer jerked his body around at the scraping sound his ears heard. A packed 'chute was shoved beneath the canvas at the rear of the tent. Goggles and a helmet were thrust through. He could hear Eddie's quick breathing—then the sound of light footfalls. The mechanic had worked fast.

He glanced at his wrist watch. Fifteen minutes. Carefully he inspected the parachute. The cable running from the rip-cord ring was well greased—he had packed the 'chute after Eddie had made yesterday's jump—had packed it with Eddie. His own had been packed two days ago. But that was out in the ship.

He got into the harness of the lobe-type silk spread. Footfalls sounded at the front of the tent. Gary stood motionless. The footfalls died—a voice sounded.

"Hey—Murphy—you inside there?"

Gary held his breath. The questioning voice was hoarse. He didn't recognize the man who called out.

A low oath reached him, then the footfalls sounded again. Gary sighed. From the right-hand pocket of his flashy coat he drew a Colt. He pressed the button on the left side of the grip-stared down as the clip slipped out into his fingers. His body stiffened.

Two bullets were missing from the clip!

For several seconds he stood motionlessly. The *putt-putt* of the gasoline pumping engine came to him, above the shrill of the music. One bullet had been in the barrel—the clip had the rest of the load. Three bullets had been fired into Walling's body.

Gary Greer swore softly. He knew that there was no bullet in the barrel of the gun he held in his hand. The gun had been in the pocket of the coat he had left in his tent when he had gone into the air yesterday afternoon. Three bullets had been emptied—had been fired. There would be three shells somewhere near the gasoline pump. Probably they had already been found. Shells from *his* gun. *Fired* from Elbow Gorringe's gun.

He dropped the gun into his pocket again. It was more of a frame-up than he had suspected. They had him—his only chance was escape. He would be turned over to the police, if caught; and Callahan was on hand—to take him back to Center City. And often prisoners had started for Center City under such police guard as Callahan's, and had never arrived alive. Attempted escape.

The irony of it was that escape was his only chance. Mechanically he fastened the harness of the 'chute pack. He glanced at his wrist watch. Five minutes left—it would take him almost that long to reach the field. He would have to move slowly, cautiously.

There was one thing he failed to understand. The frame-up had been executed with cunning, with extreme cunning. With two of his father's murderers on the carnival lot—why had he not been murdered, with as much cunning? Did the crooks want a more grim revenge. Did they want to see him suffer?

He smiled bitterly. It was not far to the field used for the take-off and landing of the plane. He would stick close to the line of tents, avoid the Midway. He would be going away from the manager's tent. There was a chance.

Parting the canvas flap of the tent, he looked out. The road was clear—he moved along swiftly. Most of the carnival people were at work. He walked with his head down, but his gray eyes moved from side to side. For the second time he was fighting out of a trap. Only there was a difference. He had the hunch that it was *known* he was fighting to escape. And they were *letting* him try to escape—for a purpose. It was a grim thought. But there was no other chance for him. They had seen to that— by the carnival kill.

IT TOOK GARY five minutes to reach one end of the small field on which the ship rested. She was headed into the wind, which was coming in gusts. Eddies of dust were being whirled up from the fairly level stretch. The propeller of the plane was turning, the engine was idling. It had a good beat. Already a small crowd was collecting around the fringe of the flying field.

Fifty yards from the ship, mingling with the crowd, he spotted Eddie Lee. The mechanic was talking with a tall, stoop-shouldered individual—one of Kelly's assistants. A sort of carnival bouncer. Gary swore softly. Eddie seemed to be arguing with the man now—he was gesturing with his arms. The stoop-shouldered man wore breeches and a light sweater. Gary could see his gun belt—the holster strapped over the left thigh. His eyes searched the field for Gorringe, Callahan. They were not in sight. Everything seemed to be going along just as it would normally. They had always furnished a guard for the plane—but it had usually been Buddy French. This time it was the stoop-shouldered man.

Gary moved out from the crowd. The 'chute pack on his back was attracting attention; as he walked swiftly toward the plane he pulled the helmet over his head, adjusted the goggles on the leather that came down over his forehead. His narrowed eyes saw that there were no blocks under the wheels.

The stoop-shouldered individual's back was turned to him. Eddie saw Gary moving toward the plane. He was talking rapidly. He bent down, the index finger of his right hand was making a circle in the mud. The stoop-shouldered guard was standing close to Eddie, looking down at the earth. Gary's heart was pounding now—he was within twenty feet of the ship. The temptation to break into a run was great.

But he fought against that. There was a good chance now. If Eddie fought for him—got the lean man's gun—

Ten feet from the plane—and he saw the guard turn. The man stiffened, called out sharply.

"Oh, Conners!"

Gary Greer leaped toward the plane. As his right foot struck the wing-step, he twisted his head. The tall man was staggering back from the blow Eddie had struck—he was going down.

In a flash the mechanic was bending over him—now he was running toward the ship!

Gary swung a leg over the fuselage side. He heard shouts from the edge of the field. Eddie's face was close to his—the mechanic was breathing very heavily.

"Got—his gun! Others—coming. Ship seems—all right. Threw out your 'chute—shroud lines—cut away—packing different! Noticed it—"

He was swinging away from the plane now. Gary nodded his head. He saw Burke running out from the edge of the field, cutting in toward the plane. Kelly was back of him—both were waving their arms wildly.

He gave the plane the gun—she rolled forward. Gary turned his head. Kelly was still running out. But Burke had stopped—his back was to the plane. He was waving toward the edge of the field. The plane was picking up speed.

It struck him then—struck him with one terrible wave of significance. His own 'chute had been unpacked—the shroud lines had been cut. Then it had been packed again. Eddie had noticed the difference in the packing—he had spotted the cut shroud lines. Why had they been cut? There was just one reason—*the plane had been crippled!*

That was why they had let him get away. *That* was why they had framed him into an escape. They had given him a crippled plane—and his 'chute had been fixed so that when the plane broke in the sky he would drop like a plummet toward the earth!

The plane was gaining speed now. In a few seconds he would be forced to pull back on the stick, to lift the plane into the air. Would she rise? Would he have the chance to get her high enough, to gain enough altitude so that he could use Eddie Lee's good 'chute?

Fear struck at him—his hand wavered on the engine throttle. He could cut—let the ship roll to a halt. He could fight it out with his gun, on the ground. But in the end, they would have him.

He was calmer now. Slowly he pulled back on the stick. The nose of the ship lifted. She got off the earth—dropped again. She bounced, and then he had her in the air. Rigid in the cockpit—he fought to hold the plane just as steady as possible—without working the controls. If he could get two thousand feet, perhaps even a thousand, there would be a chance—a chance to use the good parachute.

She was climbing. A gust of wind dropped the right wing—he let her climb with that wing drooping, pulled her back on level keel very gradually. His eyes went to the floor of the cockpit. Something white was there—something scrawled. Words on a sheet of paper.

The ship was flying at three-quarter speed. She had three hundred feet now. Gary leaned forward, lifted the paper. His lips moved as he read aloud the few scrawled words.

" *'I killed Walling—he squealed on—'* "

Gary's voice died beneath the beat of the engine. The writing was a fair imitation of his own. The name "Greer" was smeared at the bottom of the scrawl. The frame-up was still on. They were taking a chance, that the ship might not burn, that he would not discover the scrawled note. They were planting more evidence.

The ship had five hundred feet now. His shoes held the rudder bar in neutral position—the stick was pulled back slightly toward his body. He had not snapped the safety-belt buckle. The ship was almost a mile from the carnival field.

Gary Greer smiled grimly. He got the stick between his knees—with swift movements he tore the white paper in little shreds. A quick toss over his head—the prop wash was whipping half of the pieces back into the air. They would be scattered.

He laughed harshly. He might go down—but that piece of paper would never be found. His right hand was gripping the stick again—his eyes went to the rip-cord over his left thigh. The ship had seven hundred feet. That might be enough— unless something went wrong. He twisted his head.

The carnival location was almost two miles back now. Ahead was fairly rugged country. The plane was roaring toward Center City—but that place was many miles distant.

Now the plane was up almost nine hundred feet. Gary Greer was smiling with his eyes—his lips were pressed tightly together. He had a good 'chute on his back—Eddie Lee's 'chute. The plane had enough altitude for a jump. What had they done to it? What was the trap for which they had so cunningly planned?

A gust of wind dropped the left wing. He pulled the stick to the right. The wing came up slowly, a little sluggishly. The nose seemed to be getting down now—he had trouble in keeping it above the horizon. And yet the ship's engine was turning up enough r.p.m.'s. She had a steady sky roar.

He pulled the stick back another inch. The nose of the plane came up—then started to drop again. The stick was back— in the position to which he had moved it. Something was wrong—the nose was dropping—

"Elevator wire—fraying!" he muttered grimly. "She'll let go—"

His eyes went to the country below. He saw the town of Marionville, several miles to the eastward. There was a railroad winding toward it. The country below was hilly, rugged. No landing field in sight. And even if there had been—the elevator control wires were almost gone. They had been cut—the strain was fraying them out.

He stiffened in the cockpit. The nose was down a foot below the horizon now. The flying wires were starting to sing. He reached for the throttle—to cut the engine. And as he reached out—the control wires let go!

There was a metallic twang as they broke—the nose of the ship flashed downward. Gary Greer rose in the cockpit. It was almost recurrent—this action. Only, the *other* time he had not been forced to jump. It had been *his* trick—that time. And it had failed.

Thoughts flashed through his head as he straightened—shoved himself upward and outward. As he somersaulted in the air, dropping down over the tail assembly of the plane, his right-hand fingers groped for the rip-cord ring over his left thigh.

There were sickening seconds—when his fingers failed to find it. And every second counted—the ship had only climbed to a thousand feet!

Then they were touching metal—he jerked the rip-cord ring. Downward he plunged. Panic gripped him momentarily. What if they had cut the shroud lines of Eddie's 'chute, too?

What if it failed to open—let him drop—

He thought of his father, of Joyce Rawlings, of Pete

Ranning—and then the silk spread was crackling as it opened above his head.

The harness tightened about his body. He was drifting now. He twisted his head, stared downward. Already the earth was rising up—it was very close. He had fallen more than five hundred feet—before the 'chute had opened. He tried to slip away from the side of a hill—almost succeeded. He swung his body, out, twisted around as he struck. His outstretched arms broke the force of the impact. Even as he rolled over and over, down the slope of the hill, tearing through small bushes and low growth, the roar of the crashing plane reached his ears.

His arms protected his face. The harness of the 'chute, tightening around his body, stopped the rolling. The silk spread, up above, had twisted around the stump of a tree. Slowly Gary Greer pulled himself to his knees. His body was aching. He was badly bruised. But the cunning of the crooks had failed. Once again he had leaped from a plane—and was alive. Gorringe had failed, Callahan had failed—even as Gary had failed in his own effort to wipe out his name—before wiping out the other names.

He was on his feet now—there was the taste of blood on his tongue. His face was cut—his hands badly scratched. But he was on the earth, alive. He could still fight, use cunning. He would *have* to fight. He needed help now. He could get it—in Center City. He *would* get it. Three names—against one.

Slowly, painfully, he got loose from the 'chute harness. Clinging to the skin of his left hand was a bit of paper—a bit of the note they had forged. The note that was to have been his own confession of murder! Gary Greer laughed harshly, terribly. They had tried to cut things too fine—and had failed. *He* had tried to cut things too fine—and had failed. Now they were out in the open—and so was he.

He limped down the slope, dragging the 'chute after him. His lips moved slowly.

"They almost—won—on the—carnival kill!"

Back of him black smoke from the wreckage of the ship curled up into the sky. On the far side of the hill—the ship had landed. Gary Greer didn't look back. He had somewhere to go, something to do. As he moved, his eyes were narrowed, staring straight ahead. Only his tight-pressed lips seemed to be laughing. And theirs was not a pleasant laughter—it was the cold laughter of death. Death to gangster killers who had killed with laughter on their own lips.

7

River Street Death

GARY GREER SMILED faintly, leaned forward in the low, modern chair. His eyes came away; from the skyscraper bookcase, the rakish lamp. They met the dark eyes of Joyce Rawlings.

"All right, my dear," he said steadily. "It's this damn stubbornness in you that I suppose attracted me, in the first place. How much do you know?"

Joyce Rawlings narrowed her eyes. She laughed huskily, turned toward Pete Ranning.

"Shall I tell him, Pete?" she asked quietly.

Ranning was seated beside her on the divan. He did not smile, but nodded his head slowly.

"He doesn't *deserve* to know—there are too many things he didn't tell us," he replied slowly. "But he's *got* to know, Joyce."

The girl nodded her head, frowning. She turned toward Gary again.

"You tried to go it alone. Gary—and it was too tough," Her voice was low, steady. Gary relaxed a little in the chair; he inhaled cigarette smoke deeply. "You've made mistakes, Gary. They didn't count so much at first—now it's different. You wanted to work fast—and you started off like *First Place*. One of Dad's old race horses. He was great away from the barrier, Gary. But he weakened at the finish. It wasn't exactly his fault. He'd get shut off—in a large field the odds were too great."

Gary chuckled a little. "I'm still alive—" he started, but the girl interrupted him with a little gesture.

"So is Sal the Dude. So is Elbow Gorringe. So is Frenchy Lamonte. So is one detective by the name of Callahan."

Gary was sitting up straight. His eyes had widened, now they narrowed again. The girl was smiling slightly.

"*Four* names, Gary—and you only figured on *three*. Liseman and Babe Lewis. They're dead names. Oh, Gary—if you'd only—"

She checked herself, rose from the divan. She turned away from him, and he knew that the girl he loved was fighting a battle with herself. He spoke grimly.

"I only made one *bad* mistake, Joyce," he said slowly, "and that was when I implicated you. It's a game you shouldn't be playing, nor Pete, for that matter. I thought the first 'chute hop had covered me up. Almost got away with it—only I couldn't work fast enough. Had to be sure. The killer instinct wasn't strong enough."

The girl was facing him again, standing near the divan. She smiled twistedly.

"Gary," she said slowly, "you've got to go away."

He half closed his eyes. "You know I won't do that, Joyce," he said quietly. "You didn't send for me—to tell me that. You wanted me to come up here so that you could tell me something I didn't know. I've suspected that Sal the Dude was here in Center City. I don't know who he is—I've never run into a crook who could tell me, or *would* tell me. Perhaps you will, Joyce."

She shook her head. "I don't even know that he's in Center City, Gary," she said. "I know Frenchy Lamonte is."

Gary nodded. He was thinking back to the hours he had spent in New Orleans. Frenchy Lamonte—the one who had got clear with his plane. The one who had assumed the name *he* had assumed.

"Lamonte and Gorringe. Sal the Dude—and Callahan!" His voice was toneless. "Closing in for the kill, eh?" His eyes were smiling coldly. Suddenly he got to his feet. "It's *you* who must get away, Joyce. You—and Pete, here. I can't bluff any longer. They know I'm alive. They know I know the names of those who killed father. They know those names are to be wiped off the books. They're fighting, Joyce—fighting to save themselves. They'll use you—"

The girl shook her dark head. She laughed harshly.

"I won't go away. They won't use me. Pete won't go away. If you want to protect us, Gary—"

He turned away from her, moved toward a window of the twelfth-story apartment. Center City was sprawled below. Traffic sound rose in a dulled confusion. He spoke grimly.

"Four names? You're wrong there, Joyce! There are only three. I got those names from the lips of a dying man—but his brain was alert, clear enough. I'll give it to you straight, because I'm staying for the finish. There are only Gorringe, Frenchy Lamonte—and Callahan. Liseman and Babe Lewis rode in the death car—but they're out of things. Soapy Tyler rode in the death car—he squealed, told me the names. There are only three left—" The girl was facing him again. Her face was set.

"I've heard it, again and again—Sal the Dude—"

Gary Greer chuckled. It was a husky, terrible chuckle. He nodded his head. But he seemed to be staring beyond her.

"*I've* heard it again and again, too," he said slowly. "Tyler,

dying, told me 'Sal got wise.' Babe Lewis had his grim idea of a joke. Over on River Street I told him who I was. He thought that was funny. I was dead—he was sure of that. So he mocked back at me. 'Sure—an' me—I'm Sal the Dude.' I've heard the name, too, Joyce."

His smile held a peculiar quality. He was conscious of the fact that both the girl and Pete Ranning were staring at him with puzzled eyes. He spoke very quietly.

"Sal the Dude is one of three individuals," he stated. "He's Gorringe, Lamonte—or Callahan!"

He saw Pete Ranning's body stiffen, heard the girl's little exclamation of surprise. He went on, in a low voice.

"He's a fiction, created as a master mind for the gang. He never was real—not as Sal the Dude. I don't think Lamonte ran the gang—he was down in New Orleans when they were controlling Center City. But he was up for the murder of my—"

He checked himself, then shrugged his shoulders.

"No use telling you two this stuff," he stated. "You know too much as it is. I'm afraid—afraid for both of you. But don't think I'm blundering around in the dark. Only three killers are left. Four names—three killers. One of them is the boss. I made a mistake at the carnival. It came pretty close to being my last mistake. Baby Face Walling may have been a plant. They wanted to frame me—frame me right. But they won't try that again. It'll be smooth and swift—from now on. They'll protect themselves—but they're out for sudden—"

The expression in the girl's eyes stopped him. He shook his head slowly.

"Let Pete fly you over to the Coast, Joyce," he pleaded quietly. "This isn't your game. You can't quite understand it all. They don't play so fair—as I—"

He saw the scorn in her eyes; he wasn't sure of the reason. Was it because she felt he thought her a coward? He didn't, of course. Or was it because she hated him—hated him because he was fighting the murderers of his father?

Pete Ranning spoke in a level voice. He was smiling a little, but it was a bitter smile.

"They're too strong for you, Gary. There's the police—fighting you, too. You're young. We know the air game. Let's all of us wing to the Coast. Or quit the country. Try South America. A new air field—we've got the capital. We've got the ships and—"

Gary Greer laughed. It was a low, battering laugh. He could see Ranning straighten, see the girl shudder at the sound of it.

"Quit—and know that the men who turned lead loose on father's body would sit in dirty speakeasy joints, and brag about it? Quit—and know that a rotten political machine, working with crooks, had helped to send down in the mud of a street the one decent, honest prosecuting attorney they'd had in years? You want me to do *that*, Joyce? And you, Pete?"

Pete Ranning swore softly. The girl smiled with her lips. Gary could see the tears she was fighting to hold back.

"I want you to be—alive, Gary," she said slowly, shakenly. "You can't bring—Sanford Greer—back—"

She stopped—met the fury in his eyes calmly. She saw his browned fingers clench, saw his whole body grow tense. Then he relaxed. He moved toward the foyer of the apartment. She started after him, stopped. Pete Ranning called out sharply.

"Gary—wait! She's right—"

Gary Greer turned. He was smiling. His narrow lips were pressed together—the goggle scar over his left eye stood out plainly. His face was brown—he was not using the pasty make-up. His gray eyes were on those of Joyce Rawlings. He held his lean body erect, spoke in a toneless voice.

"Right? Perhaps you are, Joyce. I can't bring Sanford Greer back. But crooks and killers have a code of something that they think is honor. I have, too. They killed—and there's no justice for me to hand them over to—not in Center City. They killed—and they'd kill again. They've done it, trying to get me. I've done it, trying to get them. A lot of men were drafted during the World War, Joyce. Drafted—to kill. Code of honor. Another nation had killed. Preventive—the war to end war."

He laughed bitterly, tonelessly. Joyce and Pete were facing him, staring at him.

"They may have another honest prosecutor in Center City sometime," he went on. "I wasn't exactly drafted for this war—but I'm in it. And I'm sticking to the finish. I tried to fight the scrap alone—but it didn't work out. I don't want your help—I want you to make it easier for me by getting clear—"

Joyce Rawlings cut in quietly. She was standing very straight;

her dark eyes were on the gray ones of the man she loved.

"We'll—get clear, Gary? Will that help?"

He heard Pete Ranning suck in his breath sharply. Pete was staring at the girl now. Gary Greer nodded his head.

"It'll help—a lot," he replied simply. "But you won't—do it. And it's probably too late, now."

Joyce Rawlings was smiling a little. Her voice was steadier.

"We'll try, Gary—" she said. "We'll try to get clear."

He read a different meaning in her words. He nodded his head again. The girl was a fighter. She wouldn't run away. Pete Ranning wouldn't run away. Words wouldn't help now. Action was the only thing that would count. Swift action.

Joyce Rawlings reached for a book lying on the modernistic table near her. She lifted it, glanced at the title. Pete Ranning's eyes were still on Gary's.

"Drop in—after a week or so, Gary." The girl's tone was forced, but she was striving. "I'm running out of town— perhaps Pete will fly me out. Take care of yourself and—"

She couldn't go on. Turning, she walked slowly from the room. Pete Ranning swore fiercely.

"For God's sake, Gary—" he muttered—"don't walk out of here and—"

Gary Greer chuckled. It was a hoarse, mirthless chuckle. His eyes met those of Pete Ranning.

"Keep things at the Field going, Pete," he suggested in a steady voice. "Keep an eye on Joyce. She's damned stubborn, you know. I'm pretty crazy about her, in spite of that, Pete."

He turned up the collar of the light-gray coat he hadn't taken off on coming in. He smiled faintly.

"Kind of raw out," he stated. "Don't want to take cold. Always very careful about my health. So many things can happen—these days."

He turned, went from the apartment. Pete Ranning stood staring toward the empty foyer. His hands were clenched, his face twisted.

"Damned fool!" he muttered fiercely. "Damned—old—wonderful—fool!"

A KNIFE-EDGED WIND whipped little circles of dirt around the cobbles of River Street. Elbow Gorringe walked with his head down, his shoulders hunched forward. His eyes darted from side to side. At intervals he whistled tunelessly, off key. His right arm was rigid at his side—the hand of his left arm was buried out of sight in the pocket of his dark, wrinkled overcoat.

Once he pulled up suddenly, half turned to the left. He was looking toward the battered entrance of a River Street frame house, and he was remembering something. Soapy Tyler—and a mean room that was filled with the popping cough-sounds of a gun. Silencer choked sounds.

"Eight-fourteen!" Elbow muttered grimly, shakily. "Damn stoolie—dirty, yellow-faced squealer!"

He moved on. It had been dark for several hours—the wind blew in river sounds as he moved along the street. Tugboats signaled to each other; in the distance he could hear the metallic noise from a deck donkey engine. Steam hissed from somewhere along the docks. Elbow had a sudden idea.

"Hell!" he muttered, pulling up again. "There's the ships—a getaway. Been to sea before—guess I could stand it again."

He moved along more slowly now. In the distance, back toward the heart of Center City, there was the whine of a siren.

Ambulance or police car siren. It stiffened Elbow Gorringe's body, jerked him erect. He swore fiercely.

"Gettin' worse'n a sniffin' guy!" he muttered. "It ain't the bulls that are eatin' me. This damn River Street—smells like death!"

Eleven-twenty-two. He could see the place now. Parson Jennifer had a café on the street level. A couple of private rooms up above. But Jennifer was all right with the police—a queer character. An old sail man, religious and funny.

The building was two story, brick. Elbow walked past the entrance, staring toward the dim lights of the café. He saw no one inside. He started to head toward the door, changed his mind, went on past. He cursed himself again, a month ago he wouldn't have hesitated. Weren't the fingers of his left hand closed over the grip of his weapon? There was nothing the matter with his eyes, was there?

He turned slowly. A human limped along the narrow paving, muttering. The man was short, heavy set. He passed Elbow without even seeing him. He was muttering to himself.

"Groggy!" Gorringe breathed. "Be that way myself, if we don't do something. Be like them prize-fighters—walkin' on their heels!"

He moved back toward the entrance of eleven-twenty-two. His fingers tightened their grip on the butt of the automatic. Nothing to worry about. Frenchy Lamonte was all right. A damned fool to come into Center City. But there must be a reason. That was why he had come—to learn the reason. Frenchy was all right. Elbow could remember the smile on his face, the chuckling laughter on his lips, as he had stood beside him in the death car, spilling lead. Sanford Greer down in the mud—and there'd been the devil to pay, ever since.

First Babe Lewis. Then Fifty Mile Liseman. And there might have been others, if it hadn't been for Sal. Sal had brains. Maybe he had something to do with this meet—

Elbow Gorringe got up close to the door of Parson's eating place. The fingers at the end of his crooked right arm turned the dirty knob. The wind shoved the door open. Gorringe waited a couple of seconds. Then he stepped inside. He closed the door.

No one was back of the counter. There were pies in sight, coffee cake. The remnants of a meal rested at one end of the counter—there was no sign of Parson Jennifer, Gorringe shivered a little.

"Cold in here!" he breathed, and even as he uttered the words he knew that they were not true ones. A gas stove filled the place with odorous warmth.

Elbow Gorringe kept his left hand buried in the pocket of his coat. He used his head. But he almost slipped up, at that. He almost called out and there were humans who knew his voice. He kicked over a stool resting before the counter. It hit the wooden floor with a crash. Tin knives and forks rattled a little.

But there was no sound from the room ten feet beyond the coffee percolator. That was Parson Jennifer's quarters—the room. No sound from back there. And Elbow Gorringe felt fear strike at him. A trap—that was his thought. A trap.

He backed slowly toward the wall that faced the counter. His nerves were bad; they had been bad since they had tried the carnival kill and had failed to achieve the main purpose. The silence of the little River Street café was something he couldn't understand.

Up against the wall, he called out huskily:

"Parson! Hey, Jennifer!"

There was no answer. He'd been in the place a lot of times, and Jennifer had always been present. It was after eight. Frenchy Lamonte should be upstairs; certainly he could hear the sound of his voice. Something was wrong. Maybe Lamonte was trying to double-cross him. Maybe Callahan was getting worried. A new administration was coming up, in Center City. Maybe Callahan, in soft at the Detective Bureau, wanted to be sure that he'd *stay* in soft.

The suspicion grew. Cold anger replaced fear, somewhere inside of Elbow Gorringe. He had never trusted Callahan. The detective had told him more than once that Center City wouldn't be healthy for him, but for the fact that he could depend on Bureau help. Supposing Callahan wanted him out of the way?

"He's been actin' funny—since I got Walling, at the carnival!" he muttered in a husky voice. "He's been—"

His muttering died abruptly. Somewhere upstairs a door slammed. A voice came down to him.

"That you, Meester Gorringe? If it ees—come up—"

Elbow Gorringe swore again. Damn Frenchy Lamonte for calling out his name that way. Frenchy knew better than that. He *didn't* know who might be inside the place.

"Coming!" Gorringe muttered grimly, and started toward the stairs at the rear of the lunchroom.

At the foot of the stairs he hesitated. It was gloomy up above. He had recognized Lamonte's voice, all right. The accent was pronounced. But Gorringe had reached the point where he trusted nobody. And going up the stairs he would be a target.

His hesitation was for only a few seconds; up above he could hear Lamonte whistling. Some sort of a French-Canadian song. That one that went— "The wind she blow; she blow like hell—"

Elbow Gorringe swore softly. He started up the stairs. They squeaked under his feet. He didn't want Lamonte to think that he was scared, losing his nerve. Frenchy was only a small gun, after all. But Gorringe climbed with his eyes on the gloom of the landing above, and with the pocket material of his coat bulging just a little to the left and ahead of his body. Frenchy was still whistling—but Gorringe kept his thick lips pressed tightly together. It was funny about Parson Jennifer—he was always on the job.

GARY GREER STOOD just inside the door of the dull-lighted room in which Frenchy Lamonte was whistling. Lamonte's slender body twitched; his sharp-featured face was white, terribly drawn. He stood near the opposite wall from Greer—in his right hand he gripped a gun. It was a small-caliber automatic, and there were seven cartridges in the clip. Each of the seven was a blank.

In his right hand Gary held a Service Colt. He held it low, but the muzzle was pointed toward Lamonte's body. Gary had picked up Callahan a block from the Detective Bureau; he had tagged him to the meet with Lamonte. When the two had separated, Gary had followed Lamonte. He had followed him because he had caught the one accented word—"river." The accent had given Frenchy away. And once again Gary Greer had smeared blacking on his face. In New Orleans he had done it to save his life. He had been in a desperate situation. Now he was doing it to trap one human. And Frenchy Lamonte was the bait.

He had handled the proprietor of the café easily enough. Lamonte had entered, had come upstairs. Gary Greer had caught Jennifer with his back turned, as he was drawing a cut of the stuff he sold as coffee. The Service Colt was a convincing argument for silence. Jennifer was lying on the cot in his room below, heavily gagged, tightly bound.

Frenchy Lamonte had been more difficult to handle. He was nervous, and Gary Greer had abandoned the creaky stairs. He had climbed the fire-escape, had got a window open and slipped into the room, while Frenchy was outside, on the landing, peering down. Lamonte had backed into the room, and the small of his back had pressed against the muzzle of Gary's Colt before he had been aware of Greer's presence. After that—Gary had talked. Frenchy had listened. Fear was in his eyes; he was a yellow killer of men far more brave than himself.

And now Elbow Gorringe was coming up the stairs. Frenchy had called to him—with Gary's gun leveled at his body. Frenchy was waiting for him to come into the room now—holding a gun in his right hand. The gun had been Gary's—he had traded it for the one Frenchy had possessed. He had traded it because of the blank cartridges.

Lamonte—one of the killers who had shot down Sanford Greer! Lamonte, back in Center City for another kill. And now he was trapped, waiting for Gorringe to come into the dimly lighted room—and waiting with a useless weapon gripped in the fingers of his right hand!

Gorringe had reached the landing now. He had stopped moving. And Frenchy had stopped whistling. Gary Greer raised the Colt a little. His eyes were gray slits against the black of his make-up. And Lamonte understood.

"Here—" he called hoarsely. "Een thees room, Gorringe—"

Gary heard Elbow's breath sucked in sharply. He heard Gorringe swear in a hoarse undertone. Then the footfalls sounded. The door was half opened. When it opened the rest of the way, Gary would be back of it. And Gorringe would be facing Frenchy Lamonte. And Lamonte would be holding a weapon in his grip. That was what Gary was banking on. Elbow's reaction. The condition of Elbow's nerves—and something else—

A foot struck the door—it swung open. But even as it swung, Lamonte did the thing that Gary figured he would do. His body swung toward Gary—his gun hand came up. He cried out fiercely:

"Greer!"

The gun crashed. Red flame cut the semi-darkness of the room. Red flame from the wall against which Lamonte had been standing. And no bullet streaked toward Gary.

And then Gorringe's gun was crashing. The first shot had a pop-cough sound. The second was louder. The third was a crash, Maxim silencer worked poorly on an automatic. Sometimes it failed. It was failing now—but the lead was streaking true to the mark.

Frenchy Lamonte screamed. His body jerked forward. Wood clipped from the floor as Elbow Gorringe slanted his gun downward. Five shots he fired—and then a police whistle shrilled loudly. It shrilled from a spot on River Street, very close to the entrance of eleven-twenty-two.

Gorringe swore fiercely. He mouthed two words that Gary Greer caught.

"Dirty—rat!"

Then he swung around, started for the stairs. He went down rapidly. The police whistle was still shrilling.

Gary Greer closed the door. He turned the key on the inside, Lamonte was dead—he was lying on his face. The second bullet had penetrated his brain. There were other bullets in his body. In that last second he had tried to get Gary Greer—and the crashing of his gun had marked his doom. Gorringe might not have held fire, in any case. Not with that weapon showing in Frenchy's fingers. But when Lamonte had filled the room with gun sound—that had been stretching a point too far. A death point.

Gary Greer moved toward the fire-escape. He thought of Pete Ranning, a half block distant, shrilling the police whistle. Pete was moving away now; perhaps he was already back to the cab in which the two of them had followed Frenchy Lamonte. The rest was up to Gorringe. Police would be on the scene in a hurry. If he got away—

Gary was outside the window now. He was wearing gray gloves. On the fire-escape, crouched, he heard a return whistle—a new police sound. He closed the window back of him, slipped his Colt into a pocket. He patted the bottle of cold cream stuffed next to the face cloth. In the alley that cut off at an angle, below the fire-escape, he would get the blacking off his face. There was none on his hands.

A siren wailed in the distance. Gary started down the escape. Frenchy Lamonte was dead. He had tried to kill Gary—and Gorringe had killed one of the death car's crew. Gorringe was alive. There was a reason for that—Callahan was alive. Which one of the two was Sal the Dude? It had not been Lamonte, Gary was sure of that.

He was halfway down the escape when he heard the hum of an engine. It was not the hum of a car engine. It pulled him up stiffly, near the bottom of the ladder. He stared toward the western skyline, between two buildings that towered above the two-story structure. A ship was winging toward River Street. She was flying low!

Gary Greer swung himself to the alley. He stared up toward the tiny fire-escape. Voices reached him, from the direction of River Street. The police would be inside the café pretty soon. They would find the tied-up proprietor. Had Jennifer seen beyond his disguise, or would he report that a negro had bound him?

Gary crouched in the alley. The beat of the plane's engine had become loud, a terrific drum. He could hear the shrill of flying wires. The ship was winging toward the brick building—she would pass almost directly over it. Gary Greer cried out.

"Double—trap! Callahan—playing *his* game—"

He broke off. Bending low, he started to run along the alley. He'd gone ten feet when he saw the form ahead. He got a glimpse of something that flashed in the reflected light from a window above. A police badge. A voice sounded faintly beneath the beat of the ship engine.

"Hold up, you! Lift 'em—"

And then came the first crash. There was a terrific concussion—a blinding flash. For a split-second, as Gary rocked forward, off balance, he thought that the police officer had fired—that he had been hit. But the zoom beat of the ship's engine reached his ears as he staggered to his feet. Again the officer's voice reached him.

"Stay back there! Throw—"

Gary Greer threw himself forward. His right arm came up under the right arm of the officer. There was a sharp crack as the officer's gun let go. The air vibrated—sharp sound danced in his ears. And then came the second crash!

The surface of the alley seemed to rock under the concussion of the explosion. The police officer was hurled to one side— Gary sprawled to the alley a short distance away. There was the hiss, the whine of objects catapulting through the air. In the medley of sounds he was able to distinguish the shrill screams of a woman. And then bricks, bits of mortar, metal objects were raining down on all sides!

Gary Greer rolled over on his face. He covered his head with his arms. Something struck him heavily in the right leg. The walls of the building close to him were being battered with falling débris.

Thoughts were stabbing through his head. A ship whose pilot was dropping bombs. A good aim. The bombs were being thrown toward number eleven-twenty-two, toward Parson Jennifer's eating shack. They were striking the mark! Callahan.

He lifted his head a little. The police officer was lying motionless, ten feet away. He was sprawled on the bricks of the alley. He wasn't protecting himself. Something had hit him.

Gary crawled toward him. There was a plane engine drone in the sky—it was rapidly becoming a roar again. The pilot of the plane was coming back, winging in. He was going to make sure that the job was done right!

Callahan had known that Gorringe was going to meet Frenchy Lamonte at the Parson's place. No doubt he had arranged the meeting. And now bombs—high explosives— were raining down from the ship in the sky. And Frenchy

Lamonte was already dead. And Gorringe was out of the place!

Gary Greer twisted the officer's gun from his grip. The man had been struck over the right eye—he was stunned. The ship in the sky was diving again. There was another terrific explosion. Gary flattened his body close beside that of the police officer. Once again objects were hurtling through the air, battering against walls, pounding down into the alley.

Callahan. He couldn't be sure. He had no proof. But the timing had been so perfect. Gorringe would have had plenty of time to reach the café, to get to Frenchy. And yet there would not have been enough time for much conversation. Parson Jennifer did not count—others who might be injured did not count. It was a ruthless attempt at a double kill.

The plane was droning upward again. Objects had ceased to rattle down into the alley. Gary Greer got to his knees. He twisted his head, stared up toward the sky. He caught a glimpse of a dark shape, banking around. The officer groaned, at his side.

The ship was diving again. Gary moved toward the alley exit on the side street. He moved with a limp—his right leg was paining sharply. And the plane was coming down to lay another egg.

This time the crash was more distant. It was sharp, battering. Gary muttered to himself:

"Struck—other side—of the place!" He broke into a limping run. His breath was coming in little gasps. There was a pool of muddy water near the street end of the alley. It was several inches deep. He dropped the officer's gun into it. Sirens were sounding from several directions now. There was the clang of ambulances. He could hear the pounding of feet—shouts.

There was a doorway on his right—a musty odor, old crates and boxes inside. The stale smell of vegetables. He limped into the place. His hands were shaking as he got the cold cream jar from his pocket. But they steadied as he applied the cream to his face. The drone of the plane's engine was growing fainter now. He paused in the cleansing of his skin—listened.

"Eastward!" he muttered. "Over toward—the mountains!"

There was a cut on his left cheek—it stung as the cream cut the blacking from his face. He used the soft towel. There was only a faint light from a street lamp beyond the alley. But twice he had rehearsed getting the blacking off without the aid of a mirror. He worked fast, but carefully. There would be a great deal of confusion. That would help. It was a break for him.

Sirens were, whining steadily now. Fire apparatus was coming. Into the alley room came the first glow of red. Flames, licking up through the ruins of the bombed building. Flames— perhaps destroying the body of Frenchy Lamonte. Gorringe was in the clear, unless he had blundered into the police. But would Callahan know it?

Would Elbow allow him to know it? Gorringe was no fool. He was a cruel killer. What would he think of the bombing of Lamonte crashing a gun in the dimly lighted room?

Gary Greer smiled grimly. There was a confusion of sounds beyond the alley room now. He could hear hoarse shouts, the hiss of water under high pressure. There was the crackling of flames. Police lines would be thrown out, but he was beyond them. He would go out, walk back toward town.

Suddenly he threw back his head—he laughed. It was a terrible, bitter laugh. He was thinking of Joyce Rawlings— "You can't bring—Sanford Greer—back—"

No, he couldn't do that. They had laughed when Sanford Greer had gone down into the mud that covered the cobblestones. They had laughed as they had sprayed lead down into his body. Five killers, there had been. And one man who had held his fire, and had died because of that. Five killers—and three of them were dead. Elbow Gorringe, his fate was uncertain. Ten to one he had escaped. Callahan was alive.

Gary Greer stared out into the alley. It was lighted redly by the flames of the burning building. Gary Greer drew a deep breath. His face was twisted into a smile that was a mask of bitterness.

"Callahan—is Sal the Dude!" he muttered hoarsely. "He was—the brains—" He checked himself, shrank back behind a pile of boxes in the alley cellar room. Footfalls were sounding in the alley. Voices came to him.

"—the Parson's place. Figured he was in—with the River gang!"

Another man swore sharply. Two officers in uniform hurried past. Gary Greer straightened up. They would find the other officer. He might be able to remember, to talk. It was time for him to get out.

He stuffed the darkened cloth, the cold cream jar into a box. Fingerprints on the cloth—he had to be careful. Very careful. The walls of the cellar room were concrete. Flames wouldn't get beyond the boxes. He struck a match, applied it to some dry papers. The flames licked upward. He pulled his soft hat down low over his face.

A glance down the alley, toward the rear of Parson's place, showed him that the two cops had found the other officer. They were lifting him to his feet. The side street was five feet distant.

It was filled with humans drawn to the scene of the explosions and fire. Additional apparatus was coming up.

Gary Greer walked swiftly from the cellar room. He turned up the side street, toward the heart of Center City. He had to fight his way against those coming toward the river. He moved with a limp. Callahan and Elbow Gorringe—they were still alive. It was ironical—unless he was guessing wrong. Callahan had tried to strike at him by destroying two humans who knew too much about the man whose other name was Sal the Dude. And he had only *helped* the man whose father he had murdered.

Callahan—seeing Gorringe breaking under the strain, trying to destroy him. Trying to destroy Lamonte at the same time. Killing his killers—for self-protection.

And he had failed, Frenchy Lamonte had died seconds before the first bomb had dropped. Gorringe was clear of the place. Gary felt a sudden stab of pain as he thought of Parson Jennifer. He had bound the man, tied him securely. Had *he* escaped?

An associate of killers, Jennifer was. But he didn't deserve that sort of death. Gary's hands were clenched at his side as he limped on. *Was* he justified, after all? Joyce Rawlings' face was before his eyes. Pete Ranning's. They were involved. They might be hurt, battered down.

And yet—his father had been murdered. There had been no justice. He had taken justice into his own hands. He would go through with it—he *had* to go through with it now. In spite of everything.

He was fighting for honesty, decency. The most desperate of his father's killers were still alive. He needed more proof about Callahan. He needed no more—not for Gorringe. He moved along, muttering grim words half to himself.

"I'll get them—or they'll finish me—"

A hand gripped his arm, swung him around. He felt fear grip him, his body stiffen. The fat face of a short man was close to his. A voice sounded.

"What blew up—down there—Mister?"

Gary Greer forced a smile. His body relaxed. He replied in a husky tone:

"Don't know—sorry. Guess some one—made a mistake—"

The fat man hurried on, breathing heavily. Gary Greer moved on, too, keeping his eyes on the street. A mistake. Perhaps it had been. He hoped so. But he wasn't sure of Gorringe. He didn't know the inner workings of Callahan's brain. Only one thing was certain. Frenchy Lamonte was out of things. Death had erased one more name. One more—killer name.

8

The Squeeze

ACROSS THE DIRTY-SURFACED table Pete Ranning sat facing Gary Greer, his blue eyes narrowed and holding a worried expression. It would be midnight in twelve minutes. Outside the River Street speakeasy run by one "Touch" Dillon, the rain battered down against the cobbles of stone. A gusty wind drove it against the alley window panes of the squalid room at intervals. Ranning spoke again, in a low voice, despite the fact that they were alone in the room.

"They're out to grab you, Gary—you can't fight 'em *now*. That was a rotten piece of killer business—that bombing of the Parson's place. And with a South Side Field ship! The papers are spreading the stuff—the *News* has a column, pinning the job on you. You've got to get clear, Gary!"

Gary Greer shook his head slowly. The news had given him a jolt—a ship registered and hangared at his own airport, the South Side Field, had been used for the bombing of Parson Jennifer's River Street joint, hours ago. Jennifer had been killed—two humans on the street had been killed. And they had found Lamonte, shot to death in the room upstairs. The *News* was run by a politician named Brookers—and he was a rough rider. The administration he worked with had been the same one in power when Gary's father had been shot down by the hired killers. It was the same administration in power now. Brookers knew that Gary was alive, that Gary had started a clean-up of his own. Brookers was out to get him—and to get him properly, Gary knew that.

"My job's almost finished, Pete," he stated slowly. "Gorringe is still alive. And Sal the Dude. That's Callahan, I'm almost positive. But I've got to be sure. The gang's broken up—I'm pretty safe down here—"

"Safe!" Pete Ranning cut in sharply. "Like hell you are. Every side-walk pounder in the city has been staring at your photo. The dicks are out in force. And Callahan has his own special boys hunting you—you know that. The *News* states you're alive and wanted for "questioning." You know what that means. You've killed—and they know it. They'll get you—before you get *them*."

Pete Ranning stiffened in the chair opposite Gary's. Dillon came into the small room, smirking. He was short, red-faced. He was illiterate, and at times his mind wandered a bit. Sea men gave him trade. His graft toll was small—and the police didn't bother him much.

"Another toss-off, gents?" he muttered thickly. "Bad weather outside—"

Pete Ranning got to his feet. His face was pale; he stood stiffly, blinking his eyes. He started to say something, swore softly, thickly. His right hand moved downward, toward his right hip pocket. He swayed a little.

"I'm—feeling—rotten—"

Gary was staring at him. Dillon chuckled harshly.

"You need—another!" he stated thickly. "How about—"

He stopped. Gary was getting up unsteadily. He shook his head from side to side, swore thickly. He shoved a chair toward Pete's swaying body. Ranning dropped into it heavily. He started to speak again—his head fell forward, his body

swung toward the dirty wall beside the chair. He breathed several times, heavily—then his body relaxed.

Gary Greer stood looking down at him. He chuckled foolishly.

"Can't stand the stuff, Touch." His voice was thick. "Damn strong, at that. It's got me feelin' rocky as—"

He staggered toward Touch Dillon. There was a little gleam in the shorter man's eyes. The liquor in both glasses that he had set before the men was gone—the liquor had been doped. One man was out. And the other—

He backed away from Gary Greer. He half turned away, toward the faded green curtain back of the door. He didn't see Gary's body stiffen—he didn't see the right arm swing.

"Touch!"

The voice was sharp. It was a warning. Dillon pivoted. He tried, in that last second, to rock his head. Gary had cried out sharply, and Gary was striking. His fist caught Touch Dillon under the left ear. There was a sharp crack—Touch groaned, his body collapsed. Gary caught him—there was no heavy thud to the wood floor.

He dragged him toward the chair he had vacated, eased him into it. He turned the back of the chair toward the door. His mind was working fast.

Ranning was pretty heavy—but the spot was a bad one. Gary got him in his arms—headed for the rear of the place. All speakeasy rooms were the same in one respect, along River Street. They had an easy exit to an alley. Dillon was motionless as Gary got Pete back of the small counter-bar, found the alley door. And he'd figured Dillon was dumb!

Rain splattered into his face as he reached the alley. A gust of wind rocked him off balance. He was forced to let Ranning down. A voice reached him—a half whisper.

"Got him, Touch?"

Gary Greer grunted. His back was turned to the speaker; he swung back toward the door.

"Come on!" he muttered thickly, and went in through the door again.

Inside, he swung around. Beyond the counter he could hear Touch Dillon groaning, trying to pull himself up. The man outside had mistaken him for Touch—he had given the game away. Gary's right hand fingers closed over his Colt—he felt the safety catch. The gun was locked.

Just outside the alley entrance he could hear the heavy breathing of the man who had spoken. He was bending over Pete—Gary heard him mutter grimly.

"Ranning! That makes—all three—" The man was straightening—his form, soaked with rain, swung in through the doorway. He whispered hoarsely.

"Touch—where's the—"

Gary struck—he held the automatic by the grip. It was the

barrel that battered down on the side of the questioner's head. The man's breath came out in a wheezing groan—he pitched forward at Gary's feet.

A faint light reached the floor near the alley door. Gary rolled the man over. He didn't recognize him. He had a fat, pallid face—and the gun metal had robbed him of consciousness. From beyond the counter there was a sudden crash as Touch Dillon, trying to pull himself up, lost balance and tumbled again.

Gary's fingers went through the pockets of the fat-faced man's clothes. In the first three he found nothing—in the fourth he found two sheets of folded paper. Voices reached him, from the rain drenched street beyond the main entrance of the speakeasy.

Gary straightened, headed for the alley. He got Pete Ranning in his arms again—moved toward Third Street. Pete was breathing heavily, but evenly. Across Third Street, deserted in the rain, a green light showed faded letters above it. The letters spelled the words *Jones Hotel*. Gary moved straight toward the entrance. Fear was driving him on now. The one he had struck down with the gun had said—"all three." The man had been wrong. But who was the third. Joyce Rawlings?

He swore fiercely. He was inside the narrow entrance of the hotel now. It was a mean corridor, badly lighted. He moved along it, swaying a little. Ahead was a dirty desk—a few chairs. A figure stood and watched him come. Gary dropped Ranning's form into one of the chairs, swore shakily. He grinned at a reddish face that held only one eye. The man had white hair—a dirty white. He chuckled.

"Booze?" he muttered.

Gary was getting his breath. But he managed to chuckle back.

"It's Whitey Leems," he stated. "He's been tossin' the bad stuff away for a week. One of the South Side boys. Want to put him away—and keep it quiet. He'll take plenty of sleepin'."

The red-faced man nodded. He and Gary carried Pete up two flights of rickety stairs. They dropped him on a bed. Gary pulled out a five-dollar bill. It was old, crumpled.

"Dig up a package of cigarettes any kind," he stated. "Whitey's got to smoke when he comes out of this. He's liable to wreck things, if he doesn't have 'em. An' he's out of 'em right now. Forget we come in, see?"

The hotel man flat-footed out of the room. Gary listened to him clumping down the stairs. The one bulb in the room gave a ghastly white light. Pete Ranning was out, but he was sleeping well enough. He'd wake up with a rotten head and bad taste. Gary got his shoes off, loosened his belt—eased up the tie pull around his neck. He went through his pockets, took away a small caliber automatic, a watch that looked too good, a check book.

It had been a narrow one. Touch Dillon had tried to dope him—had got Ranning instead, on the accidental switching of drinks. He'd made another mistake—thinking that Touch was dumb. It had been a bad place for the meet. But they were out of it. He wouldn't forget the face of the one he had knocked out with the gun—and Touch wouldn't forget him. The police were tagging him; Callahan and Elbow Gorringe were fighting hard. And the girl—

Gary swore thickly. That was the next job—to reach her apartment. If the gang had tricked her, trapped her—

The red-faced man was coming up the stairs again. He was humming in a hoarse tone. It was some sort of an Irish air. He rapped on the door, and Gary didn't tell him to come in. He walked three paces and opened the door. The red-faced one tossed a pack of humps on the chair nearest the bed. He grinned with his black teeth.

Gary nodded. He spoke thickly, but slowly.

"Don't be funny with Whitey. He's sittin' next to a certain Eyetalian guy. I've paid his board—an' when he walks out—just let him hoof it."

The red-faced one looked hurt. He swore in a mumbling tone.

"I ain't seen any Whitey," he stated.

"Sure," Gary grunted. "Open a window an' let a little air an' rain in. The only thing water or air can hurt is the bugs in here. I'll be in tomorrow, maybe—around noon."

The red-faced one shoved open a window. It wouldn't stay up, so he dug up a book from the shelf of a table—the one book in the room—and used it to prop open the window. The act seemed to amuse him. He chuckled a lot, but he didn't say anything.

Gary nodded his head. He tossed a dirty blanket over Pete Ranning, and went out. Down by the battered desk a cross-eyed gent was listening to the siren on a police car or an ambulance, and grinning. The siren was somewhere in the distance. Gary went on out. He turned up the wet street toward the center of town, away from the river. The siren's wail died.

Gary walked out near the curb, and he kept his eyes opened. Pete Ranning was out of things for twelve hours, at least. They had nearly gone down together. Touch Dillon had made a mistake, but maybe there had been a reason for only doping one whiskey. Maybe Callahan knew that reason, or Elbow Gorringe.

They had used a ship from South Side Airport, for the bombing of Parson Jennifer's place. That had been Callahan's game. He had known that Frenchy Lamonte and Elbow Gorringe were meeting there. He had *fixed* the rendezvous. And the sky bombs had been dropped with the intention of blowing out two humans that might prove dangerous—to Callahan. He had failed. Gorringe had already rubbed out Lamonte. And Gorringe had got clear.

Gary had got clear, but Callahan had never known that he had been present. The detective with the beady eyes and the scrubby black mustache—was he Sal the Dude? Gary thought so. There was irony in the name—but there had been irony in many things since Gary's father had died on the muddy cobbles of a street only a few miles from the one Gary walked now.

And the squeeze was on. Gary was getting too close. Callahan was sitting inside police circles, inside political circles—and trying to smash the son of a dead man, before he was smashed. Gary had won victories—but they had cost him much. Ranning was in the fight now—and the girl Gary loved was in it. He had tried to spare them, and it hadn't worked out that way.

Two names remained on the list—two living names. Names of the death car "guns" who had battered down Sanford Greer, backed by a rotten city administration. Soapy Tyler had given Gary the names—and he had died. He had been dying when Gary reached him. Babe Lewis had gone down first. He had spoken of "Sal the Dude." Gary had tricked him; even as he had reached for his gun Gary had sent death into his body. Fifty Mile Liseman had been the second to die. His one bullet had gone wild. And now Gary had tricked Elbow Gorringe into sending lead through the skin of Frenchy Lamonte. Three names were wiped off the killer list. Gorringe was alive. Callahan was alive. And unless Soapy Tyler had failed to tell him everything—or had not *known* enough—one of the remaining two was Sal the Dude. And that man was the gang leader.

Rain dripped from the brim of Gary's soft hat. A night owl cab cruised by. Gary hailed the driver—got inside. He kept his hat brim pulled down over his face. The police were searching—cab drivers were often closely allied. They got around. He gave the address of a fashionable apartment building.

They had to cross the busy streets of the city. There was traffic. Gary Greer leaned back in the cab, tried to relax. Pete Ranning would be all right. His pulse had been steady enough; he had a strong constitution. Jensen would automatically take charge out at the airport. It seemed ages since Gary had turned over the Field to Pete—had tried to make the world believe he had died in a plane crash. Many had believed it—but after the first two killers had died, the going had become too tough. First there had been suspicion. Now they *knew*, he was sure of that. Callahan and Gorringe—trying to get him before he got them.

He smiled grimly as the driver of another cab tried to cut his own driver off. The other man failed. They were ahead now, skidding on the wet asphalt, but ahead. A traffic signal held them up. They started again—were forced to slow down for a town car just ahead. And as they turned out—the cab they had got away from shot in from the left.

There was the squealing of brakes.

For a second Gary Greer was stiff in the seat, his right hand fingers on his Colt. They were forced over toward the town car. They were squeezed. He got a glimpse of the other cab driver's head, half turned, a mocking grin on the prize ring face. His own driver was swearing grimly. The other cab went on—the town car, glistening in the rain, pulled out. They were motionless. The squeeze had been too tough—too close.

A slickered figure loomed up close to the driver's seat. A bull like voice sounded.

"What you waitin' for—three o'clock an' no traffic? You learnin' to drive—"

The cab jerked forward—the traffic cop's face swung behind. Gary was slumped low in the seat. He didn't look back. The cab driver continued to swear. Gary drew a deep breath. His fingers relaxed their grip on the gun. A traffic crash—police—recognition.

He laughed harshly. The cab driver heard him. He didn't like it.

"A lot of dirty crooks sittin' back of wheels in this town!" he stated. "A lot of ex-pugs tryin' to run things, squeezin' the decent guys out—"

Gary's voice, cold, sharp—cut in on the driver.

"Never mind that—watch your driving!"

The cab driver jerked his head to the front again. He muttered to himself. Gary's face was set grimly. He saw the apartment building ahead. It rose twenty stories high. He thought of Joyce Rawlings. He had told her he wouldn't come back until things were finished. But he had to know the truth. The one he had battered down had said "that makes—all three." For the first time since he had got control of himself, the night his father had been murdered, Gary Greer felt rage striking at him again. If they had touched the girl—

The cab swung up before the elaborate entrance. Gary gave the driver a bill, got out. He walked toward the corner. Fifty yards down the street was a delivery entrance. He went in. He had to be careful. Callahan knew about Joyce. If the place was being watched, on the inside, he would be caught. He had to go slow.

An elevator boy, off duty, came along the concrete corridor, smoking a cigarette. He was in uniform—Gary had never seen him before. He was young.

"Hello!" Gary smiled a little. "I'm from County Headquarters. Is Miss Rawlings in yet, do you know?"

The elevator boy's eyes widened. He stared at Gary.

"In yet? Say, they just took her out of here an hour ago. A gray haired guy is sittin' up above—waiting to see any of her relatives or friends. But they was City bulls that took her to jail." Gary turned away. He didn't want the boy to see his eyes. Joyce—down at the detective bureau! Joyce Rawlings—mixed up with the police because of him. He swore grimly, faced the boy again.

"Didn't go around shouting about who they were and what they were doing, did they?" he asked. "Though the City boys always make a lot of racket on a pinch."

The elevator boy grinned. "I brought 'em down with her," he stated. "She was pretty quiet—but said something about getting some people on the phone. They said it would be all right to do that from the jail—that the chief just wanted to talk with her. That's how I know who they were."

Gary nodded. He forced a grin, lighted a cigarette.

"Beat the county to it," he stated cheerfully. "I'll go up and see who's sitting up above. Don't want him to see me, though. Give him a laugh."

The elevator boy nodded. "He's decorating the red plush nearest the entrance," he stated. "You can tell him by his big feet."

Gary went up above. He stood back near the elevators—and stared toward the ornate entrance. The red plush chairs were there—but no human with big feet decorated any of them. The police didn't have a thing on the girl—and she had too much money for them to fool with, unless they had plenty on her.

There was a tired look in Gary's eyes. He could guess what had happened. Someone known to the man he had battered down with the gun, back of Touch Dillon's speakeasy counter, had run the game. The gang had taken Joyce out, but they hadn't taken her to any police station. Maybe she had guessed that they weren't taking her—maybe she hadn't. The man who had remained in the lobby hadn't stayed long. He'd been playing the game, too.

Gary went out of the apartment delivery entrance slowly. He walked away from River Street for two blocks. He took a Green cab—rode a mile westward, got out and caught another cab five minutes later. He instructed the driver to drop him off at the corner that was fifty yards from the entrance of the *Jones Hotel*, then to drive to the hotel and leave a folded slip of paper with the clerk. He said there was a message he wanted to get to the clerk. There wasn't any message. He was playing safe. He had a trail to pick up, and he wanted to do it without getting squeezed.

THE CAB SLOWED down as it crossed Bank Street, the avenue that ran parallel to River Street. Gary slipped out on the right side—he had paid the driver—fought for his balance on the slippery paving. He was out of sight of the *Jones Hotel*—the corner brick building cut off any chance of him being seen from the windows of the cheap hotel.

The cab rolled on; he could hear the wheels slush over the soaked street surface. The sound died—he heard the engine rumbling. He was close to the brick building on the corner now. He stared down Third Street. The driver was vanishing inside the entrance of the hotel. Gary waited. Then it came. From a window up above. A battering, tearing stream of bullets from what sounded like a sub-caliber machine-gun!

Glass in the cab clattered to the street. Splinters shot in the air—metal wanged as the lead tore against it. The car rocked under the impact of the machine-gun blast. It was shattered from engine hood to tail-light. The clatter died suddenly. A window slammed.

Gary Greer swore softly. From the direction of River Street men were coming—they came slowly, heading toward the cab. The driver didn't come out from the entrance of the hotel. From the direction of Second Street there was the sound of a car engine suddenly given plenty of gas, but not in gear. A police whistle shrilled, several blocks distant.

Gary swung around, headed toward Second Street. The going was tough—wind swept Bank Street, the rain cut against his face. The car engine was given the gas again, still out of gear. The driver was taking no chances—he had the machine ready for a quick getaway, warmed up. But it was clear that he was waiting for something.

Gary turned the corner. The car was near an alley that ran out back of the *Jones Hotel*, on Second Street. The wind-shield wiper was swinging; he could see the figure of a man behind the glass. He waved his hand, ran forward. It was his left hand that he waved—the right was in the pocket of his gray coat—the fingers gripped his Colt.

Gary moved out toward the street as he approached the car. He could see the driver's head, extended beyond the left side of the car. Gary was within fifty yards of the machine now. The shrilly of a police whistle, on Third Street, came clearly. The man in the car blew the horn twice. He blew it sharply.

And then, suddenly, the machine jerked forward. It picked up speed rapidly. It sped straight toward Gary!

He jerked his body to one side. There was a short flash of red from the left of the wind-shield—he heard the hum of the bullet as it cut the air close to his head. His own Colt cracked—the car swerved badly to the right, hit the curb sharply. A tire blew—the driver fought the car back into the street again. It was skidding badly as it rounded the corner into Bank Street, turning northward, and was lost from sight.

Gary faced the alley. There were muffled shouts from it—the sound of footfalls. A figure came into sight, then two more figures appeared. The second two seemed to be supporting a third person. Ranning—or the girl? It was one of the two, Gary was sure of that.

He was in an exposed position—the man in the lead spotted him right away. The getaway machine was gone. Gary saw the leading man jerk his head quickly, heard him mutter something. The two men behind him swung around with the third human between them.

Gary ran forward, zigzagging. He saw the man who had given the order, shifting his body to the side, move his left hand. There was the glint of metal. The right arm was curved at the elbow, rigid. Elbow Gorringe!

Elbow's gun spoke first. The bullet shrilled close to Gary's head. He dropped to his knees, braced his left hand on the wet asphalt. He raised the right, aimed carefully. Gorringe spilled a second shot as the wind rocked him. It gritted along the asphalt—wild.

Gary Greer was calm. He squeezed the trigger of the Colt—there was a sharp *crack!* Elbow's body jerked. He steadied himself, fired a third time. Gary didn't even hear the air-hiss of the lead. He fired his second shot.

Gorringe went to his knees. There was less than thirty yards of distance between the two men. But the light was tricky, and there was the wind and the rain. Gorringe was down, his gun arm was wavering. He collapsed forward, rolled over on his back. From River Street a car straightened out on Second, headed toward Gary. A siren was wailing again—blocks away.

Gary Greer straightened. He turned, ran toward a low wooden building that had been at his back. The building was some sort of a warehouse; steps led down to a basement entrance. He jerked his head below the level of the street as a hail of bullets nicked the iron railing above the concrete wall back of the steps.

The car slowed down. Bullets continued to splatter above his head—for perhaps ten seconds. Then the car got into high gear again—he could hear it picking up speed.

He smiled a little. Gorringe had been hit twice. They had stopped, picked him up and got him in the car. He was sure of that. But it wouldn't do much good. Gary's right arm had been steady enough. Elbow was out of the game; he felt certain of that.

Slowly he raised his head. The street was clear. Rain streaked down—the wind swept up it from the river in gusts. From Third Street came the faint sound of voices, of shouts. A siren wail diminished, dying to a low growl. Gary stared toward the alley. His body stiffened. The figure of Elbow Gorringe was still lying there in the rain! Those in the car had not picked him up!

"Trick!" Gary muttered. "Maybe they did get him—someone else, waiting for me to walk out—"

He swore softly. That didn't seem possible. The police were too close. They might come down the alley, swing around the block any second. Those in the car had discovered that Gorringe was dead—they had high-balled out of the section. They had left him. A dead gangster never counted. Center City didn't go in for expensive funerals, like Chi.

Gary moved up the steps. He kept his right fingers on the Colt—and his eyes on the motionless figure. Sounds from Third Street had died. A river boat whistle sounded above the beat of the rain. Gary went up the steps—got out on the street surface. He moved toward the figure rapidly.

Suddenly he pulled up. The right arm was flung out. It was almost straight. Elbow Gorringe had a crooked right arm. The figure lying just clear of the alley that ran through to the rear of the *Jones Hotel* wasn't that of Elbow Gorringe!

For several seconds Gary stood twenty feet distant, staring downward. Fear was striking at him. There was the strange limpness of death in the sprawl of the man's body. This was no trick. Those in the car had picked up a man—they had dropped another man!

Gary forced himself in nearer the man. There was something he recognized—the outline of the body, the build—even though the man was lying face downward. He dropped to his knees, rolled the man over.

It was Pete Ranning. Gary forgot the rain, the nearness of the police—as he stared into the white face of the man who had been his best friend. There was no expression on Pete's face. His shirt was opened at the front—he wore no shoes. Red stained the cloth of the shirt, over his heart. He had been dead for minutes.

Gary Greer got to his feet. He stood staring down at Pete Ranning's body, his lips twitching. They had found Pete, in spite of his efforts. They had found him up in the mean room of the *Jones Hotel*. And they had murdered him. Murdered him as they had murdered Gary's father.

He bent down again. He wanted to lift Pete in his arms as he had before, to carry him away from the alley, away from the rain and wind. There was no rage within him now. The hurt was too great. For the first time since he had started the fight against his father's killers the gangsters had struck back. Had struck back hard.

He thought of the girl. From between his lips came a fierce sound. They had the girl. The thought stopped him. Stopped him from lifting Pete Ranning, carrying him away.

He turned abruptly. He could be hard. He *would* be hard. The Colt he slipped into the pocket of his gray suit. He crossed the street, moved rapidly toward the river. He was fifty yards from the corner of River and Second Streets, when he heard the machine coming. An alley nearby was his only chance. He slipped inside.

The car was a detective's machine. It had the red-glassed side-light of such cars in Center City. It rounded the corner slowly, headed up the street toward Bank. The brakes squealed as it neared the alley. The sound of voices reached Gary indistinctly.

Pete Ranning—dead. Murdered as he had lain drugged up in the *Jones Hotel* room, perhaps. Or shot through the heart along the way. They had found him.

But he had not known of his death shot. He had seen no faces, felt no pain. That was the only consoling thought. The rotten part of it was that Gary had been to blame. He felt to blame. He had tried not to involve the girl, or Pete. The odds had been too great. The killers were ruthless. And Joyce Rawlings—

His body twisted, as he stood in the alley, listened to the beat of the car's engine as it waited for the men who were beside the body of Pete Ranning.

The girl had been tricked. She had been taken from her apartment. Gorringe was out of the fight. Gary could not be sure of it—but he felt that Elbow was dead. He guessed that the men behind him—the ones who had gone back into the darkness of the alley during the gun fight—had been carrying Ranning then. Had he been dead, or had they killed him after? And why had they not closed in on Gary as he had crouched on the steps of the warehouse?

The police had been too close. Perhaps Gorringe had not been dead—and they wanted to get him medical attention. Certainly they knew that Gary was still alive.

The voices had died now—the detective car was picking up speed. Gary stared toward Bank Street—watched the glow from the red light on the soaked street surface. His eyes went across the street, toward the alley. The body of Pete Ranning was no longer there.

Gary Greer waited until the detective car was three blocks distant, heading toward the center of town. Then he moved on to River Street, turned away from the direction of Third.

In the distance, over toward the city's business district, he heard the siren of the detective car. His eyes were narrowed to gray slits. Hurt slits in a pale, set face.

Callahan. His thoughts centered on the man. Callahan was the one he would have to find. It shouldn't be hard. Callahan was a crook sitting in the seat of a plainclothes-man. Callahan would know where the girl was—where they had taken her. There was only one chance now. River Street haunts were useless. There was no time to play stool-pigeons, to work inside from the outside of the circle. He'd have to get to one man— Callahan.

The gangsters had struck hard. They had tightened their grip. The girl had been taken—and Pete Ranning had died. Callahan was the only one who counted now. Gary knew less about him than he had known about the others. That was gangster creed—others always knew less about the big guy. But Gary knew that it was Callahan who had trapped Joyce Rawling, who had murdered Pete Ranning. It was Callahan who had ordered the squeeze.

IT WAS AN hour before dawn. Casal Callahan walked from the entrance of the City Detective Building, slipped back of the wheel of the battered coupé near the curb. The battered coupé was Callahan's business car. Ten blocks distant, in a certain garage, he had a sporty green roadster. He kicked the self starter, the engine rapped noisily. Callahan reached for the shift.

A figure slid up near the door—it swung open. Callahan stopped shifting. His right hand dropped toward a pocket of the coupé. A left hand struck it aside. The figure slipped into the seat beside Callahan. Something hard, metallic, pressed against Callahan's right side.

The detective's breath was sucked in sharply. There was a sickly grin on his face. His voice was hoarse, broken.

"Hello—Greer—"

Gary Greer smiled. It was a terrible smile.

"Hello, Sal!" he said grimly. "Take me for—a drive, will you?"

Callahan swayed a little in the seat. He was fighting for control, and he was gaining it. But it took effort.

"Sure, Greer," he managed shakily. "Which—way?"

His eyes went toward the entrance of the Headquarters Building. Gary laughed a little. The laugh was as terrible as the smile had been.

"One hand on the shift—the other on the wheel!" he ordered. "When you get through shifting—*both* hands on the wheel. Be very careful, Sal—we don't want an—accident."

Callahan smiled again. His eyes were narrowed a little.

"Which way, Greer?" he asked again.

Gary spoke very slowly. "Out Main—to Carlisle. West on Carlisle. Quiet street—we'll talk as we—ride."

The car jerked forward. Gary held the Colt pressed against Callahan's right side. He had the cloth of his coat over the weapon. He pulled his soaked hat down over his eyes. The streets were almost deserted.

Callahan drove carefully. The rain had become a fine drizzle.

It was colder. They went west on Carlisle. Callahan was breathing heavily. The coupé was approaching the Italian section of the city now. Wooden shacks—jammed close together. Cars parked for the night, in side streets.

"Tired?" Gary asked grimly. "You're breathing—hard."

Callahan kept the smile on his face. His was a rather handsome face, though the man's body was short, thick-set. His black mustache was uneven, badly kept.

"Had a hard day—and night," the detective stated slowly, shakily. "Trouble—on River Street."

Gary said nothing. He pointed to the left, as they approached the next street.

"Turn—to the left. Go down half a block. Pull in at the curb, near Malletti's place. Get both hands on the wheel—keep them there!"

He saw Callahan's face twist—the man's thin lips were half parted. He pulled in near the dark, wooden shack beyond a ragged curb. He got both hands on the wheel. His eyes met Gary's. Fear showed in them.

"Listen, Greer—" he started— "maybe you an' me can get together on—"

"Maybe." Gary cut in sharply. "I ran into a wop named Conti about two hours ago. Out here, in this section. I was looking for Malletti, because I knew he was after you, Callahan. You sent up his brother a week ago. Conti was drunk. I fed him five hundred-dollar bills, and he talked. Among a lot of lies, he told me one truth. He said you were sometimes known as Sal the Dude. In this section—"

He stopped. Callahan's face was white—ghastly white. Fear was gripping him.

Gary laughed bitterly. It was a low, throaty laugh.

"Don't lie to me, Callahan!" he advised. "Your one chance is—straight talk."

"I ain't—lying—" Callahan's voice was pitched too high. Fear was driving his front away.

"Is Elbow Gorringe dead?" Gary cut in grimly.

Callahan nodded. He didn't speak. His eyes were wide with fear now.

Gary spoke again. "If I send lead through you here, Callahan," he said slowly, "Malletti will burn for it. They know he's out to get you. They know you made deals with him. They know you sent his brother up. *You* know something the other don't know, Sal. You know *I've* been working under Federal jurisdiction. You know you couldn't send me up for the murder of your crooked pals. That's why you didn't come after me, *that* way. You wanted to kill. You killed Ranning tonight. I got Gorringe. Working under a rotten administration, you ordered my father—put on the spot, Sal the Dude!"

Callahan tried to speak. His words came out hoarsely.

"I swear to God, Greer—I didn't have a chance—"

"You're going to get one!" Gary's voice was like ice. "You're going to take me to Joyce Rawlings! You know where she is. If she's hurt—or if you try one trick—"

He shoved the gun muzzle deeper against Callahan's side. The man back of the wheel spoke shakily.

"I'll—play the game—Greer! She isn't—hurt. I swear to God—"

"Drive!" Gary's voice was grim. "And listen to what I'm telling you—"

The car engine raced. The engine rapped again. But something else was rapping, too. It was clattering. Beating like a steam riveting machine. A repeater rifle!

Callahan screamed. Just one word.

"Malletti!"

And then the bullets were ripping into the car. Battering against the hood. Tearing at the metal and wood, the fabric!

The car was rolling. Gary bent forward. Irony. He had brought Callahan out to Malletti's place—to drive him on. To make him realize that Gary could kill—and get in the clear. Malletti hated Callahan. And now the Italian had heard the detective. His high pitched voice had carried to the frame house. And Malletti was battering down lead to get the man he knew was in the car.

Something struck Gary heavily across the top of the head. He straightened, his body jerking. The machine-gun fire had died—the car was picking up speed. Weakness was gripping Gary. Waves of dizziness swept through his head. He tried to fight it off. Callahan was staring at him, puzzled. The expression faded.

Gary tried to tighten the grip on his Colt. But he failed. He saw Callahan's right hand streak back from the wheel—it caught him heavily under the right temple. He pitched forward.

It was minutes later when he recovered consciousness. The car was on a country road. There was a gag in his mouth. Callahan was driving slowly, a smile on his face. He glanced at Gary, but he said nothing. Instead, he started to hum. Gary tried to move his arms—his wrists were cuffed back of him, and the steel was fastened to something that wasn't movable.

The car bumped along the road. Callahan drove with a

yellow-white smile on his face, and hummed. There were two bullet holes through the wind shield. The metal at Gary's right was torn. His head ached terribly. His whole body ached. He picked out a few words of the song Sal the Dude was now singing.

" *'Sure do love to hold you Honey—*
Sure do love to—squeeze—' "

Callahan jerked his head toward Gary's. He broke off. He chuckled.

"I'm a good guy, Greer!" he muttered grimly. "You want to get to that kid of yours. By God—I'm *takin'* you!"

He started humming again.

9

Sal the Dude

CALLAHAN CHUCKLED AS he drove the ancient car off the main road, turned it up a fairly steep, rough road. There were tall trees on each side of the road—rain dripped through them. The car skidded badly in the mud; Callahan swore. Gary Greer pressed his lips tightly together, gave no sign of the pain sent through his head by the jerking car.

The fifth name—at his side, taking him to the girl, to the spot where Joyce Rawlings was held a prisoner! Sal the Dude. A crooked detective at headquarters in Center City—the man who had ordered his father put on the spot!

The car swung to the right—Callahan jerked the wheel to the left. He swore fiercely as the rear wheels failed to slide out of the rut on the right. He stepped on the accelerator—the engine clattered. But the wheels spun through the mud without moving the car forward. Sal the Dude smiled grimly as the clatter of the engine died under his relaxed foot pressure.

"Like *you*, Greer!" he muttered. "Got just so far—can't go on!"

He chuckled hoarsely. Gary Greer shifted a little in the seat—his hands were cuffed to a brace behind him. He smiled with his lips.

"Be a white man, Callahan!" he muttered. "Let the girl get clear—she's out of this."

Callahan swore harshly. "She's *your* girl, Greer!" he snapped. "And nothing that belongs to you is out of this. You know too much." Gary's eyes met those of the detective. He nodded his head.

"You can handle me, Sal," he stated. "But the girl doesn't know anything."

Callahan grunted. "I ain't that dumb, Greer," he muttered. "What I'm going to do for both of you is the right thing—*for me!*"

He stepped on the accelerator again. The car jerked forward, slid back. Callahan swore steadily. Gary half closed his eyes.

It was ironical—the way the thing had worked out. He had held his gun against Callahan, in this same car, minutes ago. Callahan knew where the girl was—where his men had taken her. And Gary had known that he knew. He had forced Callahan to drive to a curb spot in front of Malletti's place, back in Center City's Italian section. Malletti was a gun—and he was after Callahan. The detective had played him a rotten trick—and Malletti was faithful to his relatives. Gary wanted truth. He had forced Callahan to park at the curb and he had pointed out that if he didn't get the truth he could pour lead into the detective's body—and get clear. Malletti would take the rap, unless he had an alibi that was air-tight. The police knew Malletti was out to get Callahan—and Callahan knew the same thing. Gary had had him in a tough spot.

But Callahan had weakened. Fear had raised his voice. And Malletti had recognized it. From a window of his place he had turned loose a sub-caliber gun on the parked car. Only a miracle had saved them. Things had ripped loose—and Gary had been stunned by one of the things. Callahan had gotten a break. He had finished Gary—cuffed him up. And now he was taking him to the girl, to Joyce Rawlings. It looked like the end.

Gary groaned. And Callahan jerked his head toward him—laughed.

"Getting yellow?" he snapped. "Ever hear of a male and female Mexican stand-off?"

Gary felt his heart pounding. That was to be the dose for Joyce and himself. Lead pounding into their bodies as they stood with their backs to some wall!

"You'll burn for—the stuff you've pulled, Sal!" he muttered.

Callahan swore thickly. "Not if I finish off you and the girl!" he snapped. "And maybe you think the dose isn't mixed right now!"

The car jerked forward a few feet.

The rear wheels got on firmer earth—it bounced along, half off the road. Straining his eyes, Gary could see the dim shape of a house in the distance. No lights showed in the few windows he could see. The house was low and rambling. It was well obscured from the main road. And the main road was not much of a thoroughfare. It was less than five miles from the Italian section of Center City. But this part of the country was swampy, bad land. It had never built up much.

The car was making some headway now; Callahan had ceased to swear. A figure suddenly stepped out into the glare from the head-lights. The man wore a soft hat, pulled well down over his face. He called out.

"Wrong road, you—"

Callahan cut in on the other man's words. He spoke sharply.

"It's all right, Joe! Didn't have time to switch cars. Got a load of important stuff."

The man ahead stared toward the car, then waved his left hand. His right stayed out of sight. The car pulled up close to him. Callahan spoke again.

"Hop on the running-board—I may need help. Meet Mr.—" Callahan's tone was grimly amused— "Greer!"

The man on the running-board swore sharply. Gary couldn't see his face—he turned it to one side. Callahan drove toward a battered shed. He talked as he drove.

"You don't have to hide your good looks from Greer, Joe." Callahan chuckled. "What this gent sees or hears around this shack won't count worth a damn!"

The car was under the shed now. Callahan cut the engine. His eyes narrowed on the gray ones of Gary.

"You got Elbow and Liseman, Greer. You got Babe Lewis. You played Elbow so that he finished off Frenchy Lamonte. And then you had your try for me. It didn't go. Got anything to gab about?"

There was silence except for the drip of rain somewhere inside the shed, and the heavy breathing of the man who stood beside Gary, on the running-board.

"You put my father on the spot." Gary's voice was hard. "You laughed at him as you—killed. The Federal bunch were after

Liseman. They were after Babe Lewis. Both of them were murderers. I was sworn into the Federal service, before I went after them, Callahan. They both were armed. You tried to get both Elbow Gorringe and Frenchy Lamonte, with your sky bombs. I tricked Frenchy into getting his dose, that's right. He was a rotten killer. As for Gorringe—we fought that out. He didn't shoot as straight as I did."

The one on the running-board swore thickly.

"Give it to him here, Sal!" he muttered.

Callahan sucked in his breath. He shook his head.

"The other one gets it at the same time," he muttered. "Lean forward, *Mr.* Greer."

Gary leaned forward. A key turned in the steel cuffs. His hands were free. Callahan slid out of the car.

"Watch him, Joe!" he ordered. "Take it easy on the trigger— but if he acts up—give him the dose!"

Gary got down from the car. His head ached—he was stiff from his cramped position. The man beside him gave him a shove toward the rear of the car. He moved slowly; the shed was dark. Outside it was almost as black. From the rear of the house a faint light filtered through the rain. Callahan lighted a cigarette.

"Great night—" he stated grimly— "for a murder!"

Gary Greer stood close to the man who had directed the activities of the death car gang. His head was clearing; he was thinking fast.

"Five hundred grand—" he said slowly—"that's a lot of coin!"

He saw Callahan's body stiffen a little. Then the killer laughed. It was a low, rumbling laugh.

"Where *you're* going—it ain't worth a nickel!" he replied.

Gary spoke in a low, level tone.

"It would be worth something—to you."

There was a little silence. Then Callahan spoke almost cheerfully to the one he addressed as "Joe."

"Better go back down the road, Joe—don't want to take any chances. In about an hour everything'll be fine."

The other man moved off, muttering something about liking to be in "on the show." His figure was lost in the darkness. The muzzle of a gun was pressed against the small of Gary's back.

"Just walk toward that light—there's a door around the other side. And don't make any mistakes, Greer!"

Gary walked. The house was old, sagging. It was frame, and even in the semi-darkness he could see that most of the paint was gone from the wood. He moved toward a small door beyond the filtered light. Callahan spoke.

"Hit it twice—fast like," he ordered.

Gary obeyed orders. The door opened almost instantly. A white glare hurt his eyes. There was an oath. He heard a deep voice mutter.

"Jeez! It's—Greer!"

Behind him Callahan chuckled. "None other," he stated. "Show him into the parlor, boys!"

There were dim lights in the house—gas lights. Several figures stood over near a wall as Gary went in. He failed to recognize any of the men, though they made no attempt to hide their features. Callahan stepped inside behind him.

"Here we are!" he stated cheerfully. "How's the moll, Jerry?"

The man addressed was short and thick-set. He grunted.

"Damn quiet!" he stated grimly. "She ain't much on gabbing."

Callahan grinned in the yellow light. His face looked a little pasty. He spoke slowly.

"Take Mr. Greer down to the cellar," he stated. "I'll be down to see him later. Bring up a Thompson and fix her right. Keep the girl where she is. Somebody get me a drink—I need it."

A hand gripped Gary by the left arm. He was led toward some wooden steps. He was half way down when he got the final shove. But he didn't fall. A laugh drifted down as the door closed. It was cold in the cellar. Water dripped in several places. Gary drew in a deep breath.

"You can't beat—a Thompson!" he muttered grimly. His fingers twisted as he thought of Joyce Rawlings. Had the game been worth—this finish? There was just one answer—it hadn't. Pete Ranning was dead. They had the girl—the girl he loved.

"The fifth name—too tough!" he muttered to himself.

He knew too much. And yet—Callahan loved money. He knew that Gary possessed money. Five hundred grand—that had been bait. Big bait. Would Callahan give them a play for it? Or would he turn loose the Thompson he had ordered fixed up?

Gary shook his head. He thought of Joyce, swore bitterly. But she was game. She'd stand up. She wouldn't whine.

And he wouldn't whine. He had killed two killers. But he had been given the right to do that. Federal right. Elbow Gorringe had shot it out with him—and had lost. And Gorringe had killed Frenchy Lamonte. It was the fifth name that he had failed to scratch from the list of his father's murderers. Sal the Dude—Detective Callahan!

Gary Greer laughed. It was a low, terrible laugh. It didn't carry beyond the cellar. It didn't give him courage. But it helped. A Thompson sub-caliber gun could shut off the laughter. They had laughed at Sanford Greer as he had died. He would laugh at them.

From up above he heard laughter. It was mocking. He took a few steps in the darkness, ran up against a wall. A stone wall. His body relaxed. But one thought persisted.

"Five hundred thousand!" he muttered. "I might—get a play—for that!"

A YELLOW LIGHT stabbed down the steps of the cellar. Gary turned—he stood near the wall opposite the lower steps. The door slammed shut—a bolt snapped into place. A flashlight's beam stabbed downward, found Gary's figure. The man who held the light was Callahan. He descended the steps slowly, carefully. He would flash the beam on the steps—then flash it on Gary's figure. In his right hand something glistened dully. Callahan was taking no chances.

At the foot of the steps he hesitated, then snapped a switch. Dull light from an electric globe spread over the cellar. Gary smiled faintly. Up above the men had been using gas. But down here they used electricity. Why?

Callahan faced him. He was smiling a little. There was a table not far from Gary—a rough table with a stool beside it. Callahan motioned toward the stool.

"Take the weight off your feet, Greer," he advised.

He pulled another stool toward the small table. He sat down, keeping his right hand out of sight. For several seconds they sat in silence. Callahan broke it.

"Five hundred grand is a lot of coin," he stated. "A lot of coin. But if it's not in cash—"

His voice died. Gary spoke steadily.

"It's not. That's a lot of coin to have in cash, Callahan. It can be turned into cash—the paper stuff."

Callahan chuckled hoarsely. "I'm not that dumb, Greer," he stated. "I'd have to turn you loose to get the coin. You've got the goods on me. That five hundred grand won't do you any good—and it wouldn't do me any good. Not with you running around loose."

Gary smiled with his lips. "It's a lot of coin to pass up, Callahan," he repeated. "No more tracking down crooks. No more going after petty graft. You could skip the country—"

Callahan swore softly. He liked the picture. But he was suspicious. Sal the Dude, was no stupid bull. He could see the difficulties ahead. He had Gary right now. He had Joyce Rawlings. The others were out of things. But five hundred thousand—

"What's the—offer?" he snapped coldly.

Gary spoke slowly, quietly. His eyes bored into those of the headquarters' detective. Bored into those of the man who had been known to his gang only by the name of Sal the Dude, a name that didn't fit. And yet fit perfectly, for Callahan's purpose.

"Let the girl go—she'll give you her word she'll keep her mouth shut. Let me talk to her, in your presence—get her to make a quick jump away from Center City. I'll tell her you and I've made a deal. That I've got to get you the price, and that I'll meet her out West. She'll go."

Callahan was shaking his head. His eyes held a mocking expression.

"And let you follow her? You know too much, Greer."

Gary smiled slightly. He shook his head.

"You can stick to me until you've got the coin, Callahan. I tried to get you—and I damn near did it. You've got me. I can take the dose—*after* you've turned the girl loose."

Callahan stiffened. There was an incredulous expression in his eyes now.

"You mean—you'll let us rub you out, after you've handed over the coin?" he muttered.

"Just that!" Gary's voice was steady. His eyes were serious, narrowed. "It's five hundred thousand to me—to have Joyce Rawlings in the clear. You got my pal—Pete Ranning. I dragged them both into this mess. And you've got the girl and myself—got us right. I'm not bargaining for myself—I'm making a play for the girl. And—I'm on the level, Callahan."

The detective stared at Gary. But there was doubt in his eyes. He shook his head.

"You'd cross me up, Greer. You're a fighter. To get that much cash I'd have to give you too much rope."

Gary spoke steadily. "I know when I'm licked. The girl's not important to you. She don't know much, Callahan. If I tell her to get clear of Center City—she'll get clear."

Callahan was tapping the knuckles of his left hand on the surface of the table. He was thinking hard. It was a tempting proposition. Big money bait. He could go abroad, live like a prince. Five hundred thousand. And he knew that Gary Greer had it. The piece of ground that his flying field was on—that was almost worth it. Sanford Greer had been wealthy.

Gary could almost read the other man's thoughts. He spoke again, drumming in the facts.

"I'll be out of things, Callahan. Remember that. We're dealing for the girl—a damn decent kid. She shouldn't be mixed up in this."

Callahan smiled with his lips. "It's a hell of a time to think of *that*, Greer!" he snapped.

Gary nodded. "I tried to keep her out of this—from the first," he stated. "She doesn't know much, Callahan. She'll give you her word she won't talk."

Callahan chuckled hoarsely. "I don't trust any molls in that line," he stated. "But *she* hasn't got anything on me. The D.A. would laugh at her story."

"Right." Gary leaned across the table, his eyes on Callahan's. "I can have the coin ready for you by noon. You can stick with me. After you get it—you can bring me back here for the finish."

The detective swore softly. "You've got guts, Greer!" he muttered.

Gary smiled with his lips. He shrugged his shoulders.

"I've been through plenty—and I know when I'm licked. Almost got you, Callahan—but when a woman gets mixed up—"

His voice died. Callahan was thinking out loud.

"If you tried any tricks—I'd have you. You're wanted by the police. They don't know you're working with the Federal outfit. I could fill you full of lead—claim that you were trying to make a break after I'd grabbed you. You wouldn't be able to talk—and my play would be that I didn't know you were under Federal jurisdiction, had Federal authority."

"You're using your head," Gary said slowly. "You could get me before I could spout a word. Some of your boys could see that the girl gets on a train. They could ride the train for a while, even. Big money, Callahan."

Callahan's eyes held a distant expression. For a split second Gary thought that he had the crooked detective going. And then Sal the Dude laughed. His eyes met Gary's squarely.

"No good, Greer!" he stated grimly. "You're too damn clever—too damn anxious! It's not worth it. Too many chances for a slip."

Gary felt his heart sink. Callahan had seen through his game—had seen that even such bait was not worth the risk he had been taking.

"You got the boys—one by one." Callahan's voice was low, bitter. "Some of 'em weren't so dumb. You got away from us times when we had you cornered. Five hundred grand is a lot of coin—but they burn 'em hot in this State. I'd rather have you quiet-like—and the Rawlings kid the same way. I've got plenty—"

"You want more, Callahan." Gary was still fighting. "You need more to get away right. You've got some of your gang to settle up with. They don't forget. Malletti'll know he didn't get you tonight. He's got some good killers in his mob. It's a chance to get clear in a hurry—and to get clear right. And all you've got to do is turn loose a girl—"

Callahan was staring beyond Gary. He was thinking again. Thinking of Paris, Vienna, Berlin. He was thinking of Goldie Lawrence. Five hundred grand would take her away from "Spots" Deane. And Goldie was worth having.

Gary was talking in a low, steady voice.

"We can work it this way—I'll take you along with me to—"

That was as far as he got. Every muscle in his body was suddenly taut. His feet were pressed firmly against the concrete of the cellar floor. With sudden, irresistible force, he struck—struck for the point of the heavy chin.

Callahan never had the chance to get his gun up—he never even squeezed the trigger. With a sharp, cracking thud Gary's right fist hit square on the button. Callahan groaned—his fingers relaxed; his body slumped a little forward, and Gary lifted the stool on which he had been sitting and tapped the unprotected forehead. Callahan's body slipped from the table edge and the stool to the concrete floor. There were no boards for it to strike against—to make heavy sound. Gary stared down at Callahan. He was unconscious!

Gary listened. There was laughter up above—it reached him faintly. The door was bolted on the inside; he remembered that. In a flash he was kneeling beside Callahan. Blood was trickling down from the detective's forehead—his pulse was in evidence.

Gary gagged him first. He had two weapons, both automatics. Gary took both of them. He carried Callahan to a far corner of the cellar—used his belt on the man's legs. Playing safe, he used a second handkerchief as a gag. It was important that Callahan remained silent.

He straightened up. He had failed to trap Callahan one way. But the one who had done gangster killing under the name of Sal the Dude had been tricked in another way. The lure of five hundred grand had made him lower his guard—and Gary had struck.

Gary went back to the table. He put the stool beside it. He sat down. He was breathing heavily—but he was calm. Slowly, quietly, he started to speak. He played with words—and he played with them the way Callahan would utter them. His voice was pitched too low. He raised it—got away from the husky note. Callahan had a way of starting a sentence pitched high. Gary acquired the knack after a few tries. He talked sense—for those above who might possibly hear. He mocked one Gary Greer, and he chuckled the way Callahan liked to chuckle.

How many men were in the house? He didn't know that. And where was the girl? He swore softly. For the moment Callahan was out of the way. But the spot was still plenty tough. And if he failed—there would be no more dickering. Callahan would strike. It would be a finish, an end of things.

There was a sudden pounding on the door at the top of the steps. He heard raised voices. A man was swearing fiercely. From somewhere in the house there was the sound of doors slamming. In the distance voices were calling out. Something was wrong. What?

"Lay off!" he shouted, using Callahan's voice. "What in hell's the racket—"

The man who spoke from beyond the door had a voice that sounded like that of the one Callahan had addressed as Jerry. He spoke in an excited, hoarse tone.

"It's the moll, Boss—she's gone!"

Gary stiffened. He felt his heart banging again. Joyce Rawlings—gone! She had escaped from the house!

He recovered himself, swore bitterly. He moved toward the steps that led up to the door. He would have to act now—there could be no waiting. The gangsters up above would expect instructions.

"Get outside—all of you!" he called out thickly. "Get word to Joe—and search the grounds around the place. Go down to the road. And make it damn fast!"

He swore fiercely. Beyond the bolted door he heard the man Callahan had called Jerry shouting instructions. There were footfalls on the wooden floors. A door slammed—there were no more footfalls. Gary went up the stairs. He unbolted the door opened it. Gas lights gave the room a flickering yellow color. There seemed to be no one in the house. There was a heavy lock on the outside of the door—a key in it. Gary closed the door back of him, snapped the lock. He slipped the key in his pocket.

Outside he heard hoarse shouts. He was smiling grimly. Where had Joyce Rawlings been kept a prisoner? Where was she now?

He turned toward the door. There was a flashing thought in his head. If he could get clear—get away from the house and find aid, Federal aid, there would be a chance. If he could get back with help, before Callahan was found in the cellar—before the girl was caught again, that would be the finish—for Sal the Dude.

He turned toward the door that led out to the side of the house. A gray cap rested on a battered chair. He pulled it over his head—low over his eyes. And then he saw the Tommy. The sub-machine-gun rested on the floor, back of a chair. He reached it in a few strides. It was loaded—ready for action.

Gary Greer hesitated. If he only knew about the girl—knew where she was—how she had made her escape. Pitching his voice low, he called out softly:

"Joyce—Joyce Rawlings!"

There was no sound within the house. Outside he heard men's voices. Rain beat against the window panes. Gary headed for the door. He couldn't risk staying in the house longer.

There was no one in sight outside. But in the distance the beam from a flashlight cut the darkness. Gary shut the door back of him. The Thompson was not light, but he could handle it. And it was a sweet weapon to have with him.

He started toward the rear of the house, the shed into which

Callahan had driven the car. A figure loomed up close to him—a light flashed on the ground. Gary snapped out words, trying to give them Callahan's tone.

"Douse that glare, damn you!" he ordered. "That moll may have grabbed a rod!"

The light was extinguished. A man swore. A voice came to Gary. The speaker was fifteen or twenty feet off, and Gary kept him that far away.

"Bennie tied her up—but she slipped loose. Went out a window—twenty feet up. Damn if I can see how she made it—no foot-prints around there, in the mud."

Gary grunted. "Walked around the roof!" he muttered. "You birds'll get us all burned if you don't grab her again!"

He headed toward the rear of the shed. Joyce Rawlings—getting outside a window twenty feet from the ground. The roof would be slippery. And the girl was taking this chance because he had involved her in the deal. He swore bitterly. A voice reached him faintly—from the far side of the frame house.

"Joe, Benny—get up on the roof! Saw something move—up there!"

Gary stared toward the top of the house. He saw something move, too. But it wasn't the figure of Joyce Rawlings. It looked as though there had been poles up there—for an aerial. The wind had swung one loose—old wires held it up above, but gave it play.

Gary drew a deep breath. He called out jerkily—trying as desperately as he could to imitate Callahan's voice:

"All you rats—surround the house! Get in close to the walls. I'm rolling out the flivver—taking a look along the road!"

Then he was inside the shed. He didn't wait to see the effect of his words on the gangsters. This was the big chance.

Inside the car—he snapped on the lights. He swore grimly. The key was in the ignition switch—Callahan had left it there. He had had more important things to think about. The engine roared as he stepped on the self starter. He jerked the car out of the shed, in reverse. On the seat beside him was the Tommy. There was a chance now—a good chance.

Lights were flashing up toward the roof. He could hear shouts, but he couldn't distinguish the words. He was thinking about Joyce. It seemed rotten to leave her behind. Suppose she was up there on the roof? They'd find her—search for him. When he didn't come in they'd become suspicious. How soon would it be before they'd batter down the cellar door, find Callahan below? Would he get back with aid, in time to save the girl?

His face was twisted as he drove toward the road. And then, suddenly, he saw her. Joyce Rawlings! She was staggering out from the darkness on the right—her clothes were mud-stained. She threw up her right hand. He used the brakes.

"Joyce!" he called hoarsely. "It's— Gary—"

She slumped downward to the mud of the road. In a flash he was out from behind the wheel—running toward her. Back of him, from the direction of the house, he heard hoarse shouts. Some one was calling out "Sal! Something's wrong—" Gary was lifting the girl in his arms. She had fainted. He carried her to the car, swung her into the seat beside the wheel. Then he was back of the wheel—the car was jerking forward again.

He had trouble holding it on the rough road. Once it skidded off into deep mud—and he lost precious seconds getting back on the road again. Back of the car there were louder shouts. But now he had the flivver almost to the main road. He turned toward Center City—stepped on the accelerator.

At his side, Joyce Rawlings stirred. Her eyes were half opened—she was staring at him wildly. He smiled.

"Hurt, Joyce?" he asked shakily. "We're—free—"

"Gary!" Her voice was faint, a whisper. She sat up a little in the seat. Her face was pale. "They came for me—said the district attorney's office wanted me—"

"I know." Gary smiled grimly. He got his head out to the left, stared back along the road. There was no sign of pursuit. But he was sure there was another car somewhere around the house. And there would be pursuit.

Joyce Rawlings kept her eyes on Gary. She spoke again, above the clatter of the flivver's engine.

"They brought me—there. Tied me up—but they didn't hurt me, Gary. I got loose—I wasn't tied very tightly. They left me alone—I was upstairs. One of the windows wasn't boarded up—not all the way. I got outside, worked my way around the roof to the rear of the house. It was hard—work."

Gary flashed her a smile. It was a grim smile. Once again he twisted his head, stared behind. Still there were no lights on the wet surface of the road. Still there was no pursuit.

"It was—nervy work!" Gary told the girl. "They had me down in the cellar. I pounded Callahan unconscious—faked his voice. About that time they discovered you were gone. I ordered 'em out of the house—came up from the cellar. Picked up a Tommy gun—it's at your feet. I've got two other weapons. Callahan is tied up, but they'll find him in a hurry now. We're in a tight place, Joyce."

Her eyes met his squarely. "We're in it—together this time!" she stated. "Don't leave me again, Gary—"

He shook his head. "I won't," he stated quietly. "It doesn't do any good. They know they can hurt me, through you. We stick."

She smiled a little. "I had to drop—from the roof," she said slowly. "Then I ran toward what I thought was the road. I ran—into things. A tree, I guess. It was dark. But I kept trying to reach the road. Then I heard a voice calling. It was your voice, Gary—but it didn't sound natural. I recognized it—ran out toward the lights—"

Gary stared behind again. There were lights back of them now. They gleamed in the rain. He twisted his head toward the girl.

"You recognized it—and it's ten to one that they were getting suspicious," he stated. "Listen, Joyce—they're out on the road now. Coming after us. This bus hasn't much speed—they'll be up to us before we hit the outskirts of the city. They're desperate now. Callahan—he's Sal the Dude. He's the one that ran things—that had S.G. murdered. I've got the goods on him—and he knows it. They took us out there to rub us out—and they'll fight to the finish to get us. You've got to know—the truth."

Joyce Rawlings was tense in the seat. Her head was close to his. He was forced to speak loudly, hoarsely against the beat of the engine.

"They got—Pete Ranning, Joyce."

Her body stiffened—her eyes were wide on his. His face was twisted. But he went on, turning his eyes to the wet road ahead.

"He was drugged—got the stuff meant for me. I got him to a cheap hotel, near River Street. Thought he'd be all right.

But someone traced us—and when I went to the apartment, worried about you, they finished—Pete—"

His voice was shaky. He stared back of the ancient car. The lights were coming on, gaining on them. Gary turned his head to the front again.

"I wanted you—to know that, Joyce. I've been a fool—dragging you and Pete into this. But I tried to keep you out. You wouldn't *let* me—do that—"

The girl was smiling through her tears. She was game enough.

"I—understand, Gary!" She twisted her head, was staring back toward the car behind. "I tried to—stop you. I shouldn't have done that. They murdered—S.G."

Gary Greer was watching the right side of the road. Suddenly he used brakes, fought to keep the machine from skidding too badly. He twisted the wheel to the right. They were off the main road now—on the slope of a dirt road. It was in bad condition. The car slid off to the left, dropped into a shallow ditch. Gary spoke sharply.

"Outside—quick! Follow me!"

He lifted the Thompson machine-gun—slipped around through the mud, cut back into a field of low brush. The girl was right behind him. He stared toward the main road—saw the lights of the car behind swing as the machine made the turn.

"Down!" he cried sharply. "Don't move!"

They were both on their knees. He could hear the engine of the pursuing car racing—the headlights were pointed in the opposite direction from the field in which they crouched. The driver had turned too sharply—the car had swung all the way around. It was headed almost directly across the dirt road. The tail-light was in plain view when Gary lifted his head.

He spoke to the girl. "Keep low—follow me. We've got to—take a chance."

He led the way back toward the main road. Figures were piling out of the car that had given chase—but they were moving up the dirt road slope, toward the machine that had been Callahan's. And they were moving cautiously. Perhaps they were not aware of the fact that Gary had the sub-machine-gun. But they knew that he was armed.

Gary and the girl moved in the opposite direction. There was a wind across the low foliage of the field, and the rain was coming down fairly hard. Wind and rain made sound. And there was the racing engine of the pursuing car. The sound of their own movements was drowned out by the combined other sounds.

They reached the main road again. There was no sound from the searchers—but the engine of the skidded car was still racing—the rear wheels still spinning in the mud. As they crouched by the road, Gary spoke to the girl. He smiled grimly.

"We're going—across the road! They'll follow on back. Keep low—and run. Are you—up to it?"

She nodded. Her face was pale—her dark street dress was soaked. She wore no coat.

Gary got a good grip on the Tommy. There was no traffic on the road—nothing within a half mile. Straightening he started forward. The girl was at his side, on the right. Suddenly he glanced toward the car that had skidded from the main road, turning off. Its driver was backing it—he was backing into the main road. In a second the lights would flash along the stretch they would have to cross.

"Wait!" Gary's voice was grim. "You—stay here. I'm going to—get that car!"

He was gone even as the girl uttered a cry of protest. It was the best way out, and if he could get the car, get back of the wheel, there would be an end to the pursuit. It would take them too long to get his car—Callahan's car out of the ditch. And even if they did get it out—it wasn't fast enough.

The driver had the car headed in the right direction, for Gary, along the side of the main road. His head was extended from the right side—he had slipped out from behind the wheel. He was staring up the slope of the dirt road. Muffled voices reached Gary as he crept in. The Thompson was hard to handle—he had to move carefully.

He got within fifteen feet of the car along the main road, before he stood up. The engine was running, throttled down, and the driver was still staring up the dirt road toward the dark shape of the car Gary had taken from the shed.

The Tommy was swung up; he leveled it at the driver's head. Then he walked forward.

"One move—you get the load!" he snapped in a low tone.

The driver's head jerked—but not more than an inch. His eyes stared wildly toward the Thompson. Gary was at his side now. The glow from the headlights outlined his body faintly. He spoke again.

"Both hands outside the car—over the door! Fast!"

The driver's hands moved outside the car. They were empty. His face was white—his lips were twitching.

"Call to your pals—tell 'em to look farther up the road!" Gary's voice was like ice. "Tell 'em you saw something move— shout loudly, and don't make any mistakes!"

The sounds from the wind, rain and engine drowned out Gary's low words—from the men up the road. The driver took a deep breath. He called out hoarsely.

"Hey, Jerry! Go on—up the road. I seen somethin' move—"

"That's enough!" Gary swung the Tommy's muzzle a few inches. "Climb down—go up the road ten feet—wait a second!"

He thought he heard movements toward the car. For several seconds both men stood motionless. But it was only one of the searchers going on up the dirt road. It was so dark that figures were lost from sight in a short distance.

"Got a rod? Toss it down!" Gary spoke in a half whisper. "Don't be a fool—the Tommy packs a kick."

Something hit the surface of the road's shoulder. Gary took a step—kicked it into a ditch beyond the shoulder.

"How many—looking for me?" he asked grimly.

The driver spoke hoarsely. "Three," he muttered. "Don't turn that loose—I ain't never—"

"Shut up!" Gary's voice was sharp. Once before tonight a man had pitched his voice high—and there had been lead streaming toward a car. "Walk ten feet along the shoulder. Keep out of this car's headlight beam. Get down flat—face downward. Stretch your arms out. One slip-up—and you get the dose!" The man muttered something Gary didn't get. But he obeyed orders. He was down in the shoulder mud now—lying on his stomach. His arms were spread widely.

Gary slipped in back of the wheel. The car was a roadster of a fast make. The top was up. There was a rumble seat, with the back up. A voice sounded from up the dirt road as Gary got the sub-machine-gun at his feet.

"Jake—put your lights—up here!" Gary smiled grimly.

Another break for him. He could start the car now—and they wouldn't be immediately suspicious. He shouted something hoarsely—got the car under way. As it rolled past the driver he shouted at him.

"Keep your—head down!"

Then he was stopping—Joyce was climbing in beside him. They were picking up speed now—he shifted into high. The roadster was fast—and she handled easily.

"You—did it!" There was a strange note in Joyce Rawling's voice. "They can't follow—"

"Steady!" Gary was smiling a little. "We're not out of this yet. We're too—important."

He twisted around, stared back of the speeding roadster. There was no pursuit. But he knew that Callahan would not give up easily. And the man was powerful.

"We're heading for—South Side Field," he stated grimly, staring at the road ahead. "I've got enough on Callahan to send him to the chair. He knows it. But I can't fight him—not this way. I'm going to get you away. Then I'll come back—"

"No—no!" There was panic in her voice.

"Joyce—steady!" He spoke almost roughly. "Can't you see— Callahan has been the brains of this organization. It was he who murdered—S.G. It was Sal the Dude that planned all these things—can't you see that? And Pete's—out of things. He can't go on—this killer Callahan! He can't."

The girl was trying to break Gary's will with words. She shook her head.

"Can't *you* see? He's too strong for you, Gary—too powerful. And he has the police on his side. You can't—"

"He *had* the police on his side!" Gary slowed down for a

sharp turn, then sped the car up again. "Joyce—I've been working with the Federal government, since the night after father was killed. You didn't know that—neither did Pete, not until two days ago. But Elbow Gorringe was wanted by the Federal outfit. He mixed into some bad money deals. They were reasonably sure he wasn't the brains of the crook gang they were after. They couldn't get enough on him. I was sure there was someone on the local force in the gang—so I couldn't let the police get the information that I was working under Federal authority."

The girl was staring at him. He twisted in the seat again—there were no cars coming along the stretch this side of the turn, and they were a quarter mile past it now. The South Side Airport was only five miles distant.

His head was to the front again. He spoke grimly, above the hum of the roadster's engine.

"I've got to get you out of this, Joyce. You won't go—alone. I'm going to have you *flown* out. From the airport. Then I'm coming back—"

Joyce Rawlings was smiling wanly. But there was an expression in her eyes that puzzled Gary. She nodded her head slowly.

"I can't stop you, Gary. I'm tired—tired of it all. Pete Ranning—dead—"

Gary's face twisted. But there was a grim expression in his eyes.

"That's just *another* reason—why I'm coming back, after you're in the clear!"

Joyce Rawlings was relaxed in the seat beside him. Her eyes were half closed—on the road ahead. The lights of Center City gave a yellow glow in the distance, to the heavy sky. Gary turned his head, stared back of the roadster. There were no lights in sight yet. He smiled faintly as he turned his head to the front again.

Callahan was still alive. And while he lived there was danger. Danger for the girl beside him—and for himself. He stared down at his wrists. The skin was scraped, torn where the steel cuffs had rubbed. Callahan had put the cuffs on him—and had taken them off. He had been too sure. But the next time there would be no waiting. Money would not be even a temporary bait, Gary knew that.

He drove with his eyes on the wet road ahead. Already he was making plans—speed was necessary. Callahan would be desperate. And that quality would breed cunning. Joyce Rawlings must be gotten in the clear. After that—

Gary's lips moved a little. But Joyce did not hear the unspoken words they formed.

"It's my name—or the *fifth* name—off the list!"

THE GATE GUARD came out from the little house and stared at Gary. His eyes widened. Gary spoke calmly.

"Hello, Brooks—is Jensen inside?"

The guard started to speak. But he got out only a few words.

"He came in an hour ago—"

Gary nodded. He drove the car through the entrance— headed it toward the Administration Building. But he did not stop in front of the building. He swung the roadster past the entrance, drove down the road back of the dead-line. The B Hangar was open—he turned the car inside. Then he smiled at the girl.

"Stay close to the car, Joyce. Please. I've got to phone."

He was outside—moving toward the Administration Building. From the main entrance to the Field, the front of the Administration Building could be seen. And he didn't want the roadster to be parked in sight. Callahan was no fool—where was the most likely place for Gary to go? To the police? Gary doubted that the detective who was known to the gangsters as Sal the Dude would figure that way. *He* would think of the airport.

He went inside—moved toward his office. There was a faint smile on his face. He heard voices. Jensen was talking—Jensen was in charge of the Field now. He wondered if he had learned yet of Pete Ranning's death.

Gary opened the door—stepped in. Jensen was talking over the telephone—he stared at Gary. He hung up, got to his feet.

"Greer!" he muttered. "Gary—Greer!"

Gary nodded his head slowly. He spoke in a level tone.

"Right, Jensen. Not such a shock, is it? You suspected I wasn't killed in that plane wreck. Perhaps you saw me at the Field—"

"Gary!" The word came from behind him. Gary turned. His body stiffened—he was staring at Eddie Lee!

They gripped hands. Jensen came around from behind the desk—Gary was speaking quietly.

"You got away all right—from the carnival field, Eddie? You saved my neck—switching 'chutes. How long have you been in town?"

Eddie was smiling grimly. "Two days," he stated. "Looking for you—I've been out here, and got it straight just who you were, but Jensen told me I'd better not advertise the fact I was hunting you."

Gary smiled at Jensen. He nodded. He spoke in a steady tone.

"Call the gate guards, Jensen. Tell them not to let *anybody* through. I gave that same order once before—here's hoping I won't have to give it again."

Jensen moved toward the phone. He gave the order. Gary was smiling at Eddie Lee. He spoke slowly.

"I'm glad you got clear, Eddie—thought maybe they'd grab you. Burke was running out as I took off."

The former mechanic of Gary's swore softly.

"I didn't *wait* to see what would happen," he stated. "I ran for it—and they were so busy waiting for you to crack up that I got away."

Gary nodded. Jensen was at his side again.

"The police called a little while ago. About Pete Ranning—"

Gary stopped Jensen with a gesture. He turned his back on the two men for several seconds. When he faced them again there was a twisted smile on his face.

"Pete's out of things, I know that. But I've got to go on, Jensen. You're in charge here now. Who's sleeping at the Field—what pilot can I have? In a hurry."

Jensen stared at Gary. "Teddy Dorres is here," he stated. "And Cy Colon."

Gary nodded. "Get Teddy out at Hangar B in a hurry," he ordered. "I want him to fly a passenger, in a cabin ship. A *National* will do. Get the ship out—warmed up, Jensen. And I'll want a Greer Special. Got one?"

Jensen nodded. "I'll break out a crew—have 'em both warmed up in twenty minutes. You flying alone?"

Gary's eyes went to those of Eddie Lee. He spoke quietly.

"You scrapped for me once, Eddie? Want to try it again?"

The mechanic who had aided Gary at the carnival smiled grimly.

"You know I do, Gary!" he returned. "What do I do?"

Jensen was out of the office. Gary spoke slowly.

"Callahan is a killer, Eddie. He's the brains of the gang that got Sanford Greer, my father. He's wanted for a lot of murders. He damn near got me—tonight. I've got a passenger out in Hangar B and Teddy Dorres is going to fly her out of this section of the country. I want to be sure she gets clear. Callahan is desperate. Desperate enough to ride up into the sky to stop us. Can you handle a Thompson sub-machine-gun?"

Eddie was staring at Gary. He smiled faintly.

"I can handle any kind of a gun that crooks can handle!" he stated.

Gary spoke in a hard tone. "You can ride in the rear cockpit of the Greer Special. I'll fly her. It may be a false alarm, Eddie—but I'm damn glad you're here. Come on—let's get some 'chutes!"

He led the way from the Administration Building. It was a rotten night for flying. And a good night for an air getaway. But he would come back. Once again he would be forced to hurt Joyce Rawlings. But this time he would make *sure* that she was safe, out of the fight.

He glanced toward the main entrance. The guard's figure was in sight, near the glow from the entrance lights. Brooks was on the job. Gary turned toward Hangar B, Eddie Lee at his side.

"You told me—if anything went wrong—to come to this Field. But I didn't know you owned it, Gary. Jensen told me that, after I came through with my story. He said there were plenty of things he didn't know about—and not to talk."

They were nearing Hangar B. Gary smiled with his lips. He spoke in a low, hoarse voice.

"There's a lot—none of us know, Eddie!" he muttered. "But there's only *one* thing I want to know right now. And that's that Teddy Dorres gets his passenger away from Center City air safely!"

THE TWO SHIPS rested side by side on the dead-line. It was almost twenty-five minutes since Gary and Joyce had driven into the airport. The rain had ceased, but the night was black and the wind was blowing in gusts.

Gary snapped the last strap on the girl's 'chute pack. He spoke in a level tone.

"I know you don't want to go, Joyce—" he started, but she interrupted him.

"I'd *want* to go—if you wouldn't turn back, Gary—"

He smiled gently. "It's in the game, Joyce," he replied. "I owe it to S.G.—to Pete Ranning. I've got to turn back—"

She shook her head. Then, suddenly, she turned away from him. She was climbing into the cabin-type plane now. Teddy helped her, then faced Gary. The owner of the airport spoke in a low voice.

"You've got a load of gas—stay up until dawn. Try to make Connie Webster's Field at Courtneyville. If you can't do that—get down at the Rice Airport. I'll fly along with you for a couple of hours, Teddy. Get plenty of altitude. Seven thousand, at least. If I turn back at any time—you keep going. If anything goes wrong—use your own sky judgment, Teddy."

The pilot was staring at him. "What could go wrong?" he asked slowly. "Forced landing, you mean?"

Gary smiled a little. "Forced landing—or a third ship in the sky. Your job is to get Miss Rawlings out of any mess. Never mind about me. Wing westward."

Teddy Dorres' eyes were narrowed. He adjusted his own 'chute pack, nodding his head.

"I get you," he stated. "She'll get clear, all right. I'll stick close to her, until you come on, Greer."

Gary smiled more broadly. But the tone of his voice was grim.

"That's all I ask," he said slowly. "Until I—come!"

THE CABIN PLANE rolled out on the airport field, headed into the wind. The flood-lights were on. She got off smoothly on the Number One runway. Gary opened up the throttle of the Greer Special. The two-place ship was an open cockpit plane of his own design. He rolled her along the Number Two runway, lifted her from the surface easily. Her engine had power—and she climbed up through the gusty, night air at a steeper climb angle than that of the cabin ship.

Teddy Dorres was getting his altitude over the airport. He climbed the cabin ship in wide circles, keeping a mild bank. The ship was showing her running lights—but Gary banked the Greer Special wide and snapped his own plane's running lights out. Less than two feet of fuselage separated the two cockpits; Gary twisted his head, shouted at Eddie Lee.

"Like old times, Eddie!"

Lee nodded his head. In the dull glow from the cockpit lights, Gary could see that the mechanic was smiling.

His own face sobered. Pete Ranning had been a fine fellow. And now Eddie Lee was riding in the cockpit, back of him.

His eyes narrowed back of the goggle glass. Teddy Dorres was heading his plane westward. He was getting altitude now in a straight climb in that direction. Gary banked around—pulled back on the stick, nosed the two-place ship up. She was a quarter mile from the cabin plane.

His left wrist was aching—he had put the weight of the Thompson on it, when the girl and he had left the car he had taken from the shed. The automatic machine-gun had not been light. He twisted in the cockpit again.

"Lift that Tommy up—brace it against the prop wash!" he shouted. "See if you—can hold it!"

When he turned his head again Eddie was leaning the gun across the curve of the cockpit fabric, on the right side. He was sighting the weapon. He nodded his head.

"I can—hold her—all right!" he shouted above the roar of the air-cooled engine.

Gary jerked his head to the front again. It would be light before many hours. It seemed many hours since he had gone down to the River Street speakeasy with Pete Ranning.

He swore softly, trying to get that thought from his brain. His eyes went to the cabin plane. She was flying on level keel now; Teddy Dorres had eight thousand feet of altitude. Gary went up a little higher—but the ship was flying through the lower wisps of cloud. The wind was bad. He dropped down again.

Center City lay back of them now, to the eastward. A blur of yellow light in the thick sky. His eyes searched the darkness for any sign of a third ship's exhaust trail. He saw none. The night was so black that it was difficult to get a horizon. The level gauge and instinct—these were the guiding factors.

Dorres was a good pilot. He would get the girl through. Gary nodded his head a little. He would come back—for Callahan.

In spite of everything, he would come back—

He was suddenly stiff in the cockpit. His eyes had picked up the reddish color of a ship's exhaust, low in the sky, to the southward! A ship had gotten off from one of the level stretches beyond the city—was climbing up through the dark sky!

Gary opened the throttle of the Greer Special wide. He watched the climbing plane—he could see the faint outline of her now. Her pilot could pick up the exhaust color from the cabin ship. And from Gary's plane. But still she was climbing!

Against the beat of the two-place ship's engine Gary heard the shout from Eddie Lee.

"Another ship—coming up!"

Gary nodded his head. He stared downward toward the slanting reddish color trailing out from the dark shape of the plane. The ship was climbing up from the section on the outskirts of the city in which the frame house was located. The house in which Gary and the girl had been prisoners.

"Callahan!" he muttered grimly. "Never started—after us. Played safe—had a plane out near his headquarters. Someone got word to him that we'd got clear. That's it—ten to one!"

He banked the ship in close to the cabin plane. The ship coming up from the ground was in a line with the plane that Dorres was piloting—but she had altitude to get. Gary jerked his head, shouted at Eddie Lee.

"Swing that—Tommy up!"

He heard Eddie shout something he did not understand. Then he was diving the Greer Special toward the climbing ship.

He remembered that Detective Callahan had gotten a lot of publicity by coming out for an appropriation for a plane to be used by the police department. And there had been stories of Callahan's ability to fly. That had been months ago, before Sanford Greer had been placed on the spot. He muttered to himself.

"Hope she's—a single seater—with Callahan aboard!"

He pulled the stick back, banked vertically over the climbing ship. She was five hundred feet below now—and her pilot had leveled her off. Gary reached toward the flare rack. He dropped one flare—then a second. He banked wide.

The first flare burst—and the plane below banked to the northward. Gary stared down at her—swore fiercely. She was bathed in white light from the drifting flare. And on her fuselage side was a serial number, and the letters—U.S.A.M. An air mail plane!

Eddie Lee called out sharply. "She's all right, Gary! Air Mail!"

The second flare burst. The plane was banking almost directly beneath it. She was an open cockpit ship—she looked like a De Haviland type. Two men were aboard.

Gary slipped the Greer Special. Wing to the clouds above, wing to the earth—she shrilled downward. In a flash he had lost the altitude the ship had held. He kicked her out of the slip, got her on level keel, banked around. The mail ship was winging a hundred yards on the Greer Special's port side. Her exhaust trail cut through the darkness. Dorres's plane was lost in the darkness.

One flare was below them—far behind. Something had gone wrong with the other. It was extinguished. Gary waved his left hand, toward the other plane. He had made a mistake. The ship had probably been forced down, and had just taken off again. It was a bad night for flying.

He glanced westward—far in the distance there was the faint trail from the exhaust of the cabin ship. Eddie was shouting above the roar of the engine.

"She's—all right—"

And then, suddenly, the ship marked like an air mail contract plane was curving straight toward Gary's plane!

Eddie Lee's voice died abruptly. He shouted a hoarse warning, seconds later, as Gary was pulling back on the stick, trying to zoom the plane. But it was too late. Gary had seen the other ship bank—but his stick movement was too late.

Red fire streaked out from the nose of the air mail marked ship. Fabric ripped. Struts vibrated under lead impact. The Greer Special shuddered. Behind him Gary heard the sharper snap of Eddie Lee's Thompson.

The stick was limp in his grip—the Greer Special went over on a wing as Gary jerked back on the throttle. Callahan had tricked them at the finish—he knew that now. He had had his plane painted with the insignia of the local air mail ships—and he had turned loose a machine-gun mounted on the front cockpit cowling. And he had scored a hit. The Greer Special was out of control!

Gary jerked his head. "Eddie—jump!" he shouted. "No—controls!"

His head was turned to the front again. He let the stick loose. He tossed over two more flares. They might help Eddie Lee. He twisted his head again. Lee was still in the cockpit.

"Jump!" he shouted again. "Get—out of—this!"

He saw Eddie rise in the cockpit. His body seemed to float away from the slipping, crippled plane. Gary jerked his head to the front again. A shape plunged down from the starboard side.

Once more machine gun lead battered into the Greer Special. The propeller was shattered—Gary ducked his head beneath the cockpit as bits of metal from the engine pounded back.

Callahan was making sure this time! The crippled plane was in the first turn of a spin now. She was down around two thousand feet. Gary reached for his safety-belt buckle, snapped it loose. Waves of dizziness were sweeping over him. He pulled himself up from the cockpit seat. And then the killer plane dived again!

Red fire streaked toward Gary's plane for the third time— there was a stinging pain in Gary's left arm. Things were battering around in the cockpit. Glass on the instrument board was shattered. The killer plane was in very close. Her nose dropped—her pilot was going to make sure, then dive beneath the plunging plane.

It happened in the space of two flashing seconds. The Greer Special had been dropping in a spin—a slow spin. She slipped out of it suddenly. She lurched toward the earth in a slip. Perhaps an air pocket helped along.

The killer plane's propeller struck her first. The force of the crash almost hurled Gary from the plane. He gripped a wing strut—hung on. And now both ships, tangled in the sky, were plunging toward the earth! The pilot of the camouflaged mail plane had timed his last dive too finely. He had crashed.

Almost instantly the other plane was shooting back flames from the engine. The shattered propeller had smashed back against the engine—a feed line had been severed. She was a torch already.

Gary Greer, clinging desperately to the strut, stared toward the front cockpit. In the light of the flames he saw the twisted face of Callahan. The gangster-detective was trying to fight clear. In the rear cockpit there was no sign of the other man.

For a split second Callahan's face was turned toward Gary Greer. It was twisted with fear—lighted by the flames that were shooting back. Callahan was struggling to get free from the cockpit—but he seemed to be caught, trapped. The left wing-tip of his ship had buckled inward.

Heat from the flames was terrible. Gary stared at Callahan—his own face twisted. He laughed. It was a soundless laughter—Callahan slumped down into the cockpit.

Gary swung his body around a strut. He shoved himself upward. Something struck him a battering blow across the right thigh. For a second he thought he would be caught in the wreckage, dragged downward. And then his body was free—somersaulting. He counted three—jerked the rip-cord ring of his 'chute pack.

The silk crackled free. Harness tightened about his body. He was drifting now—he shook the tears from his eyes, stared downward. There was a great, red flare somewhere beyond. A dull booming sound reached his ears.

A line of trees drifted past his swaying body—he kicked his feet about. He struck. The wing dragged the collapsing silk. He was down in the mud now.

He didn't lose consciousness. The 'chute silk collapsed slowly. Gary Greer struggled to his knees. His whole body was battered, aching. Heat from the flames had seared his face. His left hand was numb, bleeding. He got clear of the harness, walked a few feet, sat down. He fumbled for a cigarette.

Somewhere beyond the field into which he had dropped there was a dull, red glare. Gary half closed his eyes.

"He—saw me—laugh!" he muttered thickly, weakly. "Calla-han—the last name—on the—list!"

HOWARD ALLING SPOKE very quietly. His eyes went from those of Joyce Rawlings to the gray ones of Gary Greer.

"Jerry Contis was riding that ship with Callahan. He lived for three hours—and he talked plenty. He said a lot of things that Callahan would never have said, if he *hadn't* been killed in the crash. With the information we have we can just about smash the present political outfit, in Center City. And a lot of them will face Federal charges." Gary Greer smiled at the Federal man. His eyes went to those of Eddie Lee.

"Joyce and I are moving out West, Eddie," he said slowly. "I'm selling the Center City airport. But I'll probably go in for another—want to come along?" Eddie Lee grinned. "You know I do," he stated. "Come on, Inspector—let's walk out and look this town over."

Alling and Lee left the hotel room. Gary Greer shifted care-fully on the chair.

"Three broken ribs are better than a lot of other things, Joyce," he said slowly. "I'm through—the job's done. Five killer names—against two that were worth a lot."

His face was suddenly sober. Joyce Rawlings moved to his side. She didn't try to tell him of her feelings, two nights ago, in the air beyond Center City. She had seen the third plane climb into the sky—she had seen Gary dive his ship. And Teddy Dorres had winged her away. It had been a terrible moment.

"I won't ask you if it was worth it, Gary," she said simply. "I know the answer—it wasn't. But you *had* to do it."

He smiled faintly. "It *was* worth it," he said slowly. *"Because*

I had to do it. Pete—would have—thought that, too." She nodded. She sat at his side. His eyes were half closed. He was smiling a little. It was a tired smile—half bitter, half happy. Five names—scratched out. Killer names. Crooked names.

He turned toward her. His lips formed a name that he loved.

"An end—" she whispered softly— "and a beginning."

Gary Greer smiled into her eyes. But he seemed to be looking beyond her. It didn't hurt him much to move his right arm. So he moved it.

About the Author

RAOUL WHITFIELD WAS one of the group of our earliest acquaintances. He was a hard, patient, determined worker. His style from the first was hard and brittle and over-inclined to staccato. Later, he became more fluent and went along, shoulder to shoulder, with the best of them. Earlier, a newspaperman, he wrote from knowledge of men, and women, and their ways.

Personal tragedy intervened in the midst of his career and death, this past year, cut off what might very well have been a brilliant future.

Whit was ambitious. He wanted to invade other fields than that of crime detection and criminal conflict.

Long and fascinating were the discussions between Whit and Dash. Whit maintained that, given characters and a general plot, it was a cinch to write a detective story. When in a spot, all you need do, is to use the well-known props. A good writer should produce a novel without any of these appurtenances to achieve effect. And Dash's comeback, "All right, if you want to make it the hard way, try writing a book omitting every word that has the letter 'f' for example."

—Joseph T. Shaw